CORRINE HUNTER IS Playing for Keeps

A NOVEL

CYNTHIA HARRIS

Copyright © 2023 Cynthia Harris

All rights reserved.

This is a work of fiction.
Names, characters, places, and events are either the product of the author's imagination or are used fictitiously. Any resemblance to actual persons, living or dead, events or locales is entirely coincidental.

The author in no way represents the companies, corporations, or brands mentioned in this book. All opinions expressed in this book are the author's or fictional.

No part of this book may be reproduced, or stored in a retrieval system, or transmitted in any form or by any means, electronic, mechanical, photocopying, recording, or otherwise, without express written permission from the author and publisher.

ISBN: 9798857642429

Cover art designed by Jared Frank

Printed in the United States of America

For my **friends and family**

CONTENTS

ONE A Promise For The Future

TWO My Scot, The Peacemaker

THREE Old Friends

FOUR Introductions

FIVE A New Family

SIX A Missed Birthday

SEVEN What Happened To Corrine Hunter?

EIGHT Mending Fences... Or Not

NINE The Return Of Meredith Cox

TEN The Parting Glass

ELEVEN Brainstorming At The Balmoral

TWELVE Plans And Prayers

THIRTEEN An Honorable Name

FOURTEEN The Suite Life In Paris

FIFTEEN The Rugby World Cup

SIXTEEN Our First Christmas Together

SEVENTEEN Playing For Keeps

EIGHTEEN The Cox Trust For The Arts

NINETEEN The Old Boys

TWENTY My Scot, The Husband

GRATITUDE

ABOUT THE AUTHOR

FROM THE AUTHOR

ONE
A Promise For The Future

The Corinthia Hotel
London, England
June 2023

I was mesmerized by my surroundings and the overwhelming sense of love in the Grand Courtroom of the hotel. It was a beautiful, late June evening and the open doors to the adjacent Garden Lounge brought in both the warm glow of a London summer sunset and a welcome, subtle breeze.

I watched my handsome man in his formal kilt complete with a Prince Charlie jacket and bow tie walk toward our table with a bottle of Champagne in one hand and two cut-glass flutes in the other. I could not help but smile at the mere thought of him. The impending promise of a glass of expensive Champagne was a bonus!

Looking into the gold-flecked hazel eyes of Liam Crichton—eyes enhanced by both the dying sunlight and reflections of the many candles bouncing off the mirrors and glass in the room—only made my dreamy smile grow.

Liam sat the bottle and glasses on the table just as the DJ started playing Adele's beloved ballad and expected wedding reception staple, *Make You Feel My Love*.

"May I have this dance, Miss Hunter?" Liam asked with his now empty hand outstretched for mine.

"You may, sir! I *love* this song!"

I took his hand and stood tall next to him, as we walked to join the other couples on the dance floor. The sentiment of the song, coupled with Adele's unbelievable voice, made it impossible not to feel all the love surrounding us in this room. No offense to the handsome grooms sharing the dance floor with us, as far as I was concerned, there was no one else here but me and my Scot.

"Did I tell you that you look stunning this evening?" Liam asked in a soft whisper in my ear as we danced with our cheeks together.

I felt my best in my cocktail dress from the fashion house of Alexander McQueen. It was a custom navy, caped, silk dress. The inside of the cape perfectly matched Liam's tartan. A detail the designers willingly accommodated. We were a dazzling couple this evening.

"You did, my love."

"Then let me tell you again. You look stunning! Absolutely stunning!"

"Thank you. You look handsome yourself!"

"You do fancy a man in a kilt."

I pulled back slightly to look at him and said with a broad smile, "That I do! My God! *Those knees!* They get me *every... single... time!*"

2

Liam kissed me passionately. I do not understand why this man smells like sugar to me, but I breathed in his sweet kiss and smiled up at him again.

He said, "Everything about today was lovely."

"Oh, wasn't it? I am just so happy for Mark and Colin and that we all could finally celebrate their marriage together. They are such dear friends!"

Dr. Mark Ramsey was a longtime friend of my deceased fiancé Dr. David Bryant, and my publisher Kate Woodhouse's husband, Dr. Luke Matthews. The trio became best friends in medical school and worked together at the same pediatric hospital in London. Mark's husband, Colin Peterson, is an interior designer and a gifted one at that! He helped design and decorate our new house in Edinburgh and made it truly feel like home. They are both lovely men and even better friends.

Mark and Colin have been a couple for over fifteen years and married in the middle of the pandemic. They postponed their wedding four times because of lockdown restrictions but decided not to wait any longer. They planned this reception for well over two years and their hard work was evident in every thoughtful detail.

"Did ye see Kate and Luke?" Liam asked.

"I saw them get seated on the other side of the room just as the ceremony started but haven't talked to them. They were on the dance floor earlier, but I don't see either of them now."

"Do ye think that the *Loch Leven Peace Accord* has held?"

I laughed slightly remembering our awkward moment at the dinner party we hosted at Crichton House on Loch Leven where Liam unexpectedly offered to buy Kate's publishing company—a company that she had no intention of selling. The unwelcome offer resulted in a bit of a row between friends. While everything was resolved, this is the first time all four of us have been in the same room together since that weekend.

"I do!" I said laughing at his phrase. "I promise, they are not avoiding us. They just arrived late."

"Luke is an incredible partner for her," Liam said with Adele's powerful voice still resonating throughout the room.

"They are a perfect match for sure! You already know this, but after David died, these four—Kate, Luke, Mark, and Colin—were the only people on whom I could truly rely. They not only honored the memory of their dear friend, but they honored and protected me. They cared for me when I wasn't sure I wanted to be cared for. They loved me when I wasn't sure I wanted to be loved. And admittedly, when I wasn't sure I had any love left in me to give back to them in return."

"Then I thank them! *All of them!* That includes David."

I smiled up at him and thought about how grateful I was for this man to respectfully honor the man that came before him along with my dearest friends. I believed that David became a protector the minute he left this life, and our friends helped me recover from my deepest despair. We shared our grief together, but they all saved me. Without them, I would have never found a new love with Liam. And without him, I would have never finished my latest historical fiction novel, *The Old Boys*.

Only by opening my own heart again did I find the heart of an incredible story set in Scotland during World War One. My last two novels failed miserably, and *The Old Boys* may single-handedly salvage my reputation as an author. I am excited every time a new novel is published but this book and story is without a doubt one of my proudest achievements.

Breaking the spell of remembrance of a love lost, dear friends, and my upcoming novel, Liam said, "Colin is an incredible talent! You can see his creative imprint on everything about this reception, from the venue to the flowers."

"Oh yes! I am certain Mark had a say, but Colin is an incredible talent. I am positive they garnered additional help once they made the selection of this magnificent hotel. They certainly know how to do weddings here."

"Perhaps... Colin should plan *our* wedding reception."

I pulled back and looked at the man with narrowed eyes. I think we were both conscious of how quickly our relationship progressed, but marriage was not a subject we ever broached before. Our future was always just being together. We were content with our life in Scotland and admittedly, we were both still carrying some of the pain of how both his marriage and my previous engagement ended. We felt lucky to have found each other and enjoyed every bit of happiness that came with that unexpected discovery. We were not ready to ask for more. Perhaps we did not dare wish for more!

"I am not asking you to marry me on the dance floor at the wedding reception of your dearest friends! And I have no ring in my sporran, love."

I smiled as he kissed my cheek. As much as I wanted to think about the future, I was relieved that he was not asking me to marry him... at least not tonight.

"But it *will happen*."

I could only smile at the thought of his words and promise. I stroked his close beard and kissed him just as the song ended. The last lines of Adele's beautiful song echoing in our ears and in our hearts:

I could make you happy, make your dreams come true

Nothing that I wouldn't do
Go to the ends of the Earth for you
To make you feel my love
To make you feel my love

Make You Feel My Love, *Adele*
(Songwriter: Bob Dylan)

Liam Crichton made me feel his love from the moment we met and now he offered me an even greater promise of a future together. I could only hope to make him feel my love for the rest of my life.

+++

"Corrie, my girl!" yelled a very dapper Dr. Luke Matthews in his traditional black tuxedo as Liam and I left the dance floor. I believe that I love a man in a tuxedo as much as I love a man in a kilt. I smiled at the thought before laughing to myself for a moment. No. As dashing as men look in a tuxedo, those bare knees peeking out of a kilt will always win my heart!

"Hello, my friend! I am sorry we couldn't speak earlier!" I said as we kissed each other's cheeks. Luke instantly reached to shake Liam's hand just as my man handed me a glass of Champagne from the bottle he delivered to our table before our dance.

"It was my fault, my darling," Kate said, kissing both of us on each of our cheeks. "I have struggled the last few weeks getting myself together, so we were late on our arrival to the ceremony and weren't able to speak to a single soul beforehand. Not even Mark and Colin!"

"Are you unwell?" I asked, touching her arm gently and with a genuine look of concern. Kate looked stunningly beautiful as always, albeit a little pale.

"Well," she said as she looked at her husband before answering my question fully, "if you consider being pregnant unwell, then yes!"

"No! Are you serious?" I exclaimed before immediately hugging my dearest friend. It was then that I saw that her Champagne flute was filled with sparkling water. Liam reached again to shake Luke's hand and kissed Kate's cheek once more.

Kate was a tall, blonde, blue-eyed beauty and always dressed in the latest fashion. She stood before us in a lovely, yet voluminous, black and lace babydoll cocktail dress with her signature Christian Louboutin heels. Tonight, however, she had a black wrap around her shoulders that was not only heavy for June, but clearly trying to conceal any hint of her tiny baby belly.

"I have struggled not to tell you, but I am older and have been so nervous that this could end at any moment. I could not say the words. Honestly, Luke and I just told our own families a few days ago."

"This is incredible news! I am so happy for you both! Do Mark and Colin know?"

"No, we could not tell them! They should have every happiness and I thought we could confess after they return from Capri. We have gone this long... what are a few more weeks?"

"That is fair. But you know that they will absolutely be over the moon for you both!"

Luke chimed in and said, "We know! It has taken everything I have to keep my mouth shut to Mark. He is one of my dearest friends and surely knows I am keeping something from him. I can see it in his eyes every time we speak with each other!"

"He is also a doctor, so I am certain he has put it all together, my darling!" Kate said to her husband who nodded in agreement. "But our friend has respectfully not said a single word or asked a question of either of us."

Liam said, sweetly and with respect, "Then we are honored that you told us tonight."

"We are! Truly honored! When?" I asked, eagerly wanting to know more. Now that Kate was openly sharing this wonderous news, I had to know every single detail!

"If everything stays healthy, then we are looking at early September. Liam, I am not saying it was why I completely lost my senses at the house on Loch Leven, but apparently, I was pregnant and didn't know it. So, the wine hit me *hard* that night!"

"We resolved everything then and there. Dinnae think another thing about it, love! I am so happy fer ye both!"

I smiled at Liam for both his reassuring sentiment and how even a little Champagne made his Scottish accent more pronounced. It is absolutely one of the most charming things!

I said to them both as I took Kate's hand in mine, "You will be such incredible parents!"

"Incredibly *old* parents, you mean!" Kate replied, reaching for Luke's arm.

"You will be just fine, my love!" Luke said kissing his wife's cheek. Kate was not yet fifty, but Luke was David's age. He had to be approaching sixty. They were getting a late start for sure, but I was happy for them. They are a loving couple and will make loving parents.

Just then we were joined by the grooms and shared in another round of hugs and kisses. I watched Kate stealthily place her faux Champagne on a passing tray. We would have to table this joyous conversation for now and focus on the handsome couple standing before us.

I said immediately, "My loves, I don't think there was a dry eye in the room during your vows!"

Kate said in agreement, "They were masterfully written!"

"Thank you! Colin and I tried to channel your talent, Corrie. We both spent weeks and weeks writing and editing those vows. I do not know how you do it! And for a full novel no less!"

"I told Mark I was going to outsource my vows to you, love, but he said that was cheating and unfair."

"It is cheating, Colin! But also, unnecessary. You both did beautifully! I cried through the whole thing."

"Speaking of novels, congratulations to *you* and to you *Missus Publisher Extraordinaire*," Mark said changing the subject and nodding to me and Kate in succession. "When do we finally get our hands on your latest, love?"

"Thank you," I answered quickly. "Kate can correct me, but initial reviews and articles should start coming in toward the end of July and the publication date is the seventh of August."

"That is right. Pre-orders will be made live early next week and tested before the first reviews and promotional articles hit starting at the end of July. Everything seems to be trending positively based on what I have seen and heard so far. But this is all due to Corrie and her incredible talent! Well... and maybe her beloved Scot," Kate replied beaming proudly to both me and Liam. She knows better than anyone how Liam opened my heart and his connection to Dr. Andrew Marshall made my novel come to life. Everyone smiled at Liam who tenderly kissed my hand that he held tight in his.

"Colin and I watched you and your Scot on the dance floor, and I told him that I wished we had a bouquet of flowers to toss to you tonight! Surely you *must* be the next to marry!"

Liam and I did not respond to Mark's statement. We just smiled at each other upon his words.

Liam said it will happen, and I believe him.

It *will* happen.

TWO
My Scot, The Peacemaker

After a celebratory wedding weekend in London and the indulgence of five-star, penthouse hotel living, Pilot Nate collected us at London Luton airport. We were seated for the quick, one-hour flight home to Edinburgh in short order. While we enjoyed our stay in town and shared in the happiness of our friends, we wanted nothing more than to return home. Our new house in the Stockbridge area of Edinburgh's New Town had quickly become a welcome respite and comfort to us both.

"Corrine, if I may interrupt your reading."

"Of course," I said as I closed my book. I was researching my next novel focused on a lost Scottish distillery in the 1920s and could use a break.

Liam poured us both a whisky and handed me my glass. He just looked at me but said nothing. I could tell he seemed nervous. Not since he told me he was married and in the process of divorcing in The Colonies pub in London had I seen him in such a state. He seemed unable to find his words. The whisky was either meant to be liquid courage for him or a stabilizer for me. Depending on the nature of this conversation, our beloved dram may serve each of us equally today.

"Babe... what is wrong?" I asked, while taking off my glasses and narrowing my eyes in search of some indication for what was troubling him so.

"Nothing is wrong. I just...need to talk about the lads... and suddenly I feel *nervous*."

I leaned toward his chair opposite mine and took his hand. "You feel nervous to speak to me about your sons? Please, don't! Go on!"

My words and my tone were reassuring but I did sip gingerly from my glass just in case I needed it. I had no idea what would make him so unsettled, but it was starting to make me feel the same.

"Well, the school term ends the last of June and the lads will move into our house for a month."

"Then they will finally get to see their new rooms! How exciting!"

"Aye, but they will live with us and... well..."

"Say what you need to, love."

"They have not met you yet. I would like to take everyone to dinner to make introductions before and... erm...I would like to... erm... invite Sarah."

I sat up tall in my chair and breathed in before taking another—and much larger—sip of whisky. He was wise to give me this glass. My first and only interaction with Liam's ex-wife was an embarrassing scene in the middle of Boots on Princes Street in Edinburgh where she not only called me a mediocre author and a whore but accused me of stealing her husband in front of everyone in the entire shop. It was unfortunate and it hurt. It still hurts. I do not know what to make of this plan.

"I understand..." I said stoically, and without emotion. I knew well enough that my face was likely betraying my words. And if not, then surely the shift in my energy was. I could feel all the embarrassment from that first encounter with Sarah along with a fresh dose of anxiety at the thought of a second.

"I know it will be uncomfortable, but I do not want Eric and Ewan to feel like they are in the middle of their mum and me. If we can make introductions and maybe mend a bridge between you both it will only help you develop your own relationship with my sons."

"Do you think Sarah will agree to this?"

"I do not know. She may not, but I believe it is the right thing to do. I must make the offer."

Despite his honorable conviction, all I could muster was another weak, "I understand."

"*Please* say more than that, love!"

I could tell he was frustrated by the repetition of my simple words in response, but he also wanted some semblance of support that I was clearly reluctant to give. I sat quietly for a moment trying to determine what I truly felt and what to say back to him so that he could understand. I needed to respect his family and his intentions as a father and a peacemaker, but I may have innocently hoped I could avoid Sarah a little while longer. Now, suddenly I am the one that feels nervous.

"*Please, Corrine!*"

"Liam, I do not have children. I cannot image all the emotions Eric and Ewan must have about their parents' recent divorce or what meeting me will add to those feelings—good or bad. I respect your intention as a father to bring everyone together at the start. *I do!* Like you said, it is the right thing to do."

He nodded as I continued with my voice suddenly sounding emotional, "But all the same I do not want to meet your sons for the first time seated across from a woman who screamed and cursed at me. *There!* That is the truth of it! It feels like we are making an already emotional situation potentially volatile. I cannot quite see this going the way you want it to."

"That was months ago and..." Liam said calmly.

"And thankfully I have not seen the woman since!" I said, loudly interrupting him. I instantly regretted my emotional outburst, no matter how honest my feelings were at this moment.

Liam just looked at me and I could feel the tears start to well up in my eyes. They dropped one by one onto my red-hot cheeks. I do not know if I was emotional about the embarrassing memory, the fear of seeing Sarah again, or that I wished I had not said the words I just did. I know he was silently asking me to be the bigger person and I wanted to. I *should* be the bigger person... even just for him. But I was finding it difficult.

"No, no! I am sorry!" Liam got up to hug me and rubbed my back. "Please do not cry! It was not my intention to upset you."

"I am sorry to be emotional. I want to support you... I just... I just *really* want your sons to like me, and I am afraid I will not have that chance with their mother glaring at me from across the dinner table the very first time we meet!"

"I know Sarah hurt you, but she will not want the lads to see her be so rude to another. They are very respectful to us as parents, and they know we will not stand for rude or disrespectful behavior to anyone."

I thought about Elaine Preston's words to me at Crichton House on Loch Leven that Sarah had no trouble berating Liam, even in front of their sons. Perhaps there was some hope that she would restrain herself in front of an outsider. Well, one could only hope that would be the case. However, knowing how she treated me in Boots didn't really instill much confidence.

It took me a minute to calm myself as I said stoically, "Then let's see what Sarah says. If she agrees, then I can do the same. I will be respectful, of course."

"Och thank you, my love!"

"But..." I said, taking his hand again and looking him directly in the eyes, "if it all goes sideways, I will not cause a scene, but I *will* excuse myself."

"That is only fair."

+++

Over the next several days, Liam went back and forth on his plan for introductions with Sarah. He said little but from what I could tell, she may have been as reluctant to have this family dinner as I was. The lengthy negotiations told me that much. I did not press the topic and waited for him to come to me when it was all finally decided.

After my day at the National Library of Scotland and Liam's at his office, we decided to meet at The Balmoral Hotel for drinks. We arrived at the front door to Bar Prince at the same time.

"Well, hello! That is perfect timing!" I said as Liam grabbed me by the elbow and kissed me quickly. He ushered me through the double doors into the refreshingly cool room. It was a sweltering summer day in

Edinburgh and while the walk from Old Town to New Town was short and mostly downhill, I was more than ready for an ice-laden, white wine spritzer, and the cool comfort of air conditioning.

Once we were seated by Alessandro the bar manager at the end of the bar-top rail, Liam asked, with his arm on the back of my chair, "How was your day, my love?"

"Very productive actually!"

I was eager to share my day with him as the bartender delivered my spritzer kit and our rice cracker bar snacks almost instantly. Liam's martini was not far behind. Assembling my own drink, I continued, "I found some local newspaper articles detailing the impact on various communities across Scotland when a distillery closed. But the most incredible item I found was the handwritten journal of a distillery owner, Duncan MacLeod of Glenammon on Skye."

"Glenammon is a fine whisky."

"I only made it about half-way through as I am not allowed to take photos of the journal. I took as many notes as I could so I will go back tomorrow to try to finish it. Duncan was the namesake of the distillery's founder in the late eighteenth century. The man was detailed in his documentation and devastated not just for his family and their legacy, but for the impact the closing had on the entire island. At the time it was the largest employer on Skye. What is incredible is that the Glenammon brewery and distillery were revived fully by MacLeod descendants in 2013. I have more research to do but it is leading to such a positive story, and one that is completely family-led. That has opened so many story possibilities for me."

"Wasn't your first novel about Clan MacLeod on Skye?"

I smiled at him before taking his hand in mine, "Yes it was! It means so much to me that you remembered!"

He kissed me quickly on the cheek before we clinked our glasses together. I am certain Liam has never read any of my novels, but he was right, my first novel *The Ruins Of Dunmara* was a fictional take on the descendants of Clan MacLeod and this connection to my next novel was not lost on either of us. In fact, as an author it has opened an entire network of connection points between research and writing I had already completed.

"I think that is why I got so excited at the library! The connection between my historical fiction novels is starting to span the centuries! I want to see Andrew again, if we can."

"Aye, and I am certain he would be happy to speak with you again. Scottish history aside, the man not only loves whisky, but he also has a thing for *you*."

We laughed together about our friend but if I learned anything during my time in Scotland over the years is that nearly every Scot loves their whisky. You can take me and history out of the equation. Though I freely admit that Dr. Andrew Marshall is quite a charmer! I might have a little thing for the man myself. His gift of inspiration made my upcoming novel come to life in a way I never expected, and I will forever be indebted to our friend.

"Perhaps you should also spend some time with Meredith Cox."

"Meredith Cox? Really?"

"Aye! I told you that she grew up in a whisky empire before marrying into two other well-known whisky empires. She knows more than most about the history and business of whisky and could be a help to you. It might also be good to keep her on your side."

"*My side?* Why?"

"I know you do not care about social politics, but she could be an excellent ally for you here in Edinburgh."

I thought for a moment about his words and while I understood them, it was the first time he indicated that I should be more involved in Edinburgh society. I did not press further on the notion if for no other reason than I had my own career and could not see myself being part of the *'ladies who lunch'* crowd. But the impending meeting with Sarah also told me that I had to figure out the balance between my independent career as an author and my new role as Liam Crichton's partner.

"How was *your* day?" I asked politely while clearly changing the subject.

"It was productive as well. Tommy and I are preparing for the board meeting this week, so I may have a few late nights to finish the deck. We will host him and Elaine for dinner at the house on Wednesday when it is all said and done."

"Of course! It will be good to see them both again!"

"We are still testing chefs but think the current one... Stephan... can certainly manage burgers, chips, and beer."

"He is not Dan, which is a fact! But I agree."

Since arriving in Edinburgh, we went through a few new chefs. None met the high bar set by Chef Dan or won either of us over enough to make a permanent hire. Stephan is an eager young chef from London. He started working for us part-time while he was also working at Gleneagles. Since he became the frontrunner at Crichton House, he left his other job to avoid the commuting time required between the two. Liam, however, was still actively searching all the restaurants across Scotland for the future of gastronomic creativity to bring to the house. The man was on a mission!

Finally, Liam said, "I think I have a plan for Friday."

"Friday?" I asked instantly before remembering that Friday marked the end of the school term. The day snuck up on me. I always said that we would have to deal with this at some point, and here we were. I corrected myself and said over my glass, "Oh...of course! *Friday.*"

"Aye, Sarah agreed to deliver the boys to the new house in Stockbridge. I thought more about it and told her that I wanted her to be comfortable with where they would be living. I also know they would want her to see their rooms. So, I changed the plan from having dinner at a restaurant to having dinner at home. I think she felt a bit wary at first, but then said she was happy to be included. She saw that I was respecting her but also easing the lads into the new house. She may not care about *me* but would want to support *them*."

I just kept sipping my drink nervously but did not say anything. He saw me trying to process his words and the shift from having dinner somewhere together to having Sarah *in our house*. This was almost more than I could bear.

"She knows that I will be there? I mean, she knows that I live in this house... with you?"

"Aye, she does. And I told her this was another transition for our sons and one that we needed to do respectfully... *for them*. This is a new home for the lads, and they will be with us for a month this summer and then off and on next academic term on the agreed schedule. We all need to adjust to our new reality... *together.*"

I admired how Liam was trying to be a peacemaker and positive male role model for his sons. I also appreciated him including me in this *new family*. But I was still nervous and tried my best to hide it. Despite my apprehension, I could not avoid this significant and unavoidable milestone in our relationship and needed to reset my attitude.

"Then if everyone has agreed on the plan, I am in! You have my full support!"

I know Liam could tell by my weak smile and the quick gulp of the last of my spritzer that I was still uncertain. Once again, my face and energy betrayed my words.

"Corrine, it will be fine! We do not have to suddenly all become one big happy family in an instant, but *we do* need Eric and Ewan to feel comfortable in the house that they will share with us. I want them to be happy there. I want them to feel like it is their home. If they sense that it's you and me versus their mum, they will be miserable. And then all of us will be *fucking miserable*!"

I am not certain I had heard Liam curse before. My sharp look back at him showed that his choice of words and tone shocked me.

"Also, I need Sarah to feel comfortable about where the lads are living away from her for the first time. We have a lot to learn together, but I take her willingness to come to the house as a positive sign. Let's build on the positive."

He looked at me in a way that almost willed me to agree with him but did not wait for me to respond. He continued, "I asked Dan to prepare supper that night. He is going to do something casual so he can leave it with us, and we will cook for ourselves. I thought involving everyone in our own meal could be a casual exercise in getting to know each other and the house. That also allows the man to get back to his restaurant for dinner service. I could not ask this of our other chefs in rotation. He knows us all so well and wants to help. He is the right man for the job."

I nodded in understanding and said in agreement, "Everyone knows that the kitchen is the heart of any home, so that is a good idea. I can be at the house to help Dan, if needed."

"Wonderful! Normally, I would just have the house manager meet Dan so he can prep, but I don't want people hovering about. I will also work from home that day. We will both be there to greet our friend."

I just nodded in agreement with the plan. Liam took a sip of his drink before saying, "I can tell you are still apprehensive, love. Please do not be!"

"I am being honest with you, Liam! I *am* nervous because I have never had to deal with ex-wives or children before. I want to support you, but I suddenly feel out of my depth. I don't want to fail you."

"Och, Corrine," he said hugging me tight and kissing the top of my forehead. "You will not fail anyone! Be yourself, love."

THREE
Old Friends

Crichton House
Edinburgh, Scotland
June 2023

I walked into the kitchen to find Chef Stephan prepping for our dinner guests and Liam pouring himself a pint from the beer tap. Much like the house on Loch Leven, we had our own pub in this kitchen as well. It was a feature I had grown to love. Liam always said sometimes you just want a beer with a friend, and the new Crichton House in Edinburgh was more than prepared to welcome friends.

"Hello, love! Can I pour you a pint as well?"

I kissed him quickly and said, "Maybe in a bit. I would really like to have a glass of wine first. It has been a long day of research and writing."

"Of course, I think Chef already has a bottle in the chiller for you."

"Aye, sir! Here you go!" Stephan said, quickly handing Liam the chilled bottles of Sancerre and soda water. Liam knew how to make a spritzer and handed me the perfectly crafted glass. We walked to the bar stools at the end of the island to wait for our dinner companions.

"What time are we expecting Tom and Elaine?" I asked sitting down next to him.

"Tommy said he would return home, pick up Laney, and they would likely get here around six o'clock. I think after long days at work he will have his driver deliver them here so they can enjoy themselves tonight."

"It will be good to see them both again! I assume the board meeting went well for you."

"Aye it did! We have a few follow-up tasks—mostly due to our last deal—but nothing unexpected. It is so much work to prepare for the meeting! We are both relieved it is over and can look forward to relaxing tonight and taking a little more time off this summer."

"You are certainly due a well-deserved break!"

+++

We walked to the front door to greet our guests just after the bell rang. As soon as Tom and Elaine walked in the entryway the smiles on each of our faces grew. These old friends make Liam so happy. You can see it on his face and hear it in his voice. They all default to nicknames, as old friends do, which instantly lightens his mood and puts him at ease. In the brief time I have known them, I can say they make me feel the same. For that I appreciate them both!

As usual, Elaine came carrying her signature bottle of Champagne, but this time also carried a gift basket that had the largest bow I had ever seen!

"Both of these are for you with our compliments and in celebration of your beautiful new home! You did not say if you were going to have a housewarming party, so I took the liberty of bringing a gift."

I took both from her and said, "Oh my! How thoughtful! You did not have to do that!"

"I hope the items I chose will work for the house, but upon first glance... just here in the entryway... I think I may have done right by you both. *Everything* in the basket is handcrafted in Scotland!"

"That is lovely! As you will see, Elaine, we have tried to do the same here in the house. Come in! Let's get you both a drink so that Liam can take you on a house tour."

Liam took the basket from me and placed it on the kitchen island as I handed the Champagne bottle to Chef Stephan for a quick chill.

Tom said as Liam handed him his pint, "Oh Laney! Look at that back garden!"

"It is exquisite!" Elaine said. "And in the heart of the city, no less! This reminds me of the house at Loch Leven to have such light coming in *and* to have the beauty of nature accent the décor and design on the inside!"

Chef handed me and Elaine a perfectly chilled Champagne flute as I said, "It does feel like an extension of the room, doesn't it? My dear friend Colin Peterson, who you both met at our dinner party at Loch Leven, designed the whole thing for us—including the outside garden landscaping. He is an incredible talent!"

Liam agreed saying, "Aye, he is! And he made the move so easy for us. Corrine and I had our own art, books, and clothes but extraordinarily little else. The house needed absolutely everything, and Colin and his team not only made it beautiful but kitted it out—right down to cutlery and linens!"

"Liam will agree with me, but because it all was so new at the start, we felt like we were staying in a hotel or someone else's house. But within days, it was ours!"

"I do agree! It is *our* house now!"

Liam took the Prestons through the entire house, pointing out advanced technical, security, and design features. I answered basic questions about décor and working with Colin and his team. Liam apologized for not showing the boys' rooms as he explained that he wanted them to be the first to see the completed versions. We all respected this request, but he gave Tom and Elaine an explanation of how Colin used a bespoke questionnaire to involve Eric and Ewan in the design and décor of their own rooms. He assured us that they both reflected each lad's wishes but still miraculously matched the overall design aesthetic of the house. And of course, their computer desks and gaming stations had the most advanced tech as well.

Elaine said as we walked back down the stairs, "I think you both have created a beautiful home! I may want to speak with Colin about ours."

Tom added, "Aye, and I think the tech advancement alone is worth a relook! Can you imagine, love? You would never get me out of the bath with a telly built in the damn room!"

"What are you talking about the *bath*? You mean the *toilet, man*! But aye, I would never get you out of *either* with a telly in direct line of sight!"

We all laughed loudly together as Liam refreshed each glass. Elaine and I joined the men now with pints of our own in anticipation of our supper of burgers and chips.

"*Sláinte,*" we all said in unison as we clinked our pint glasses together.

"Let us get out of Chef's way here in the kitchen, and it is still light outside," Liam said, moving us all out to the patio and nodding to Chef Stephan, who seemed somewhat embarrassed to have us all standing at the kitchen island watching over him.

The warm summer night on the garden patio as the sun began to set over the trees and hedges framing the garden made for a great night of pleasantries about the weather, the house, and the drive here. Eventually the men moved to talk business down by the end of the garden, leaving me and Elaine together on the patio.

After a moment, Elaine said, "I am so glad to be here with you, Corrine. I felt the shift in our friendship with Lee the minute we met you, and then even more so with the invitation to your lovely dinner party at Loch Leven. You both were so kind to include me and Tommy. I feel like we are all reclaiming what we had before, and it makes us both so happy! The world has shifted beneath our feet... in a positive way. Thank you for that! If he hasn't said the words himself, I believe Liam thanks you for it as well. He is a lighter version of the man we know. You have made him happy once again."

"I appreciate your thoughtful words and the love you have for your friend. I know Liam is happy to have restored his friendships," I said, reaching out and clinking my pint glass with hers. I looked at Liam speaking with Tom on the other side of the garden and smiled at my handsome man as he smiled back at me in return.

"The house is stunning! It is incredible that it does not just look like an interior designer's dream… it is cozy! It is technologically advanced and thoughtfully designed, to be sure, but it is a comfortable home. It feels like you and Liam have lived here for years! Your friend Colin is an incredibly talented man!"

"Aye, Colin is talented! Much like Crichton House on Loch Leven it has thoughtfully blended the old and the new. But along with Colin's incredible creative talent, it is worth noting that every decision was easy because Liam and I have the same tastes. There was little debate on key decisions which made the process go even faster."

"Well, if you are comfortable, I would like to get Colin's email or mobile so that I can reach out to him myself. We love our house here in Edinburgh and the one we have on the River Dee near Banchory, but both could use a facelift on the inside. I can tell Tommy is already thinking about all the tech and security improvements. And what I wouldn't give for a back garden like this in the city!"

"Consider it done! I am happy to connect you both."

"When do we finally get our hands on your next novel? I told Tommy that I was chomping at the bit for it."

"It is about to be set for pre-order to coincide with the first reviews and articles. The book will be released on August seventh. Come with me back to my study and I will show you the author proof copy."

"Och, how exciting!"

We walked around to the next patio and through the French doors to my study. I took the book from the desk and handed it to her. "You are one of the first to see it!"

"This is incredible! I am so envious! I mean, that you work in such a creative space and can see the output of that work manifest itself. An actual novel! What is this one? Twenty?"

"Close. Twenty-one, in fact!"

"You must be so proud! What does Lee say?"

"Well, look at the dedication."

She flipped pages forward to read the dedication that I had presented to Liam months prior.

For My Scot
who helped me find my heart again
and with it, the heart of this story

Elaine immediately teared up as she said, "*Och, Corrine!* That is lovely! Does he know? And if he does, please tell me the man cried like a baby... like me."

"He might have shed a tear," I said smiling and thinking about my Scot who got emotional when he read the dedication himself when we played *the game* at The Balmoral Hotel for the second time.

"Well, then I cannot wait to read it! As soon as the pre-orders are available, I will be first in line!"

"Thank you! Bring it next time we get together and I will sign it!"

It was then that I suddenly realized that while we had the excitement of my newest novel, we also had to deal with the adjustment of our new family meeting at the same time. Elaine saw my face shift from a sense of pride and accomplishment to worry and perhaps even fear.

"What are you worried about? It will be fine! I can tell you put so much work into this one!"

"No. I mean... yes, I did. Thank you! But suddenly I was thinking that with all the excitement about the book and reviews starting in the next few weeks, we have a personal adjustment happening here at the same time. Liam's sons arrive on Friday and will stay with us for a month."

Elaine nodded in understanding as Liam mentioned it in talking about the boys' rooms. Finally, I added the source of my real apprehension, "And that starts with a family dinner on Friday... *with... Sarah.*"

"Och, Christ!"

"Liam wants us all to have dinner together here at the house. He also thought that the boys would want her to see their new rooms. And I think he wants her to feel comfortable about where they would be living away from her and their childhood home. This is another major milestone in the transition after divorce."

Elaine just nodded and said, "That is respectful, and it sounds like Lee. Tommy told me what happened in Boots. I hope you don't mind, but Lee asked him for advice. The man truly did not know if the way he tried to reassure and defend you was correct, and Tommy wanted my own advice."

"I don't mind. Liam is thoughtful and I should expect that he asks his friends for guidance or reassurance when he needs it. That is what friends are for. We are both dealing with emotions and situations we never had to navigate before. But I confess… I am *so nervous*!"

"Corrine, I think you will be fine! You are a kind-hearted person, you love Liam, and he loves you! *Everyone* can see it when you are together!"

I smiled at the thought of people seeing what I felt every day from my beloved Scot. We do love each other. Part of my angst was because I love him so much that I do not want to fail in embracing all of him, including his sons and yes, perhaps even his ex-wife.

"You already know what I told you about my own opinions of Sarah. I will not expand on those thoughts other than to remind you of two things. First, without a doubt, Sarah loves her sons, and they are beautiful lads. You will love them, and they will come to love you. I have no doubt that the divorce has affected young Eric and Ewan, but they *will* love you, Corrine. Just give them time."

"Thank you, Elaine," I said softly under my breath.

"And second, this is your house! Remember that! Sarah tried to lead where she could before, but she cannot lead here, love. This is *your house*! *Not hers!* I believe she will be aware of that and will not be ugly to you in front of Liam or her sons under this roof."

"I appreciate that reminder," I said almost tearing up at the thought. Elaine took my hand in hers for a minute and gave me a comforting smile. I nodded back to her and silently thanked her for reminding me of the small nugget of confidence I still had deep inside.

I am not a passive participant in this extended family, and I had the power to help drive how this first meeting and introductions would go as she said… under my roof. This is *my house*, and yes, as hard as it might be at first, Sarah Crichton was welcome here.

+++

Liam was correct that it was difficult to mess up a traditional burger and chips, but Chef Stephan took his menu one step further by offering an assortment of toppings like crispy bacon, crumbled blue cheese, and caramelized onions. He also added a choice of sauces beyond the standard fare including a sweet chili ketchup that I gravitated to instantly with my chips. He also made batter-fried onion rings with a spicy ranch dipping sauce that may have singularly made Elaine's entire evening.

While Tom stayed traditional with his choices, the rest of us tried everything. I admired the man's ambition to secure the Head Chef role at the new Crichton House in Edinburgh. I don't know that this night put Chef Stephan ahead in the running, but Liam ensured the young man knew we were all more than pleased with the variety of options he presented.

Much like our introductory visit together at the house on Loch Leven, they all told more stories about their lives, and we laughed together. We laughed a lot! Liam was once again just a lad with his best mates and his mates had clearly become my very own.

It was nice to have such a casual, and relaxed evening. Liam often says that sometimes you just want a beer with a friend and tonight I felt surrounded and supported by friends.

When the evening ended, we walked Tom and Elaine to the front door together. Tom spoke first, saying as he took my hand sweetly, "Thank you both for another grand dinner and even better conversation. It was so nice to see the new house! It is gorgeous!"

Elaine agreed and said as she hugged me, "It is that! Send me Colin's contact information, and we will see if the man is up for another assignment… or two… in Scotland!"

"I will do it straight away! I will make an introduction by email and send you a link to his company website so that you can see his other work. Thank you again for the thoughtful basket. We all must do this again!"

"We will and perhaps host at our house next time!" Tom exclaimed as they walked out the door to their waiting car.

As Liam shut the door and took my hand, I said, "I adore them! Should we have one more beer and talk?"

"Absolutely, love!"

+++

FOUR
Introductions

Crichton House
Edinburgh, Scotland
June 2023

When Liam and I settled into the new house in Stockbridge, we slowly developed a daily routine. Much like the house at Loch Leven, my own study proved to be a comfortable retreat when I wanted to write. On sunny days I could be found on the garden patio outside my French doors which offered its own source of relaxed inspiration. Another gift was that wine and beer were no longer fueling my work. A glass was now a welcome reward at dinner or at the pub at the end of a solid day's effort.

There was a small knock at my half-open door followed by the soft Scottish voice of our house manager, "Miss Hunter?"

Mrs. Iris Clarke was a lovely woman in her early sixties but unlike Miss Betty, the house manager at Crichton House on Loch Leven, had no divided loyalties between Liam and his ex-wife Sarah. She was a warm, motherly figure in our home and managed her job duties well. Everything was clean and stocked just the way we preferred, and her presence was unintrusive and respectful. I thought I would be uncomfortable with someone coming in and out of the house during the week, but she has proven to be a quiet comfort for us both.

"Oh, come in, Mrs. Clarke!"

"I dinnae mean to disturb ye but wanted to let ye and Mr. Crichton know that Chef Dan has arrived."

"Oh wonderful! Thank you! I will wrap up everything here and join him straight away."

She backed out of the room as I hit save on my manuscript and leapt up to follow her eagerly down the long hall. I was keen to see my friend! Surely his presence this afternoon would be a reassuring comfort. Liam met me in the hall and kissed me quickly before we walked together into the kitchen where we found Dan unpacking a large cooler on wheels filled with our dinner provisions.

"LC! Miss Corrine!" Dan said walking toward us. Liam went to shake the man's hand and then they hugged each other. Dan immediately kissed me on each cheek and said, "I feel like I haven't seen you all in ages! It has been at least a month if not more, aye?"

"Aye! That is probably right," Liam said in agreement. "We haven't made it up to the house at Loch Leven in a while though we keep telling ourselves that we need to come back to Mythos and see how you are faring."

"It has been an adjustment for sure, but our first few reviews have been positive, and after a few growing pains which are typical for a new restaurant, we are starting to find our rhythm as a team. I am pleased!"

Liam patted the man on the arm and said, "I have seen some of those reviews and you should be proud! We commit to visiting again. You know that the lads are coming to stay here for a month, but I thought we would spend the last week at Crichton House. You know the loch and grounds are so beautiful during the summer!"

"Aye! Just give me a head's up! The garden patio is open, and I would love to have the lads see the restaurant and host you all."

"Of course!"

I chimed in and asked, changing the subject, "What have you prepared for us tonight, Chef?"

"Aye, Miss Corrine! It is pizza night at Edinburgh's *new* Crichton House!"

I laughed at the thought, and said, "Brilliant!"

The paved garden patio off the kitchen had a woodfired pizza oven along with the elaborate built-in grill, fridge, and stovetop. Nothing says interactive cooking like a make-your-own-pizza night. Liam said he wanted something casual that we could all do together, and he got it.

"I have the dough measured out for individual pizzas and all the sauces, toppings, and cheeses based on everyone's preferences here for you," Chef Dan said, as he handed me and Liam the small menu cards detailing all the topping choices, cooking instructions, and suggested combinations. "Miss Corrine, I hoped that by knowing some of your preferences that you have everything you need for a custom pizza."

"Chef, I see the prosciutto and black olives here on the list, so I am set! Well done!"

Liam smiled at me and shook his head, likely mocking my simple tastes. He said, "Dan, walk with me and let's ensure that I know what to do with the pizza oven. I would hate for my incompetence to be the reason no one has a properly cooked pizza tonight."

"Aye! It isn't as complicated as it looks, LC!"

+++

After the bell rang, Liam sat his pint glass down and took my hand as he said, "Even though I know you want to, you cannot hide here in the kitchen. You should join me at the door. Come with me, love."

He was right, but I was so nervous that I could not speak. I just walked quietly with him to the entryway. He let go of my hand to open the door where he was met instantly by two enthusiastic young lads who ran in and hugged him together. He kissed each of them on top of their heads over and over.

It was a heartwarming scene. I smiled broadly at their reunion and the genuine love that they shared. This family reunion had to be worth all the nerves and apprehension I carried for weeks. I knew that Liam was a loving father. He showed it every time he spoke about his sons, their individual accomplishments, or even about their talks during Sunday lunches together. But *seeing* Liam as a father before me for the first time made me only love him even more.

Just behind this loving trio stood Sarah Crichton and I swallowed deeply but desperately willed the smile to stay on my face. Liam kissed Sarah on the cheek and asked her as he shut the door, "You didn't have any trouble finding the house?"

"Not at all! Though parking is a bitch here. I completely gave up and blocked your garage. Why don't you have a gated drive?"

Liam and I both laughed at this as he said, "Well, then I guess there is no chance of a hasty retreat tonight! We've put in planning permission to remodel the garage, enhance the utility room, and gate the drive. It just hasn't been approved yet."

Pulling me forward, Liam said pointing to each of them I assume to help me know the difference between the boys, "Sarah, Eric, and Ewan, may I introduce you to Corrine Hunter?"

"It is a pleasure to meet you all," I said eagerly. I heard the pitch of my voice, and it was much higher than usual and much more Canadian in contrast to the four Scots standing before me. I tried to hide my obvious nervousness behind an enormous smile. In a way, I was relieved. I could no longer sit and worry about this first meeting. The first part was over, and they were all finally here in our house. Now we all just needed to survive the rest of the evening together.

We all shook hands before Sarah said, clearly willing kindness and graciousness from the same depths I was, "It is nice to meet you, Corrine."

I appreciated that Liam ignored the fact that technically Sarah and I had met during the unfortunate confrontation in Boots in May. Perhaps this was his way of ensuring we were both starting with a clean slate. For me, perhaps it was a chance to also show some forgiveness and grace. Like I told Liam at the pub, I hope Sarah got what she needed in the moment, but we all knew the truth. I *was not* the reason for their divorce, and I *did not* steal her husband.

Following their mother's lead, both young Eric and Ewan shook my hand politely. Ewan spoke for both boys and said sweetly, "It is nice to meet you, Miss Hunter."

"Corrine, please."

I hoped Sarah and Liam would forgive the informality. I know Ewan was simply being well-mannered and respectful in addressing me, but I could not imagine us all living under the same roof and having them call me *Miss Hunter*, like a schoolteacher, constantly.

Ewan and Eric Crichton were handsome and tall, like their father. They had his gold-flecked, hazel eyes and the three standing before me made a decidedly handsome trio. I smiled imagining Liam being of the same age. I could instantly see the difference between the twins and knew that I would have no problem telling them apart.

As much as they looked alike, Liam's descriptions of them were accurate. Ewan was clearly bigger and had a much more athletic build than his brother. His sporting look was enhanced even more as he was dressed in a Scottish rugby jersey, shorts, and trainers. Eric was smartly dressed in a lime green Ralph Lauren Polo shirt, khaki shorts, and loafers. Upon first impressions, I liked them both. I might have some work to do to win them over in the end, but our first meeting seemed to be positive. As Liam reminded me, we should build on the positive.

"Leave your bags here at the bottom of the stairs, lads. I will take you all on the quick tour of the house so you can get your bearings and then I think we must see your new rooms upstairs!"

"We cannae wait, Da! You stopped sending us photos and we are dying to see our bedrooms!" Ewan said, eagerly, almost bouncing on his toes.

Sarah added, "Aye! They are so excited! It is all these two talked about on the drive here."

I chimed in and said, "I am dying to see them too!"

Ewan asked innocently, "You haven't seen them, Miss Corrine?"

"No! I mean, I saw the early work that you did but only your father has seen the final version of each room. He felt like you should be the next to see them and determine how your visions came to life! But I promised Colin I would let him know what you think when you do."

I turned to Sarah and explained, "You may already know this, Sarah, but my friend from London Colin Peterson designed the house and worked with the boys and Liam on their bedrooms."

"Yes, I know," she said somewhat flatly before looking at her boys and correcting her words and her tone. "Erm, I saw the questionnaire and thought it was brilliant. I loved that Colin and Liam involved the lads in planning. They are of an age now to have more of a say in their rooms. We are *all* excited to see what they created together. Aren't we lads?"

"Aye, mum," the boys said together in agreement.

I smiled at Sarah and tried to imagine that even though she was the one to file for divorce first, this evening still had to be awkward for her as well. Here she stands in the house her ex-husband now shares with another woman. A woman he moved on with the instant their divorce was final. A woman she confronted aggressively in public months ago. But I could also see that while we were both nervous, we were trying to be calm and cordial for her sons. There was some sort of silent agreement on that shared goal between all the adults standing in this entry hall.

Liam conducted his house tour much like he did for Tom and Elaine pointing out all the rooms on the ground floor, including the large primary suite, which thankfully we did not linger in. We spent a bit more time in the large open kitchen and living space as everyone caught up with Chef Dan and then marveled about the view to the garden and patio. We quickly noted the formal dining room along with a sizable butler's pantry, powder room, and the utility and laundry room off the garage. Liam told the boys that they were responsible for bringing down their own dirty laundry in the baskets from their ensuites. Mrs. Clarke would leave their clean clothes for them to pick up there and return to their rooms on their own.

The opposite end of the house was fitted with a large guest suite, complete with a sitting room, and large ensuite bath. It was right next to my study. Much like the house on Loch Leven, the sitting area had a small bar and coffee station. I loved that bedroom and joked with Liam when we moved in that if he ever angered me, I would essentially occupy my own wing of the house.

Outside the suite, Eric said dismissively, "Och, that looks like a *girl's* room!"

On occasion Sarah just politely said, "That is lovely." But I could not tell if she meant it or was just trying to fill in the awkward silences during our house tour.

Eric was about to burst and finally asked his father bouncing on his toes much like his brother, "Can we go upstairs *now*!?"

We quickly looked at two more large guest rooms with ensuites upstairs, and a small window nook in the hall that looked like a cozy spot to read a book on a rainy day. It was, in fact, surrounded by bookshelves. Colin added my own novels amongst the remaining books that did not fit on the shelves in my study. I smiled in appreciation of my friend's show of solidarity and support.

Finally, we found ourselves standing outside Eric's door. Sarah and I looked at each other and couldn't help but smile as Liam opened the door and ushered the lad in. We all gave him a moment and then followed the happy boy into his new room.

Eric just stood there surveying his surroundings with his mouth and eyes wide open. He could not speak he was so in awe. I winked at Liam signaling we might have a winner with this one.

The room was a neutral and comforting mix of ivory, gray, and tan. It felt modern but in a subdued way. Pops of green in pillows and woven, woolen throws made the room feel like it belonged in any of the fine hotels I choose to stay in. The subtle color palette amplified the colorful art on the walls—all Eric's own creation. Liam saved and framed everything his son made for him, and the room served not just as his bedroom but as a mini gallery for the young artist. We watched Eric and Ewan eagerly go from one corner of the room to the next together in amazement!

"Da, I love it!" Eric said as he hugged his father. Sarah and Liam shared a glance and a quick smile. Despite everything, they love their sons. In our short time together, I could tell that there was no doubt about that.

"I am not sure if you noticed on our tour lad, but I placed my favorite painting, one of your Edinburgh Castle acrylics, in the dining room."

"No! I missed it! I will look again when we go back downstairs!"

Ewan patted Eric on the shoulder and said, "This room is *so you!*"

Eric had a wall mounted television, a desk with computer, and gaming station, along with a full painting area near the window. It looked out to the same back garden view I have from my study on the floor below. It had an easel, an assortment of papers and canvases, brushes, and paints. He went straight there and marveled at everything. Even his ensuite bathroom was a wonder. Like ours, he had a heated tile floor along with built-in audio and television in the room.

Sarah and I gravitated back to the gallery wall together. The artwork was impressive. Eric Crichton had a natural talent and a boy of his age and skill could only continue to improve over time. He was prolific across mediums and while he was still determining his own artistic style, his love of Scotland's landscapes and castles was apparent. They served as the primary focus for his work on display.

I said softly to Sarah, standing next to me, *"You must be so proud."*

She just nodded. I chose to believe that she was not ignoring me in the conversation, but that perhaps she could not speak to me without emotion. I do the same thing, so I tried to give her some grace. I could tell she was proud of her son and his impressive artwork in his new bedroom. She wiped a tear from her cheek before turning around to her son and said, "This is incredible isn't it, love?"

Eric hugged his mother with sincere and loving gratitude as he said, "Aye, Mum! I love it! Thank you, Da! Thank you! I cannot wait to sleep here tonight but it is so perfect I do not want to mess it up!"

We all laughed with him, but his sentiment was sincere. The lad was happy with his room, and I could see every bit of that happiness and pride in Liam's own face. He was proud of his son and the bedroom they created together.

"Should we share with Colin? He is dying to know about the room reveals today and has already texted me in anticipation!" I asked as I brought my phone out of my pocket.

"Aye! Miss Corrine, can you please send the photos to me so I can share them with my friends?"

"Of course, but you must have that impressive art gallery in the background of at least one picture!"

I took the photo of a happy lad with his original paintings behind him as he held his arms as wide as his grin. I took another of him sitting on his bed so I could get a wider shot of the rest of the beautiful room. We exchanged mobile numbers so that I could send the images to him directly.

"Are we ready for the next room reveal?" Liam asked, ushering us back to the main hall as Ewan's room was just across from Eric's.

Ewan started bouncing up and down and yelled, "Aye, Da!"

As soon as Liam opened the door, the boy yelled, "I LOOOOOVE IT!"

We all laughed as he eagerly ran into the room looking at and touching everything. The room was in stark contrast to his brother's and suited the lad perfectly. This was exactly what I expected for the bedroom of a fourteen-year-old boy. It was decorated in brighter hues of Scottish blue and white with subtle accents of navy and gray. It looked modern but with a sporty edge. His gallery wall was filled with what looked like every rugby jersey the lad had ever worn. At the center of a sea of Crichton jerseys was a large framed Scottish Rugby jersey signed by Stuart Hogg.

I could appreciate that a proud father saved his son's team jerseys but knew little of Scottish National Rugby. Ewan politely explained to me, "Miss Corrine, Stuart Hogg is a full-back. He plays for Exeter but is a brilliant player for Scotland! He will retire after the Rugby World Cup in France this year. I never expected to see his signed jersey on the wall, but he is why I wore mine today. I knew it would be perfect for what I told Da and Colin!"

I realized in that instant that young Ewan Crichton inherited all his father's Scottish charm and thought his explanation to me was his own way to bring me into his world. He helped put me at ease and I silently thanked him for it. I smiled at Liam across the room and hoped he saw the same kindness in his son that I did at that moment.

We all laughed at his coordinated outfit as I said, "Oh my! Thank you for giving me more rugby insight. This must be an important jersey then."

"Aye! It is! I never expected it!"

Liam just looked at me and said, "I pulled in a favor and thought it would be perfect for the room."

"Looking at this wall Ewan, I believe you planned your attire—and your room—*perfectly*!"

"Aye! I did! Can you believe it? I match my own room! Miss Corrine, let's take some photos for Colin!"

"You got it! And I will send them to your father so your parents can have them as well! Colin will be so pleased that you are both happy!"

I spent a few moments on my phone sending images of the room to Ewan, Colin, and Liam as the boys ran back and forth sharing what they loved about each room and discovering new features and wonders with each trip.

Sarah politely said to me, "If the lads will be here, in this house, then you should have my mobile as well."

"Of course, and you should have mine!" She was correct that we should not solely rely on Liam as a middleman, but I was still shocked she offered. We exchanged numbers and she quickly confirmed that she received the images of the boys in their new rooms.

She finally said, patting Liam on the arm, "The rooms are lovely! I am happy that the lads will be comfortable here."

+++

FIVE
A New Family

When we returned downstairs to the kitchen, Chef Dan had left us for the evening. We had instructions and all the ingredients well-placed on the kitchen island with floured boards set for each of us to create our own pizzas. He even left me and Liam a small notecard that wished us good luck this evening.

"Dan is incredible, isn't he?" I asked, touching Liam's arm for a moment of connection, and offering a subtle sign that I thought that all was going well so far.

"The man certainly is," Liam said in agreement.

The boys were still talking to each other about their rooms. Eric took a minute to go back with his brother and mother to the dining room to see his large painting of Edinburgh Castle holding pride of place over the sideboard.

While they were gone, Liam said as he kissed my cheek, "Let me check the pizza oven and you can lead the drinks."

Liam was reassuring me that I had a role to play here as hostess for our guests. I could tell he was also happy with the way things were progressing so far.

When the others returned from the dining room I asked immediately, "Sarah, may I offer you a glass of wine, a pint, or anything else to drink?"

"Aye, I think a glass of wine would be lovely. I will have whatever you are having."

"I have a Sancerre here in the chiller. What do you think?"

"Perfect!"

I knew that she likely preferred a Chardonnay but thankfully did not ask for one as we do not have that varietal in the wine cellar of this house. I like my white wine, but I do not care for Chardonnay.

Liam chimed in saying, "Corrine, I'll take a pint and will find out what the lads want."

+++

Once we all secured our drinks, Liam set about informing us of all of Chef Dan's instructions for making our custom pizzas from the printed menu cards. He pointed out each of the ingredients in the middle of the island between us. It was quite an assortment! He also noted that we had a Romaine salad which we could incorporate any of the toppings in to customize as well. And to follow, we had a platter with a variety of small cannoli bites and cheeses for dessert.

Sarah said over her glass, "This is so great because it is interactive and doesn't need a chef, but I must admit that it's an unexpected choice as you *hate* pizza, Liam!"

Before I could even think, I said loudly across the island, "What kind of person *hates* pizza?"

Sarah immediately smirked upon my words said with incredulity. Liam looked at me in a way that told me this was a point of judgment he did not expect. But it was something about him that I did not know until now, and I was genuinely shocked by the revelation. I mean this is the man that taught me that sometimes you just want a beer with a friend. What is better for a casual supper than pizza?

I tried to redeem myself and said, "Perhaps, you just need to find the combination that works for you! Dan has given you many appetizing options here on his menu card."

I think I was forgiven as he said laughing, "Wait until you see what these two lads put on a pizza, and you will understand my aversion."

Sarah and I both laughed with him as he said, "I can only cook one at a time? Who is first? Eric?"

"Aye, Da! Here you go! Mine was easy to make!"

I leaned across the island and asked, "Alright! What do we have here for the first pizza?"

"It is a pineapple and ham pizza," he said proudly as his father and I both immediately made a face clearly hesitant about his choice of a Hawaiian pizza.

"Well, Eric, I might have to agree with your father on this one."

"You are both *wrong*! It is *so good*!"

I said back to the boy, "Then you can thank Chef Dan for those options! He clearly knows your preference."

I knew that I would never have to fully plan for a single meal in any of Liam's houses on my own. But pineapple and ham would not be first on my ingredient list for make-your-own pizza night. Now I know!

"I will take this *monstrosity* to the pizza oven. It only needs six to eight minutes according to Chef Dan. Decide amongst yourselves who is next, so it is ready when I come back."

Liam left me and Sarah with the boys and suddenly took some of the conciliatory air out of the room with his departure. We all fell into an awkward silence.

It took a moment before I could say, "You should be next Ewan! The adults can wait. What have you prepared for yourself?"

"I made a pizza pie of meat and cheese. I love the ham, pepperoni, and spicy sausage especially!"

The lad's pizza dough was laden with an absurd amount of meat to the point that I am not certain how it would even bake. Not to mention it did not have any sauce. None. It was literally meat and pizza dough with a smattering of cheese on top. If this concoction baked in the oven at all, it would most certainly be filled with grease. Now I understand! If I were Liam navigating pizza with these two, I don't think I would be a fan of it either.

I joked about the meat pie with Sarah and said, "If this thing *bakes at all*, we are after Ewan! What have you selected?"

"I have a white pizza with feta, tomatoes, kalamata olives, artichoke hearts, and red onion."

"A Mediterranean pizza! Alright! Alright! Finally, that is a combination I can support!"

"As you know, Dan is a master of Mediterranean cuisine. He made it for me once and I instantly fell in love with the flavors. Now, whenever I have pizza, I find that I choose a Greek combination first. And you?"

"I have gone a tad more Italian with a simple pizza with tomato sauce, mozzarella, prosciutto, and black olives."

Sarah nodded and said politely, "That does sound good."

"It is simple compared to everyone else's. But I will add red pepper flakes to it when it comes out of the oven to give it some heat. Like you said, I have tried other things, but find I gravitate to this combination time and again."

Liam came back in with Eric's perfectly cooked pizza, looked instantly at Ewan's, and said, "Och! Christ above, son! Mum and Miss Corrine will never get a pizza trying to bake this thing!"

Ewan laughed and instantly high-fived his brother. In that moment, I wondered how much of his creation was based on his own preference or perhaps a cheeky attempt at testing his father's ability to manage the woodfire pizza oven on his own.

Before walking out, Liam said as he passed me, "Take note, Corrine!"

Liam managed beautifully, and I cannot confirm it, but he may have stripped the pizza of a few layers of meat before baking the thing. I admired him for cooking all our pizzas when he could have asked Chef Dan to do it. He wanted to do this for us all and so far, seemed to be faring quite well as our executive chef for the evening.

Once the boys had pizzas and sodas in hand, I cleaned up their preparation boards. It appeared we were all comfortable with pizza night on the island and not the dining room. I always said the kitchen was the heart of every home and wanted to stay here myself. It kept our evening as casual as the meal we were sharing. Sarah insisted at some point that each boy add some salad to their plate. They did so willingly, while almost replicating their pizza choices on top, but I made note of the expectation.

"Liam, please take Sarah's next and I will refresh our drinks."

"Go ahead and put some ice in mine like you have, Corrine. Liam going in and out to the garden has brought the summer air in and made it warm, hasn't it?"

I appreciated her attempt at small talk and desperately needed a task since the boys were eating and she and I were just waiting for pizzas. I said, "Of course! I will place the Pellegrino here just in case you want a full spritzer or some sparkling water on the side."

Liam delivered Sarah's pizza and said, "Only two left!"

I quickly cleaned up Sarah's area and delivered her plate, cutlery, and napkin as I said, "Please, eat it while it is hot, Sarah. No need for formality tonight. Ours will be ready shortly."

"Thank you," she said as she also added salad to her plate.

"And how are you boys doing?" I asked.

"It is *so… good!*" Ewan said nearly choking on his bite. Eric also had a mouth filled with pizza and just nodded his head in agreement. It was too early to judge the evening, but I happily took two boys thrilled with their rooms and filled with pizza as a positive. Liam asked me to build on the positive and I accepted every bit of positive surrounding us tonight.

"I am glad. If you want anything else to drink, you can get it in the drink cooler there next to the fridge. There is a larger one in the butler's pantry if you do not see what you want."

Liam tried to bake our pizzas together and I think his simple Margherita pizza got a little dark in the back of the oven, but we could all finally sit together. If all five of us did not have mouths filled with pizza and salad, I would have thought the silence uncomfortable. Everyone seemed happy and content with their supper.

As soon as the boys finished their meal, they leapt up and Eric asked, "Da, can we go back to our rooms?"

"What are you supposed to say and do when you leave the table?" he asked in return.

Both said reluctantly and in unison, *"May we be excused?"*

"Aye! Dishes in the sink please."

I took note of this point of parenting and the expectations of manners. I respected it immensely. I would have offered to help put away any pizza leftovers for them, but neither boy had anything left on their plates. They both devoured every bit of the pizzas and salad they made. In some way, I was shocked these growing boys did not ask for more or even look at the dessert tray. I think their new rooms were a bigger draw than supper. Perhaps the boys knew they could raid the sweets later in the evening.

"You all had nothing left to save but Dan gave us a little extra of everything so if we want to try pizzas again tomorrow, we can."

"Thank you," Ewan said before the boys ran up the stairs. And I mean they *ran... up... the... stairs*. I think this might be one of the things I have to get used to with teen boys in the house. Once they left, Liam poured Sarah and I another glass of wine and sparkling water before he refilled his own pint.

I broke the silence between us and said, "I do not have children of my own, and I know this is awkward for us all, but may I ask you both a question?"

Liam and Sarah both looked at me in a way that made me nervous. They were clearly unsure what I might ask them. I took a large sip of my spritzer and continued, "I just witnessed one rule, if you want to call it that, on using manners to ask to be excused from the table and the expectation of clearing their own plates. I also freely offered the drinks cooler to them, but I should have asked you if that was appropriate. Do you have any other established rules and restrictions that I am not aware of? I want to respect and uphold them in this house."

Liam smiled at me in a way that showed he respected my question and that I was honoring him and Sarah as parents. I did not know much about teenage boys, but I did not want them to feel like this was a holiday house where no rules applied. I knew that I could rely on Liam to guide me, but I wanted Sarah to hear my request so that she could see my own respect for her role in raising these young men. She should tell me what she expected in the care of her sons.

Liam waited for Sarah to speak first, and she finally did.

"Thank you for asking. I am sure Liam will help you here as he is probably the stricter of us both."

I smiled at him, and he nodded his head in agreement as she continued, "The lads have been brought up with the expectation of being respectful to each other and kind and respectful to others, especially adults."

"Aye," Liam said in agreement. "These lads have *everything*, and they *know it*! There is much those two do not have to worry about. But I think Sarah will agree, we would be devastated as parents if they were so entitled that they could not be kind and respectful to others. They should use the manners they were taught. They should not be making any demands. And I do not care how many people work in our houses, they are not to expect that someone else cleans up after them all the time. This goes for what is expected at the dinner table, in the care of their rooms, and you heard what I said to them about their own laundry."

I nodded to them both just as Sarah added, "I appreciate you asking about the sodas. I tried for a long time to limit sugar and would still argue that should be the case. Especially with Ewan as he is so focused on his sports and of the two can get the most hyped up on caffeine and sugar. But as they have gotten older it has become more difficult to limit. It was easy when they were five to put a glass of milk in front of them and say that is it, lad! Drink up!"

Liam and I laughed instantly before he said, "Aye! As teenagers, they are more vocal and insistent on their own preferences. I think the only thing I would say is trust your gut, Corrine. You know what acceptable behavior is and not. They both showed you who they were today, and you will learn even more over time. You do not have to have all the keys to teen knowledge, nor do we all have to be best friends on day one."

"Thank you," I said laughing. "I think I am still nervous."

I raised my glass to the middle of the kitchen island. They both met my glass as I added, "But I thank you both for making me a little *less* nervous."

Sarah joined Liam upstairs to say goodnight to the boys. I chose to wait for them downstairs in the entryway. They did not need me hovering about during their farewells.

Sarah said at the door as she shook my hand, "Thank you for a lovely evening, Corrine."

"You are most welcome! You have my mobile if you need anything."

"Aye! And you have mine."

Liam walked Sarah out to her car, and I went back to the kitchen to put everything remaining in the fridge or the dishwasher before I made myself one more spritzer. It was a welcome respite after a long evening. Admittedly, this pour might have been a little wine-forward.

I do not know how to gauge the evening but celebrated that it was over, and we all survived. An ex-wife left our house without incident and two boys were enjoying their new rooms upstairs. I was not just relieved; I don't think I could feel any happier!

+++

"Well, that was an absolute triumph!" Liam exclaimed as he refreshed his pint once more, kissed my cheek, and sat next to me at the kitchen island. I could feel his relief because I shared it.

"We all survived at least. No one raised a voice, and you have two happy sons upstairs in their gorgeous rooms!"

"I knew that the rooms would be a hit."

"They are amazing! Colin is thrilled that they loved everything. I just texted and told him that the first thing they wanted to do after dinner was not dessert... it was to *go back* to their rooms."

"That is quite the endorsement! I think you will find that teenage boys mostly want to hang out in their rooms, and they sleep a lot. *A lot!* I bet they are up there playing Xbox. And they are probably playing together... while sat across the hall from each other!"

"Do you know what the best part of the night was for me?"

Liam did not answer my question but looked at me intently waiting for me to finish my thought. I stood up and took his face in my hands and kissed him passionately. "You have always been a proud father but to *see* you with your sons for the first time... was amazing! I could see how much love you have for them and how much they love and respect you in return. It made my heart so happy! I did not think I could love you more."

"Och, my love, thank you! Let's go to bed."

We got ready for bed and Liam checked that all was set on the security cameras and monitors. We had to keep the motion detectors off since the boys could come downstairs at any time and realized that we never discussed the security system in detail with them. They do not even have a passcode.

Once in bed, Liam kissed me and started pulling up my night shirt as he made his way up my thigh. I stopped him as I whispered, *"No... Liam, your sons are in the house."*

"They will be with us for a month, Corrine!"

He was only slightly joking, but his incredulity was laced with the slightest fear that I might be saying sex was off limits in a full house. A house that would be full for a month.

"It is their first night in a new house and I am certain it will take some getting used to."

"They are fourteen, not four! Believe me! These two can adapt," he said while kissing my neck and working his way down my chest.

Before I could respond to his welcome attention, there was a polite knock at the door followed by a soft voice who asked, *"Da? Da, are you awake?"*

I tilted my head toward Liam with some sense of vindication as the unexpected visitor just proved my assumption. Liam wrenched his face and bowed his head to my chest as he whispered, *"Christ above! I have just been cockblocked by my own son!"*

I laughed at his ridiculous statement and said patting his head, "Get up and go to him, silly!"

Liam opened the door to young Eric who looked at me and then his father multiple times before finally saying, "Da... erm... I need some water."

"Aye! Come with me, lad!"

+++

I almost fell asleep twice while waiting for Liam to come back to our bedroom. After about thirty minutes I began to worry about what could be keeping him.

I immediately sat up as Liam finally opened the door and asked, "Is everything alright?"

"Just give me a moment, love."

Liam walked into the bathroom. But, when he finally came to bed, he just sat on the edge next to me instead of getting in. I could tell he was unsettled. I could tell he was emotional.

"What is it?"

Liam sat silently for a minute and shook his head. He clearly could not find the words he needed.

I put my hand on his knee and asked again, "Your silence is making me uncomfortable. *What is it, love?*"

"I just had a very *interesting* conversation with Eric."

"And?"

It took Liam a moment. I could tell he was processing everything that they talked about, but his prolonged silence along with the pained look on his face was unnerving.

"Babe, is Eric alright? Is he not feeling well? Is he not comfortable in his new bedroom?"

"He is fine," Liam said with a deep sigh. "I showed the lad how to get the filtered water from the dispenser in the fridge and he was noticeably quiet. I knew today was an adjustment, so I decided to walk him back to his room. I helped him get into bed and showed him that we could modify the light levels on the panel if he needed since it was the first night in a new place. I rambled on about when we stay in hotels for the first time or return to a house we haven't been in for a while… it just takes some getting used to."

"Of course," I said in agreement. "I am fifty but still sometimes leave the light on in the bathroom my first night in a hotel. Just as you said, it takes some getting used to new surroundings."

"That was not it."

"*Oh.*"

"The lad asked… why *you*… were in *my* room."

"Wait! *What?*"

Liam just looked at me but did not answer my question.

"You told them about me last December, right?"

"Aye, I asked the lad what he thought when we talked last Christmas, and he told me that I said you were my *friend*. Love, I *did* say that word. We had not even been together for a month at that point and whilst things were moving quickly; they were so new. I did not know how the lads would react to the news of a new woman in my life so soon after the divorce."

I just looked at him and nodded as he added, "You also know that I cannot say words like *boyfriend* and *girlfriend*."

"I do and I agree! It sounds like we are teenagers ourselves. And who after only three weeks together wants to say a word like *lover* to a teen boy?"

"I don't think I could say that word to them no matter how long we are together," he said laughing. "But something about that conversation, the Christmas hamper you sent, and even my words about you over the last several months have not connected for him in *any* way. I have tried to understand it, but the lad believed that you were my *friend*. He seemed genuinely shocked that we were in a relationship that was anything more than that! He only saw *friendship*."

I looked at Liam with narrowed eyes trying my best to understand a young boy's mind and how after six months, he could not understand that his father had a new love. As much apprehension as I had initially about the prospect, perhaps we should have all met before these boys were in this house with us.

Liam continued, "Remember on the tour when we saw the guest suite next to your study and he commented that it looked like a girl's room? He somehow thought it *was ... your... room*."

"I remember him saying that but took it as a remark about the décor of the room. It does have a lot of floral."

We sat silently for a moment as we agreed the room décor did look more feminine. Finally, I said, "All of this confuses me. Are we just friends and roommates then? You are an incredibly successful man, why would he think you would have your *friend* living here? To help you pay for the utilities?"

"I asked the exact same thing," he said laughing. "Remind me to send you a bill."

"I dare you, mister!" I said laughing back with him. I took his hand in mine. Despite his humor, I could tell he was still unsettled.

"I don't know how it did not register for the lad in all our discussions, but somehow, he thought it was *your room*. So... he was shocked to see you in here... and..."

"*Oh, God!*"

I am not sure I wanted to hear the rest, but somehow, I knew what was coming for us both.

"He then asked if we sleep together in the same room.... well... more specifically... he asked if sleeping together meant that we have... sex."

I buried my face in my hands as I said, *"I am mortified!"*

"I answered him honestly that you were my *partner* and that I loved you. He just stared at me blankly and finally I had to say you were my *girlfriend* because he still seemed unsure based on my word choice. Corrine, no other words seemed to resonate for him!"

We sat in both stunned silence and shared embarrassment as Liam continued, "I told him that we do have sex and then he asked about us not being married."

"Really?"

"When the lads were much younger, I was tasked with answering the *how babies are made* question and apparently, I mentioned being married as a condition. I think I blacked out during that talk, to be honest, but could have said it if for no other reason than I was married at the time. And perhaps I didn't want either of them to think that they should be having sex the minute they started dating. There is a responsibility in raising lads! I have answered many questions since and have spoken of consent, love, respect... but if I added *marriage* to the mix in that first conversation... then I suppose I did."

I just nodded to him as he declared, almost in resignation, "Christ above! No one prepares you for having that conversation with your own children! But this lad seems to remember every word I said that day!"

I quickly kissed his cheek in support. For all the things that are supremely natural, there are still many parts of life that we have made difficult and uncomfortable to talk about. Facts and biological science are weighted with responsibility and often these parts of life are shrouded in secrecy or shame by a lack of honest and open communication. That goes especially for our bodies, reproductive health, and sexual pleasure. I couldn't imagine having to explain it all to another myself.

"I understand," I said. This is my typical reply when I cannot find my words and need a moment to collect my feelings and thoughts. I have learned over time that Liam is frustrated by this non-response, but I said the words anyway. I tried to correct myself and asked, "What did he say after that confession?"

"The lad asked if I was going to marry you, and I told him that I hoped to, but had no timeline for such a thing. And then he asked... he asked through tears that broke my heart, love... if I would have more children in my *new family*."

"Oh, Liam! The poor boy!"

"I know," he said as we both teared up at the thought of his son's genuine fear and sorrow that Liam moving on with a new love meant leaving his sons behind or worse yet... that they could be replaced. I got up to get tissues from the bathroom.

When I returned, I stood before him on the bed. I ran my hands through his thick hair and hugged him tight with his head to my chest as I said softly, *"You know that ship has sailed."*

"It has for both of us! With much admiration for our friend Luke, who is roughly my age, I do not want to be nearly sixty years older than a child. But it broke my heart that the lad saw our being together could potentially result in replacing him and his brother. His words and his tears about a *new family* knocked me back on my heels."

Seated on the bed and with his head still resting on my chest, Liam put his arms around my waist trying to temper his own emotions. He was holding on to me for comfort and reassurance. I held him hoping I could offer what he needed. Finally, I said softly over the top of his head, *"Listen* to me! You know that the lad has gone through a great deal of change in the last year. Some children of divorce often secretly hope that their parents will find a way to get back together. Your clarification today and my being here probably made him realize that fantasy was not going to happen. It had to hurt him."

"*Aye,*" he said with an exhausted and emotional sigh.

"*And as a teenager, he may also be thinking more about sex and what that means in terms of connections and consequences... like babies. We think they all understand everything in this modern world, but clearly Eric is still quite innocent and naïve.*"

Liam just held onto me and nodded his head in agreement as I continued, "*What I love most is the honest conversation you had with your son.*"

"I agree. As awkward as it all was, it was honest and open. I appreciate that. I do."

I kissed the top of his head before moving back to bed and asked as I slipped under the duvet, "Do you think Ewan has the same questions?"

"None that I have seen or heard yet. Remember he told me that he could tell I was happier."

"Yes, but that was an honest observation of *your* demeanor and behavior. That could be a result of the divorce being final or a new *friend* could make you happy as well."

"Fair. Honestly, between the two of them, Ewan is the last one I would worry about. He has always been perceptive and aware. He was the first-born and is the more mature of the two. Sometimes to the point of causing me more worry as a father, especially where lasses are involved. He alone may be the reason I added marriage to *the talk.*"

I laughed for a moment at his words. The lad had already proven that he had every bit of his father's charm, so I did not question Liam's assessment of his son.

"Will you speak to Sarah about Eric's questions?"

"Aye! I will call her in the morning and see what she thinks. I do think the lad's confusion shows that perhaps she has said little to them about her own opinion of us and our relationship."

"Perhaps like us, she assumed they understood the situation. Though I do appreciate she hasn't made me out to be a whore to them both."

"I should expect that he may also want to speak to her about this arrangement and I do not want her to be blindsided. I also want her to know what I said to the lad."

"And at some point, should she find a new love herself, she could get the same questions and concerns... about a new family, I mean. He may need some reassurance from both of his parents."

"Aye," he said in resignation. "We will just go forward with this understanding. The lads will see us together over the next four weeks. Subtlety and vague words are not going to work with this lot, especially Eric. While we are not married, I want you to remember that this is your house. We should behave respectfully but we need to be clear that we are in a relationship and love each other. We are *not* just roommates!"

"I agree, and I do love you. Come to bed."

"Och, my darlin'! You must know I love you more!"

I held Liam tight until he finally fell asleep. We were both emotionally spent with the events of the day. As I drifted off to sleep myself, I realized that this first summer with Liam's sons may be more challenging and complicated than I ever imagined.

+++

SIX
A Missed Birthday

Crichton House
Edinburgh, Scotland
July 2023

Our first weeks together were uneventful after Eric's confusion about the relationship between his father and me. Liam was right. Teenage boys like to keep to themselves and do in fact sleep a lot! On occasion, they had friends over to the house to play Xbox or football in the garden but that was about it. In the beginning, Liam was insistent that we should have supper together and try to talk or watch movies after, but most days, Eric and Ewan were not particularly interested. I took no offense as this would be my expectation of teenagers. We planned to take our final week with the boys at Loch Leven free of the pressures of business empires and novels.

I walked into the kitchen, laptop in hand, with the simple goal of finishing my current chapter before Liam got home. He had been working so much lately on another deal that I missed the man and wanted to greet him the moment he walked into the house. Unexpectedly, I found Chef Dan and the boys gathered around the island.

"Hello friend! I did not expect to see you here today!"

"Aye, Miss Corrine!" Dan said as he kissed me on each cheek before handing me a piece of fresh-baked bread. The man learned over time that I was a sucker for the simple delights of bread and butter. I tried to limit it as much as I could, but I could not turn down the gift of warm bread and creamy, salted butter this afternoon. "I didna expect to see you either! The lads texted and asked me to do something special for LC's birthday."

"Of course," I said calmly while simultaneously realizing that I had absolutely no idea when Liam's birthday was. I felt the red-hot embarrassment flood my cheeks as it must be today... July twenty-fourth.

"And what did you clever lads decide?"

Eric read my falsehood instantly and asked incredulously... and quite loudly across the island, "You *live here* but *don't know* when Da's birthday is?!"

His question, coupled with the subsequent shared laughter between the brothers at my ignorance took all the air out of my lungs and forced even more blood to my cheeks. I could not respond to either of them. I could not look at either of them. I just stared at Dan with wide eyes, silently willing him to save me from this moment of utter humiliation being served unapologetically by two fourteen-year-old boys.

I breathed in anxiously as Dan said with a reassuring smile, "We are going to make LC's favorite grilled langoustines. I thought you would be at the house on Loch Leven. The lads told me it was supper for three tonight."

"You are right! *Just three*. I am on my way to the lake house so tell me you have some cheese and crackers for me, or I can stop at Tesco along the way," I said with a forced smile. I prayed the boys would not say another word or I would surely start to cry.

"You should be set! I helped Chef Stephan get used to everything in the pantry, kitchen, and wine cellar along with everyone's preferences, so we did inventory and some shopping ahead of your arrival on Friday. Outside of fresh deliveries planned for tomorrow the house is well-stocked. I apologize that I did not ask directly about you being there early or I would have done more for you tonight myself before coming here. I would also be more than happy to call the restaurant and have something delivered to the house, if you want."

"No, no. You have done more than enough, Chef! Liam will love having a special birthday dinner with his sons, and you know he absolutely *loves* your langoustines! He deserves this celebratory feast!"

I walked out of the kitchen the instant I finished my words. I took my computer and placed it in my bag in the hall. I heard Dan call out to me on my way to the garage. I could not look back at the man. I just had to get into my car and leave this house and Edinburgh as quickly as possible. I had to leave the utter embarrassment and rejection I felt in that kitchen. I prayed on the drive that I had enough clothes in the wardrobe to get through the night.

+++

"Corrine!" Liam yelled as he entered the front door to Crichton House at Loch Leven. I leaned back in the barstool where I sat at the kitchen island with my wine and my computer to look toward the entryway and the man rushing frantically into the house.

"Why are you here, Liam?"

"I could ask you the same," he said as he stood in the kitchen instantly refilling my glass and securing his own. "Why didn't you answer your mobile or texts? You gave me absolute fits! I have been so worried that I rushed all the way here! It is a wonder I did not get pulled over by the police for speeding!"

I sat silently as Liam looked at me over his wine glass patiently waiting for me to answer his question. I could tell that he was genuinely worried about me. I intentionally left my phone in my bag because I knew he would be calling me the minute he arrived home and found out the birthday plan did not involve me. I could not speak to him for all the humiliation I felt, and I did not want to shame his sons in the process. I just bit my lip and stared at him.

I took another sip and finally asked my own question in response. I asked with tears forming in my eyes, "How did I not know today was your birthday?"

"Because my birthday is not important to me... other than I suppose I am grateful to have another one," he said laughing. I do love that this man tries to make me laugh when I get emotional. I could not help but smile and shake my head in rejection for the forgiveness he was offering me.

"I'm so ashamed," I said hanging my head low, unable to look at him.

"Why?"

"The boys knew, and I didn't, and they quickly made note of that fact in front of Dan. I feel like I failed you. I failed you all! This could have been something that we planned together for you. It could have been a point of connection between me and your sons... *for you!*"

"You did not fail anything!"

"You are being kind."

He saw my tears fall onto my cheeks and said before I could finish my thought, "Och darlin'! I *never* told you when my birthday was!"

"And I *never* asked!"

Dinner planning aside, I was mostly embarrassed that I did not acknowledge Liam's birthday myself. In fact, I was distraught most of the evening over that fact alone. My words were correct. I failed. In all our talks, I somehow knew that he would be fifty-seven on his next birthday and yet *never once* asked when that day would be. And if he told me at some point, clearly it did not register or find its way into my calendar. Some *girlfriend* I was!

"Dan tried to give me some grace... I know that! The minute I walked into the kitchen we both realized that I was not invited to supper, and I had to leave. The boys... they not only knew what I did not, but they had a plan. They just had not figured out what to do with me, so I helped them by taking myself out of the equation. And honestly, if for no other reason than to save both me and Dan from the crippling embarrassment that only seemed to grow by the minute!"

"Dan called me in the car on my way home and told me what happened. He was... let me say... *uncomfortable* with the situation. You know that I respect the man as a friend. He had known my lads since they were about nine and he knew that they had not been honest with him... or you... about supper. He never said his words in judgment or criticism, but I appreciated him telling me the truth from his perspective so I would be aware of what I was about to walk into. He was also worried about you because he knew you left the house hurt and embarrassed."

I sighed and nodded as another tear fell onto my cheek. I know that Chef Dan was as shocked to see me as I was to see him. He knew that I left in an emotional state and Liam's words only proved my original assessment of the man. He could have bowed down to these boys and the money that supported them, but he did not because he has integrity. Like Liam, Chef Dan Garrett is an honorable man.

"When I arrived home, Dan had dutifully fulfilled his task and left us. I had a delicious meal waiting for me and two eager lads at the table in the dining room wishing me a happy birthday. I tried to accept what they offered with the genuine kindness it was given, but as soon as we started, I asked if we should wait for you to join us for supper. I could see there were only three place-settings but wanted them to answer my question. It took them a moment before Eric said you were on your way here, like it was all part of the plan. But I knew better! I knew there was no understanding between you. They just capitalized on the fact you removed yourself. Then Ewan added they wanted to be with me, just the three of us, and they knew I would only want Dan's cooking."

"That last part is completely fair!"

"Aye, it is!"

"I do not want your sons to feel like they did anything more than plan an incredible dinner, with your favorite chef and dear friend, *for you!* Their hearts were in the right place. It is not their fault I did not know today was your birthday."

"I appreciate you saying that, and everything the lads did, but I told them if we were to be in the house together, not including you or at least telling you what they wanted to do for me was not only unfair, but it was also *unkind*."

"*Love,*" I said shaking my head as he said the words.

"Let me tell you everything, Corrine," Liam said as he topped-off our glasses once more. I nodded to him. There was more to this story, and Liam needed me to listen to him. He wanted me to know everything. My understanding ended the minute I walked out of the house. I breathed in deep, sipped my wine, and tried to temper my emotions as he spoke the truth of the rest.

"I told the lads we could have had the same dinner together, just the three of us, but to not tell you that was their wish, was not fair. I admitted this was all new and explained we do not have to do everything together. I told them I appreciated time alone with them, but they should not make you feel excluded or uninvited and they did exactly that."

"How did *that* go over?"

"Eric was sad, and it showed on his face and in his silence. I am not sure how much was actual regret for their foolish plan or how much was reaction to my scolding them over birthday langoustines. Ewan, who is generally more vocal, tried to argue for a moment but could not find the words he needed. Finally, the lads agreed that they should have told you what they wanted to do for me. I told them you would have given them exactly what they wanted but they did not need to shame you."

"I would have," I whispered above my wine glass.

"I know, love! I reminded them that I met you in September of last year and we did not become a couple until December after the divorce was final. We dealt with holidays and other events but never had to deal with my birthday. It just somehow never came up in conversation. I told them that their plan also put Dan in an awkward position. How was he supposed to know you had no supper? His shock that you were there in the house at all was genuine!"

"I know that! I do! Honestly, Dan did his best to help me. He even tried to call me back into the house, but I *had* to leave!"

"I asked what they were thinking with this plan… did they honestly think you would never come out of your study when I came home?"

"I think I would have surely started crying if you were standing there in the kitchen."

"I wish I had been because I would have never let you leave like that! They clearly did not think their plan through."

"*I know.*"

"Eric then said you could have taken your plate to your study, and I never thought I could be more disappointed in the lad. It took everything I had to remain calm before them both, after hearing that blatant dismissal."

I felt the tears well up in my eyes again as he continued, "I asked him if he thought I would allow you to take a plate to your study in your own house? And the fact that both boys said yes saddened me. Eric said that you lived there and did not even know it was my birthday. He tried to shame you again... this time to me directly! I am not proud of it but admit I shamed them myself. I asked how they had been in the house for over three weeks and had not noticed once that you were allergic to shellfish and oftentimes could not have what we did for supper and certainly couldn't have langoustines."

"*Oh Liam,*" I whispered as I put my hands to my face trying my best to temper my red-hot cheeks and stop the tears from falling.

"The lads looked at each other and I said sarcastically that I guessed it *never... came up... in conversation*!"

I know Liam was frustrated with his sons and admired how he was defending me. But all the same, I regretted that we were even in this situation. The last few weeks had moments of expected awkwardness as we tried to get to know each other under the same roof, but it feels as if it all turned negative in the span of an afternoon.

"I told them that I hoped that their mum and I were raising young men that would be more considerate of someone else's feelings. Eric responded rudely by saying...well... something along the lines of... *Mum hates her too!*"

"They *hate* me? Is this what it is all about, Liam? Your sons *hate* me?"

"I told the lads they had just laid it all out and were finally being honest! It wasn't about being with me, it was about hurting you, and for that I was disappointed. I thanked them for the birthday dinner, and I told them I expected better from them as honorable Crichton men."

I hung my head and whispered through my tears once again, *"Oh, Liam!"*

"Then I said I would leave them to come here and bring you back to your own house. I told them they were old enough to figure out how to make it right with you. That is my expectation, Corrine. They are old enough to figure it out. I expect the lads to apologize to you in an acceptable and respectful manner... either as individuals or together."

"Do they... do they... really *hate* me?" I said through my own halting sobs. My heart was already broken with the shame of not knowing Liam's birthday, now it was even more so with this revelation. Despite a positive start, everything I feared seemed to be coming true.

"No, my love. Please do not cry. I think between Eric's confusion about our relationship and a shared need to protect their mum, they do have an opinion. Perhaps *resistance* is a better word. They have a *resistance* to the change happening around them. Sarah and I deserve that, not you! I also believe Ewan may be protecting his brother in some way, though he remained quiet toward the end. But no, I am not convinced either of their actions and feelings are *truly* hateful. Misguided, aye! But not hateful."

Liam's assessment was correct, this had nothing to do with me or anything I have or have not done in getting to know his sons. I was pitted against their mother from the start. Even if she were not glaring at me across a dinner table, we are not the same. I never expected that we would be, but somehow, we were all silently choosing sides and it made me sad because all sides put Liam square in the middle. Until we finally find a life together that works for us all, the poor man would always be in the middle of everyone he loved. My initial embarrassment and shame turned instantly to sorrow. I no longer cared about my own feelings. I only felt for Liam.

"Corrine, I know we are coming back here in a few days for the end of our summer holiday, but you cannot hide out here waiting for us. We must go to Edinburgh tonight. I told the lads I would bring you back to your own house... and *I will!* We will retrieve your car when we come back at the weekend.. I will text Miss Betty and have it cleaned and stored in the garage until then."

Liam set expectations with his sons, but he was doing the same with me. He was asking me to let this nonsense go for the moment. I needed to let it all go and find the strength to walk back into our house with my head held high and not with the immense shame I walked out with. I nodded in agreement as I joked, "Well, from here on out, I guess I will never forget your birthday! I should have known you were a Leo!"

"Why is that?"

"A Leo is a natural leader, highly confident, and passionate. We are an incredible duo... a Libra and a Leo!"

Liam walked to my chair and put his hands around my face as he kissed me. He said softly, *"I am sorry about today, my love!* You have done everything that you could to get to know my sons and I am sorry they hurt you."

"I will live. We are all adjusting to something we have never had to deal with before. All of us! Clearly, we just need more time to figure it all out… to figure each other out."

He kissed me again and put his forehead to mine. He whispered, *"Before we go home, I would like a moment with you alone if you would not mind… and in a house not filled with lads."*

"I was hoping you would say that!" I said, kissing his cheek and then his neck as I ran my hands slowly down his back. *"Considering I did not know today was your birthday, I have little else to offer!"*

"Corrine!" Liam lightly scolded me as he took me by the hand, and we laughed together all the way to the bedroom.

It was true! I had no other gifts to offer the man I loved on his birthday and to be honest, also welcomed that we had this house to ourselves for a moment.

+++

SEVEN
What Happened To Corrine Hunter?

Crichton House
Edinburgh, Scotland
July 2023

I eagerly accepted the unexpected and early morning call on my mobile phone. I was standing in the kitchen with Liam as we were both trying to wake up with our morning tea and toast. Mrs. Clarke, our house manager, had not yet arrived for the day and Liam's sons were still sound asleep upstairs. Much like our time before the fire at the end of the evening at Loch Leven, we found that the quiet mornings together in the city, especially with a full house, to be a suitable alternative. I put the call on the speaker so he could hear what I did.

"Good morning, Kate!"

"Hello, my darling!"

"Please tell me how you are feeling, love!"

"I am well! We are counting down... just two months to go! I feel strong but weary at the same time. Pregnancy is a miraculous thing, but at this stage it is mostly... *exhausting*! My God! I only want to sleep but cannot get in a comfortable position to sleep, so I feel even more tired. I suspect Luke feels the same as I toss and turn throughout the night. I feel for the man and have some sorrow that he must seek respite in one of our guest rooms ahead of busy days at the hospital."

I laughed at the end as I said, "I am sorry to hear that, but I suppose you are both preparing yourselves for sleepless nights with a newborn. I am glad to hear you are healthy, though! Remind me... when do you go on leave?"

"At this rate, probably when I am giving birth!"

"Kate! Don't say that! You must take care."

"Well, first, you know me! I do not know what to do if I am not working. I also have a bugger of a new novel to publish and then I can finally focus on my family."

I knew Kate was being cheeky with me and I also knew that she had more to say. I smiled at Liam as I said, "Well, let me not add to your stress level today. What has prompted this morning's call?"

"Corrie, my darling, I know it is early, but I could not wait! Your first review for *The Old Boys* came in from Patricia Brookside at *The Guardian*."

I knew who Patricia was, as she was one of the harshest critics of my last two novels. While I was proud of my latest, I was uncertain about the plan for hers to be the first published review. There will always be a spectrum of feedback for a novel, but initial pick-up from the first review will generally follow the original in sentiment and tone. Patricia Brookside could determine how this novel performs from the very moment her review posts. If she still has a negative opinion of me or my writing, I could be doomed from the very start.

"As you know, based on her reviews of your last two novels, we chose to give her exclusivity for the first post. We saw this novel as a point of redemption and the offer as appreciation for her viewpoint as a well-respected voice in the media."

"Understood," I said staring at Liam hoping he could feel my nervous reticence.

"Patricia's review will be posted online at ten o'clock this morning, promoted on the wire and social media, and then printed in tomorrow's paper. The embargo will be lifted at five o'clock tomorrow. More news and trade publications will publish reviews and articles over the next days, weeks, and months. I will just read the first few paragraphs. Are you ready?"

"Oh God, I guess so! I am certain you can tell that I have you on speaker because Liam is standing here with me in the kitchen. I want him to hear what Patricia has to say as well!"

"Good morning, Liam!"

"Good morning, love!" Liam said over his tea.

"Alright, let me have it!"

I held onto my own teacup and shut my eyes, awaiting Kate's reading of Patricia Brookside's judgment live over the phone. Liam lovingly put his hand on my back, silently reassuring me as she started reading.

"The Old Boys by Corrine Hunter review—a triumphant return via Scotland's forgotten history

An author's redemptive tribute to the honourable service and sacrifice a generation of Scottish lads made during the Great War

Three years ago, after reviewing two back-to-back contemporary romance novels that did not live up to her reputation as an author, I drafted an additional article with the stark and biting headline—<u>What Happened To Corrine Hunter?</u>

Like many devoted readers of her work, I was left disappointed and confused by the novels before me. I was lost in her writing. I was unable to connect to her characters or follow her meandering plotlines—both of which were equally anemic and depressing. I could not recognize any association with the skillful author that had been a joy to read for nearly a decade. Admittedly, I accused Hunter of capitalizing on her name and reputation by putting out insignificant novels during the pandemic because she could. That was exactly how it felt! I know that my judgment and my words were harsh, but the contrast these novels had to her previous body of work was not only noticeable... it was jarring. My original question was valid:

What happened to Corrine Hunter?

After reading her most recent historical fiction novel <u>The Old Boys</u>, I found Corrine Hunter once again! By returning to the historical fiction genre, in which she excels, Hunter has triumphantly emerged from the ashes of her previous failures for a story that deserves to be told. She rediscovered her voice with a little-known piece of Scottish history from the first World War. I can say with certainty this tale was one she was uniquely qualified to tell and does so with such dramatic reverence, heart-wrenching emotion, and lyrical prose that I encourage you to keep tissues nearby as you read it."

The headline and sub-head sounded positive at the start. Liam squeezed my elbow and smiled at me. I started crying in the middle and handed my phone to him so that I could retreat to the powder room in the hall to grab tissues. I leaned against the wall outside the kitchen so I could still hear everything Kate said. For some reason, I could not go back into the room with him. I just wanted to take in every word on my own for a moment. Kate continued,

> "Starting with the dedication, Hunter tells the reader exactly what they should expect from this remarkable novel. This story has heart. It lays bare the heart of Scotland and its people during a time of war and great societal change. It champions the heart of the undeterrable human spirit, heroic sacrifice, and enduring love. But this novel ultimately shows us the author's heart and it will uplift and break yours in equal measure!"

"*Corrie?*" Kate asked, sounding as emotional as I was. I could not speak, and I could not move from my place in the hall. If I am completely honest, it was from the full combination of reliving the emotions behind my last two failed novels, the pride I felt of this one, and this beautiful review. I could *not* speak. I could not answer her. I just dabbed my eyes and tried to catch my breath.

Finally, Liam responded sounding somewhat emotional himself, "She understandably had to take a moment in the middle, Kate. That was *brilliant*! I don't know what she missed. Can you read it once more when she comes back?"

When I could finally recover, I returned to the kitchen. Kate read the passage as we all embraced and cherished every word once again.

Kate said through my audible sniffles, "Liam, I know Corrie cannot answer me on the second reading. This is the best novel she has ever written and will get more attention as more reviews are published. Every positive review is going to mean that more people will want to speak with her. We may even recommend additional press because of it. She must be prepared. She may need your help. *Bloody hell, man!* I may need your help!"

"You both have it!" Liam said, kissing the top of my head as my tears of relief flooded his chest. I could only anticipate the rest of the review if this was the start! It was glorious! I no longer questioned Patricia Brookside kicking this off and thanked her for the honest recognition of the novel before her and my recovery from past failures.

I finally said haltingly through my tears, "Thank you, Kate. I will do… what you need. I… I believe in this novel… this story."

"The rest of Patricia's review is more detailed on the history, characters, and your writing… and it is bloody fantastic! It is an absolute reclamation of your reputation as an author! Right out of the gate! Prepare yourself for nothing but goodness, respect, and validation for weeks to come. You deserve it! You deserve every *fucking* bit of it, my darling!"

"*Thank… you,*" I said haltingly through my tears.

"I will call with the next review when it posts tomorrow, and we will send all article links to your email when they post live so you can read them in their entirety. As you already know, pre-orders are live across all retail sites and are trending modestly… mostly followers and fans that got notices of the novel's pre-order availability from their retailer of choice. These reviews and the marketing campaign will only expand your reach and sales. So, starting this Friday, Gemma in marketing will email us both at the end of each week with a report on sales numbers across sites and geographies. Congratulations again, Corrie!"

Liam said as he hung up my phone, "Aye! Thank you, Kate."

I buried my head in Liam's chest as he kissed the top of my head and held me tight. He whispered, *"I am so proud of you, love! Well done!"*

While this was only the first review, I knew that this novel was going to do everything I hoped it would. It will honor the old boys of Aberlour Orphanage and it will also restore my reputation as an author. I was so overwhelmed that I could not speak. I could only cry tears of joy and relief in the arms of the man I loved. The man that opened my own heart and made this all possible.

+++

After the debacle of Liam's birthday, we spent the next few days preparing for our holiday week at Loch Leven. Well, to be honest, I spent *my* days preparing for our week away. All the Crichton men had closets and chests filled at the house and needed to take little more than their toothbrush and any clothing that they wanted to leave there. Sarah had new swimming trunks delivered directly to the house for the growing lads.

I needed summer clothes to take to the lake myself, so spent a few days shopping in town. It gave me an opportunity to spend time on my own away from the house, and perhaps away from some of the awkward tension that unfortunately still lingered there.

Chef Stephan had been contracted to care for us and was now taking orders from both Liam and Chef Dan. Dan needed to focus on his own restaurant, Mythos, but we all had some sense of comfort that our friend who knew us best was still invested in our care in some small way. His mentorship of Chef Stephan was something he took as much pride in as helping us himself.

Liam told the boys that they had to make it right with me, but they instead decided to act like nothing ever happened. I am not sure if that was belligerent resistance or if they were afraid to come to me. But with each day that passed, I could tell Liam's patience was wearing thin. I asked him to meet me at the Rose & Crown after a day of work and shopping so we could talk about the growing wedge of frustration and disappointment he seemed intent on building between us and his sons.

Fancy a beer with a friend?

Always!

Meet me at the
Rose & Crown.

Give me a moment to
settle work and I'm
on my way!

"Hello my love!" I said as Liam joined me at my table with his pint in hand. We kissed quickly before he sat down. My God! I love the smell of this handsome man! It is pure intoxicating sweetness! We sat quietly for a moment under the watchful eyes of Flora MacDonald sipping our pints. Her portrait has always been a welcome comfort for me in my favorite pub.

After the normal sharing of the events of the day, Liam spent a good amount of time passing judgment about the number of shopping bags I had under the table and on the chairs next to us. When he found out that I had more being delivered to the house directly from Harvey Nichols, he just shook his head. I deserved the scolding as I had clearly spent a fortune but told him that my shopping day made me happy, and with that, he could not fault me. He could see that I was relaxed and said nothing more about it other than Paul would drive us home versus walking. To be honest, I am not even sure how I managed to carry this many bags on my mile-long walk across town to the pub from St James Quarter!

Finally, I confessed the reason for our meeting here today, "Liam, I wanted to talk to you about something... outside of the house."

"You did not just want a beer with a friend?"

"Always! But I wanted a moment to speak with you before we go to the lake house on Friday."

He just nodded and waited for me to continue. I assume he knew exactly what topic would drive a conversation to the pub.

"I know that you asked the boys to make it right with me. And every day that passes, I can tell... no, I can *feel* your disappointment that they have not done that in the way—or when—you hoped. In fact, we can all see and hear your frustration. Frustration that only seems to grow each passing day."

"*Corrine...*"

"Babe, you know I am right! You are protecting me, and I appreciate it so much! I *love* you for it! But I do not want you to lose your temper with the boys. Perhaps we should just let this one transgression go. We can enjoy our last week of the summer together and continue to grow over time. I believe it will take just that... *time*."

"No."

I waited a moment to see if he would expand on his definitive response. He did not. He meant what he said. He set his expectation with his sons and until that expectation was met, he was not inclined to back down. He was not going to let this go. His answer was *no*.

"*Liam...*"

"No. I am trying to raise considerate and respectful young men and they have shown me with every day that passes, that I have *failed*."

I shook my head in disagreement and said, "They love and respect you. They are struggling in a way that you, me, and even Sarah need to understand. But I do not believe that they are still trying to hurt me."

Liam shook his head, clearly disagreeing with my own assessment while simultaneously trying not to argue with me in the middle of the pub. Interactions in the house had been cordial but I could still feel a distinct difference between me and the boys since Liam's birthday. I just wanted us to get past this difficult start, but sadly that is where we all remained. We all remained in limbo of awkward politeness and forced tolerance.

"I want you to know that I am fine with where things are now. I am begging you... *please* let this go."

"No," he said flatly again. "When I talked with Sarah, she said that she would reinforce with the lads the same guidance... that they make it right with you."

"Really?"

"Aye, and Ewan asked her how best to do that. She gave them several options but said what I did not. And that the best thing to do was to simply take a private moment to apologize to you. *Christ above! Just say the words!* The fact that they have not made any attempt to do that simple task—as individuals or together—is a great disappointment to me."

"I understand, but the apology has not come. And with every day that passes, your fuse is only getting shorter. They can do nothing right, and your anger is apparent to all of us."

"I am not angry. I am disappointed."

"Well, that disappointment is palpable, and it *feels* like anger to everyone around you. I do not want you to go to the house on Loch Leven looking for a fight."

He laughed at my choice of words, and I explained further, "That is exactly how it feels! You are just waiting for them to say or do the wrong thing so that you can take out all the frustration you have built up on them. You are teetering on the edge. Please do not do that... not for me! Not for this! Let's just move on."

"I admit that I *am* angry, and that it is showing outwardly to you all. But..."

"But nothing! Please let this go. That is all I ask. And if you cannot, then say what you need to direct the boys on their task again."

"I do not want a *false* apology because I forced them to say the words. I want them to learn the lesson here, be responsible, and do the right thing."

"That is fair." I breathed in acceptance of his position as a father and continued, "Listen, you have one more week together then you are all on the off-and-on schedule for the next academic term. You told me yourself that we did not have to completely understand each other and be one big happy family from the start. Give it some time. Give *the boys* some time. The same time you afforded me at the outset."

Finally in resignation, he agreed with a simple, "Aye."

I took his hand in mine and said, "We will have a good week together and enjoy some time off by the water, my love. You know how much I love being by the water! That alone may be the healing remedy we *all* need."

+++

EIGHT
Mending Fences... Or Not

Crichton House
Loch Leven, Scotland
August 2023

The four of us travelled to the house at Loch Leven in relative silence. It was a short trip to a most welcome destination. Our travels did not feel angry, but certainly felt like we were all still disconnected. Four souls in the confines of a Range Rover not engaging with each other. Occasionally the lads argued with each other or their father over the music selection but mostly the boys spent the short ride focused on their phones.

Despite his words to me in the pub, I could tell that Liam was still lamenting the birthday situation, to the point that he could not find anything to talk about on the drive himself. This moody version of Liam Crichton was unsettling. To break the tension, I reached over the console and took his hand in mine. He brought it to his mouth, kissed it gently, and offered me a weak smile.

I finally said, "Chef Stephan texted me and said that he was preparing to grill tonight. He will have steak, chicken, and fish to order with sides, vegetables, and salad."

"That is a good plan for a summer night on the water," Liam said. I squeezed his hand as he continued, "I am in the mood for a steak myself and if the weather holds, perhaps we can sit on the patio instead of the dining room."

"I would love that! I think I will see what fish he has, but now that you mentioned it, I could easily go for a steak myself."

"I am not sure I told you but I had Dan show Stephan what to order for the wine cellar so we would not have to go into town."

"Bless you!"

Things were tense and emotional enough that I did not need to add the judgmental wine merchant, Mrs. Giles, to the mix. On our first trip to the lake house together, she made it perfectly clear that she disapproved of Liam having a new female houseguest so soon after his divorce. I would be fine not to ever step foot in her shop again.

Our conversation remained just on the surface, but it was obvious he was trying his best to meet me in the middle... even for small talk about weather, food, and wine. There are surely no more benign topics than that!

"Da?" Eric asked while kicking the back of his father's seat in the car.

"Aye?"

"What day are we gonna play golf?"

"We can go to Gleneagles any day you lads want. Perhaps we make a whole day of it. We can play golf while Corrine is in the spa and then we can all meet for a late lunch at The Dormy before returning home."

"Can I invite a friend?"

"I would prefer that you did not. We are already a threesome… unless Corrine wants to make it a foursome."

"I can putt, but I cannot golf. And I am not certain I am prepared to learn on the immaculate courses of Gleneagles!"

Liam smiled but before he could say a word back to me, Eric sighed loudly and threw himself back into his seat forcibly in frustration as he yelled, "Och! You *never* let us do anything fun!"

Liam looked at me as he said flatly in return, "No, I can't imagine playing golf with your Da at Gleneagles is *any fun,* lad!"

I squeezed Liam's hand once again trying to temper his sarcasm and apparent frustration. He winked at me before trying to correct himself as we pulled up to the automatic gate to Crichton House on Loch Leven. While waiting for the gate to open, he said looking back in the rearview mirror at his son, "Let's decide when we are going to golf so Jenny can book a tee time and make the other reservations. Perhaps you can have a friend come up and join you for the final weekend."

Ewan took his headphones off immediately and said, "If he gets to invite a friend, then I do too!"

"Aye," Liam said in resignation. He looked at me almost apologetically about the prospect of a house filled with teenage boys for our final summer weekend.

The permission to invite friends seemed to placate the boys for a moment. But I could tell in the confines of the car that things were still not right with Liam. I had never seen the man so miserable, and it was breaking my heart. What he said in the pub resonated more with each day that passed. He felt like a failure as a father that his sons had not politely corrected themselves.

Liam had been immensely successful in his work life, but a failed marriage and now two sons that cannot seem to apologize for hurting someone else were weighing on him. For everything he said about feeling my energy, I could feel the same from him. I wanted his sons to feel the same so that we could end this unfortunate stalemate.

We were immediately met at the front of the house by Miss Betty and her two still unnamed lads. After rounds of hugs and handshakes from Liam and his boys, I said politely reaching out my hand, "It is good to see you again, Miss Betty."

"And you as well, Miss Hunter," she said with a short shake of my hand.

I am not certain either of us were really all that pleased to see each other again, but perhaps the fact that I was still with Liam and now here with his sons in tow, she couldn't dismiss me completely. Miss Betty was another woman that did not take my appearance here at Crichton House on Loch Leven so soon after the divorce well. Like the judgmental wine merchant, her loyalties were clearly still with Sarah.

I said to Liam and Miss Betty, "I think most items in the boot are mine. Just delivering to the room should be fine. No need to worry about them. I can sort it all out later, but I may need the steamer iron handy."

"Aye! Consider it done!" Miss Betty said, clearly relieved not to have to help me any more than she needed to. Liam said nothing to me, but I could tell he wanted me to let Miss Betty handle the unpacking and steaming of clothes. But he had certainly learned over time that I am not particularly comfortable with someone else managing my things and honestly, it would not hurt for me to have a task.

"Miss Sarah had clothes and swimming trunks delivered for the lads. They are all hanging in their closets. Miss Hunter, all parcels delivered this week to your attention have been placed in your closet."

"Fantastic! Thank you!" I am not certain at this point if that was the closet in the guest suite, or Liam's. I could not find my words to ask for clarification before Eric and Ewan. Surely as house manager she knew that I had moved into Liam's room long ago and only worked in the guest suite.

Liam asked with a wink and a smile, "You ordered *more*?"

"You already knew that I had some items delivered directly from Harvey Nichols, but the rest is mostly toiletries and puzzles from Amazon to keep here."

"Puzzles? Jigsaw puzzles?"

"Yes, I wanted something to do while you lads were boating, swimming, and golfing. I could work all day long, but I wanted a holiday myself this week. Things are going to be mad after publication. This might be my last chance to relax... and I *love* puzzles!"

"I am learning something new about you every day!"

He kissed me quickly on the cheek and shook his head in mock judgment at my choice. He did not say the words, but I could only assume that Sarah spent a lot of time on other pursuits during vacation and that did not involve completing jigsaw puzzles.

+++

Chef Stephan, well trained by Chef Dan, had a plan to grill all manner of protein and vegetables to order this summer evening. Liam and I chose the filet mignon that he easily accompanied with fire-roasted fingerling potatoes, and asparagus. He also had a charred Romaine Caesar that was incredible on its own but made even more perfect with the steak. Both boys chose grilled prawns with all the fixings to make tacos. Liam insisted that they find some salad and vegetables. He told them that salsa did not count and that made everyone laugh, briefly breaking the lingering tension between us all. Ewan, the athlete, had no problem eating a large salad with his tacos. I have not seen over our last few weeks together that this growing young man had any trouble eating anything put before him.

Dessert consisted of a cheese plate and mini-fruit tarts. Liam and I naturally went for the cheese as the boys ate nearly all the tarts before their father finally cut them off. He told me with a laugh that the last thing we needed was a sugar-fueled evening with teenagers. I believed him.

+++

Liam had my instrumental soundtrack music playing in the background over the house speakers, yet I was surrounded by three men still not fully speaking with each other. The boys were on their phones in one corner of the kitchen island and Liam was sulking with a glass of wine on the patio, alone.

Looking at the boxes before me, I finally decided that the first puzzle on this summer holiday would be the challenging image of Mealt Falls backed by Kilt Rock on the Isle of Skye. It was a beautiful image, but with over a thousand pieces, the uniform colors of the rocks, land, and sea in the image made it even more challenging.

I poured out the pieces on the coffee table in the middle of the room and sat on the floor in front of the fireplace alone. If no one was going to speak to me or to each other, I could at least try to alleviate the tension I felt in this room with my own focused task. And what better way to start a holiday, than with a challenge?

I was seated on the floor between the sofa and the coffee table turning all the pieces over trying to separate corner and edge pieces to the side. Liam said little but when he came inside, he did his best to keep my glass full. Each time he did, I just smiled up at him, trying to silently reassure him. I am not sure he noticed. He was clearly lost in his own feelings of anger, resentment, and parental failure.

Soon I had a companion appear on the floor with me. Ewan Crichton suddenly seemed interested in what was happening here with the puzzle.

"Hello, there! Do you want to help me?"

"Aye, but I don't think that I have worked on a puzzle since I was a wee lad."

"Alright!" I said, handing him the box cover so he could see the image of our shared goal. "It is Kilt Rock on Skye."

"We have been there to see the waterfall!"

"It is lovely, isn't it?"

"Aye! What do we need to do?"

"So first, we must turn all the pieces over to the image side and then you can see that I am putting all the edge pieces like this to the side. You will want to find the corners as well. They are most important."

I showed him an edge piece and a corner that I had already collected. He nodded his head and said simply in understanding again, "Aye!"

"In my opinion, it is easiest to start with the corners and edges and then work in. Once we get them turned over, sometimes I start to group them by color according to the image. Like these pieces here, you can see with the white that they are all part of the waterfall and then the places where we have green."

"I can see that."

"Here, you oversee the edges. Build the frame for us."

I handed all the pieces I had already gathered to him, and he began building out the corners and edges so that we could have the border of our image. We worked silently, save for the occasional words about edge pieces found or the difficulty of the image that had so many of the same colors.

I was thrilled that Ewan remained working on the puzzle even after his brother retreated to his own bedroom upstairs. I looked at Liam when he replaced my spritzer again and smiled hoping that he could see that his son was trying to connect and make it right with me. Even if the boy did not say the words expected, he was making a point to connect in a quiet and respectful way. I hoped Liam could see what I did and forgive his son on this kind effort alone.

I leaned in and said like I was sharing a secret well within earshot of Liam behind us, "Your father clearly has no patience for puzzles."

"Aye, Miss Corrine! I cannot see Da sitting still for this. It is all business, all the time for him!"

"Your father and I both like to work, that is true."

"You are an author, right?"

"I am and my latest novel is coming out next week. Do you know that your father helped me finish that book?"

"He did? *Really?*"

"Yes, he connected me with a Scottish historian that made my story come to life, and I am so proud of it."

I did not dare approach the fact that his father changed me and opened my heart in a new way. Liam made me whole again with his love and it is apparent in my writing. I do not think I need to speak with young Ewan about my wounded heart and his father's love... at least not tonight.

Ewan just nodded his head and then finally said, "I think I have all the edges together."

"You do! Look at that! Well done! And so fast! You are a natural, Ewan! Thank you for helping me get this far."

"Erm, I liked it. As Da likes to say, it is *logical work*. And... well..."

I looked reassuringly at the lad who seemed to be nervously searching for his next words as he stood up from the floor. He looked at me with the same sweet, gold-flecked hazel eyes of his father and bright red cheeks as he said, "Erm, I wanted... I just wanted to say... that I am verra sorry about Da's birthday."

I breathed in his words and said stoically with a broad smile that I could not contain, "I know, love. Thank you for saying that to me. Can I count on you to help me with the puzzle again tomorrow?"

"Aye!"

"Then I will stop right here with you myself so that we can work more together. I will not progress any further without your help. We are a team!"

"Goodnight, Miss Corrine!"

"Goodnight, Ewan. Sleep well!"

I watched as young Ewan ran up the stairs. Oh! How these boys love to run up and down the stairs! The lad finally did exactly what his father expected of him. I could not see where the man was behind me, but I knew he was there, and I hoped he heard every glorious word his son said.

+++

Liam topped off my wine spritzer before helping me up from the floor. Now that both boys were upstairs, we claimed our rightful place on the sofa before the fireplace. I love these moments with him and thought fondly of our first few weeks together here. This room will always have a special place in my heart for that reason alone. A new love formed on this very spot.

"I assume you heard our conversation?" I asked as he put his arm around my shoulders and kissed the side of my head.

"I did," he said smiling over his glass. "You were correct, love. I have no patience for puzzles."

I turned to him immediately and yelled, *"Not that part, Liam!"*

He laughed as he said, "Aye, I heard the apology I expected to hear, and it made me proud."

"He was kind and apology aside I appreciated the time to work on the puzzle. It was the first time we just sat and talked together on our own. Having a shared objective made that easy."

I could tell Liam was a little more relaxed as he said with a smile, "Now perhaps I understand this puzzle business."

"I can assure you there was no other intention with the puzzles than offering me a means to relax in a way that did not involve my laptop. But I see now that it offered me a connection to Ewan. I appreciate that he was interested, and it opened the conversation. *You* should appreciate that, as well!"

"I do."

"Perhaps it will help me connect with Eric the same way."

"I think he is going to take more than a puzzle."

"Why do you say that?"

"He seems to be carrying more emotion from the divorce. His questions about a new family told me that much. I told you that I thought he was the more sensitive of the two. You taught me to think about them as individuals and how they showed their feelings in different ways."

"I remember that conversation."

"As I have observed Eric more, the lad is not only naïve, but of late, I can see his emotions turn negative at a certain point. It seems this son of mine is carrying pain and resentment his brother is not."

"Honestly, that could just be called being a teenager," I said over my glass. Liam just looked at me with a furrowed brow as I continued, "I do not discount his feelings in any way about the circumstances surrounding your divorce, and it has been a while, I distinctly remember how everything—good or bad—felt magnified at that age. Your hormones are raging through your body, and you cannot control your emotions because you cannot quite understand them. At least as a young teen, I can tell you that I felt *everything!*"

Liam said nothing back to me but seemed to be thinking about my words. Perhaps he was remembering being a fourteen-year-old lad himself.

I said laughing at my own teenage memories, "I felt everything in the most dramatic fashion! A lot of my feelings were angry and misguided. I am certain that my poor mother took the brunt of my emotional outbursts."

Teen years are a rite of passage to be sure! I cannot imagine adding divorce, new homes, and shared time between parents you love to the mix. The boy must be all in his feelings and consumed by emotions he cannot yet control. I wanted to give the lad some grace and understanding. I wanted his father to do the same.

During our shared reflective silence, I finally asked, "When can you let this go, love?"

"Never. Ewan learned to do the right thing and I expect nothing less from his brother."

"I will leave it to you as a father, but I feel incredible about the apology I received tonight, and I do not need—nor do I expect—anything else."

"The lad will learn. I will see to it."

We sat silently for a bit before I said hopefully, "Perhaps he will come around if his brother tells him that he said the simple words of apology, as their mother advised, and they were well received."

"I doubt it," Liam said flatly.

I just looked at him and took in his words as a marker of his continued disappointment in Eric and I did not want to push him any more on the topic. I learned instantly that Ewan Crichton was every bit of the charmer his loving father was but needed to find a way to connect with Eric. It may not happen in our final days together this summer, but I would make it my mission. Perhaps, in the process, I could help the lad find a more neutral ground with his own father.

+++

Sarah arrived at the new Crichton House in Edinburgh to collect her sons after a month with us. We managed our way through puzzles, boating, golf, and spa time, followed by teenage sleepovers during the last weekend at the lake.

I asked cheerfully as they barreled down the stairs, "Do you lads have everything packed and ready to go? Of course, as this is your house as well, please leave anything you want to keep in your rooms."

"Aye, Miss Corrine," Ewan said quickly before sweetly hugging me. "I left all my clothes, Mum."

"That is fine, love," Sarah said winking at Liam. "Just know that if you left anything you are going to want next week, you need to remember it is here."

"Och! Let me get my rugby jersey!"

"Aye, lad, get your jersey," Liam said laughing at the boy already running back up the stairs. Surely, he would need that important item when school resumes next week!

"I have everything I need," Eric said to his mother. He said nothing to me but hugged his father briefly from the side before walking out the front door straight to his mother's car.

Reading the situation perfectly, Sarah asked Liam once both boys were finally out the door, "I assume Eric did not complete the task?"

"No. No, he did not," Liam said absolutely and with his still palpable disappointment in his tone.

I smiled weakly at them both. I honestly hold nothing against Eric for not apologizing to me. I will always cherish Ewan's apology and stand by my original statement—I do not need another. I let the entire situation go the instant the sweet boy said his words and only wished Liam could do the same.

"Then let me apologize," Sarah said.

I responded instantly, "There is no need for that!"

"No, there is," she said. "I apologize for our first meeting. A meeting Liam either *conveniently* forgot or *kindly* ignored upon our introductions in this entry hall a month ago. If I instilled any resentment in my sons, that was not my intention. I *was* angry about being left out of the annual Cox Arts Benefit and yes, that Liam moved so quickly to find another. I took all my own frustration and resentment out on you in the middle of Boots. And for that I am sorry, Corrine."

Liam nodded his head in understanding, before taking my hand in his to show that we were receiving her apology together.

"Thank you, Sarah. I accept your apology."

"I cannot ask my sons to do something I did not do myself. And I do not want them to be as rude and disrespectful to you as I was. That would mean my failure as a mother, and I cannot bear it."

"Sarah, you should know that Liam helped me understand where your feelings were coming from at the time. So as embarrassed as I was in the moment, I let it go. But I thank you for your words of apology. We are in a good place, and we are all learning how to navigate this together. We have a lot to learn, but I do not feel like enemies. You need to know that!"

"Exactly! I don't feel that way either! In fact, your experience is only going to help me... erm... as I have a new love myself! Liam, you need to know that it is Jordaan, my yoga instructor. He is a good man. He is a single father to a wee lass, Polly. She is just three years old. Her mother died young of bowel cancer, shortly after her daughter's birth, and had no family of her own. Jordaan's mother helps when she can, but she is not in the best health. He is raising this lass alone."

"I cannot imagine," I said in sympathy.

Liam said nothing. He suspected both her tennis coach and yoga instructor as lovers. Now I guess he knows where she landed. I do not know her well, but she seems genuinely in love with this man and his young daughter.

Liam finally said admirably, "That does sound tragic to be the single father to a wee lass."

"It is! But can I tell you how much having a young girl in my life has shaped me in such a brief time? I never thought I would want anything more than the beautiful lads we have! But I love this wee lass to bits!"

We both nodded back to her and her open show of raw emotion. I felt her sincere love for Jordaan and Polly. In hearing her softness when speaking of them, I was genuinely happy that perhaps Sarah had found her own path to happiness after divorce.

Liam said, "I appreciate that, but you are headed straight into the same questions we just had. I told you that Eric was especially uncertain and unnerved about *new families… new children*. You are not just adding a partner, you are adding a three-year-old lass to the mix."

"Aye! I know these lads are coming for me! And I am ready for it! I want you both to know that I plan to introduce everyone on Friday after the school term starts. I have also asked Jordaan and Polly to move into our home.'

I could feel Liam's tension both in his hand still holding mine and his deep breath upon Sarah's words. A new love was expected but he seemed to bristle at the thought of this unknown man and his daughter in the same home as his sons. Sarah was moving as fast as we were. We could not judge her on that fact, but things were now becoming more complicated.

We just nodded silently as she said finally, "I will not include you, out of respect for the lads. Well, meaning that I want this moment with my sons on my own before introducing you to this new *expanded* family. But you should prepare yourselves for any aftermath."

Liam nodded and said, "Understood."

I just gripped his hand in mine and said, "I defer to you both. But you have my support. This may be a positive thing though."

They both looked at me confused, as I continued, "This may be positive because Eric felt like his father moved on quickly, and he saw that as a slight against his mother. But if Sarah moves on to new love, it may *'even the score,'* so to speak. He may need to accept the changes happening around him in a different way. Perhaps he will see that he and Ewan are a part of families that are not a replacement for the old, they are an *expansion*, just as you said, Sarah."

They both nodded in agreement, or at least in consideration of the modest possibility of my theory.

I continued, looking at Sarah, "And if this sweet girl is part of the equation, perhaps Eric and Ewan will come to love her the same way you have."

"Och, Corrine," she said with tears in her eyes, "that is *all I want! Thank you!*"

We just nodded to her as she said, before walking out the front door, "We are all moving forward but I must admit Liam, I am not completely certain our lads are moving with us."

+++

NINE
The Return Of Meredith Cox

Palm Court, The Balmoral Hotel
Edinburgh, Scotland
August 2023

The host outside Palm Court escorted me directly to a half-moon table at the center of the room. Despite the many eager guests celebrating traditional afternoon tea in Edinburgh's finest hotel under the green leaves of palm trees, the sparkling glass dome, and the Venetian chandelier, it appeared that everyone working today was singularly focused on my companion. As I approached the table, they all stepped aside to let me sit with the woman herself—the beautiful and enigmatic Mrs. Meredith Cox.

I always thought that I had a good relationship with the staff at this hotel, and my connection to Liam only added to the positive attention and care I received here. But nothing compared to the attention being offered Meredith Cox! The entire staff was almost falling over each other to ensure she was happy and content. And in the first few minutes since my arrival, I could see her connecting politely, but also directing the servers for our tea.

"Mrs. Cox," I said putting my hand out for hers when I arrived at the table.

"Miss Hunter," she said in return and taking my hand in both of hers. "I have ordered a Champagne tea and personally selected the assortment of sandwiches, savories, and pastries against the standard fare. I admit that they know I especially like caviar. So, I told kind Octavia here that we might enjoy a *little extra* to start."

Octavia, our server, nodded in her understanding of the ask and silently walked away presumably in search of said caviar. I said, "You had me at Champagne and caviar, Mrs. Cox! Who needs tea?"

She laughed and said, "I agree completely and please, call me Meredith."

"Of course, and please, Corrine," I said as we both clinked our instantly filled cut-glass Champagne flutes together.

I have never seen anything like it! Every employee of this hotel is clearly fawning over the woman. There is no doubt that she has an opinion on both what she wants and what she expects and yet, she stays humble and gracious to each person in such an honest and genuine way.

"If you do not mind me saying Meredith, I see how much respect you have for the staff here and they clearly have the same for you."

"Well, while it feels like I have been coming here as long as the iconic clock tower has been standing, I can assure you that I was taught by my parents a sense of respect for those in service. I hear my own words and they sound both antiquated and entitled, but I mean respect for others, regardless of role. That's it! My parents taught me to always be kind and respectful to others."

"I agree! I was taught the same by my own parents, which is why I took notice. I also had a former colleague in New York City who taught me to always know my bartender's name. It was a simple piece of advice at a moment in time, but that advice has worked well for me across the globe. The foundation is simply human kindness and respect. The Golden Rule of bars and restaurants, I suppose. Treat others as you want to be treated. We all deserve that much in life."

She nodded to me in agreement just as the bar manager, stopped by our table to personally top off our Champagne. He said, "Good afternoon, Miss Hunter, and Mrs. Cox! I heard you were here today and wanted to greet you myself."

"Hello Alessandro! It is good to see you again, my friend!" I said as eagerly I shook his hand.

"Always a pleasure! Always a pleasure! Please let me or the team know if we can bring you anything else from the bar."

Meredith said, "Thank you! The Champagne is perfect, sir!"

"Then you will not mind me sending you an extra glass." Alessandro said to Meredith with a wink and a smile.

"I would never turn down a full glass of anything, love! That is for certain!"

We all laughed at her remark and as Alessandro went to retrieve our extra glasses, Meredith said to me, "I think we share the same philosophy. They clearly respect you as well!"

"Well, I confess that I have spent a lot of time *and money* in Bar Prince during my stays here in Edinburgh!"

"I have no doubt, but I believe you spent *kindness* there as well."

I appreciated the sentiment. I did spend kindness there with my friends. Changing the subject, I finally said, "I brought you a copy of my new novel, *The Old Boys*, published just last week. I signed this copy for you."

"Och, Corrine! You must feel such a sense of accomplishment to see your hard work manifest itself in physical form. I cannot imagine seeing your own name on the cover of a book! What a remarkable thing!"

"While this is my twenty-first novel, it feels exactly like the first! To see it completed makes me proud. I have a sense of accomplishment but I also, like you said, love seeing the research and effort in those words manifest themselves onto the page and not just in a computer file. It is fulfilling *and* rewarding to hand you a solid, physical book!"

She nodded and sipped her Champagne as I continued, "This novel holds a special place in my heart. The story came together in a way I could have never imagined when I started it."

"I can see here by the dedication here that Mr. Crichton had a hand in that."

I blushed slightly and nodded to her, "The man did, and I will forever be grateful to him. Do you know Dr. Andrew Marshall?"

"I know his name, but I do not know the man. We may have met at some point but forgive me if I do not remember."

"He is a Professor of Scottish History at The University of Edinburgh. He is lovely man, a respected scholar, and an incredible ambassador for Scotland and its rich history. He is a well-known author in his own right. I was writing a novel about Scotland during World War One and he gave me such a gift with the story of the old boys of Aberlour Orphanage. This story made my novel come to life! I will forever be grateful for his gift of inspiration."

"Well then, I cannot wait to read this beautiful book! Though I must confess that while I treasure this signed copy, I will read it on my Kindle so that I can make the font a little bigger. My eyes are not what they used to be."

"I understand completely! I just reluctantly traded my glasses for progressive lenses as I needed readers more and more myself! No one tells you that when you hit fifty, you can no longer see!"

"Some of us came to that realization in our forties, lass! So, you can imagine how bad it is by the time you hit your *seventies*!"

We smiled at each other as the servers replaced our tea pots. The team here knew we were both going to make the most of the Champagne first but did so only in case one of us suddenly tipped a pot for tea. If either of us did, it would be hot!

+++

"Corrine, thank you for joining me here today! Of course, I enjoy the opportunity to get to know you better. But I must confess that had another reason for asking you here."

"Oh?"

"Aye, as you know that the Annual Cox Arts Benefit is planned for February each year. We may adjust the timing slightly if we change venues, but we have a standing hold with the National Galleries of Scotland, who have been an incredible partner for us. We have found the Portrait Gallery on Queen Street to be a favorite."

"Of course, I remember the last event fondly. And that is one of my favorite galleries as well. It is a beautiful venue and is just so intimate!"

"That is right! I believe it was your debut in Edinburgh society!"

"I guess you can call it that. Though the words make me feel like a debutante on display and well… I am too old for that."

"I can imagine that it feels that way, but Edinburgh and Scottish society... regardless of age... is not always welcoming to outsiders. Your debut as a Canadian and an unmarried attendee were both notable."

"I suppose being on the arm of the most eligible divorcé in Scotland helped."

"It did," she said instantly. I was being a tad impertinent with my response throwing her own words back at her, but she was not joking. Being with Liam Crichton that night was the endorsement I needed to be welcomed into society without question. It did not matter that I was unmarried and Canadian. I was with Liam, and *I was in*!

"I wanted to ask you if you would be willing to co-chair the annual benefit with me this year."

"Me? Really?"

"Aye! I am not getting any younger, that is a fact! But, in the initial planning meetings, I kept feeling like something was missing. Everyone seemed focused on doing what worked before and placating me and my earlier decisions. I do not believe that will be enough this year. We certainly made advancements in the social media space over the last few years, but that is about it. The event exists as it has for nearly a decade. Some of that was worsened by the COVID pandemic restrictions we had for years which kept us from holding the event at all. I believe your perspective as an author... a creative artist yourself... along with Liam's name can help revamp this charity and benefit."

I knew well enough that Liam's name and money were a draw more so than my own or even my ability to help the charitable event. But I genuinely believed that Meredith did in fact see that a new and perhaps younger perspective could be of benefit to the goals of the charity. I also knew enough about society politics to know that this was her way of endorsing me and supporting me. If I am to be with Liam, I must accept that this part of his life is now part of my own. His name and being on his arm got me into this prestigious group, but Meredith Cox's endorsement was the one I needed if I was going to stay.

"I will help you in any way you need! I confess, however, that I have never done anything like this before…"

She interrupted me and said instantly, "That is exactly why we need you, Corrine! A fresh perspective and new thinking. I am confident you can give this benefit new life."

"Then I am all in, and I am honored!"

"Wonderful! I will send a message to the team responsible for the event and let them know that we will lead this year's benefit together. My only ask is that you not hold back on your questions or thoughts about what is being planned. Let me be a tad more direct! I want—and expect—you to be disruptive! I want you to ask all the questions, bring your own point of view. Even if you do not want to request a specific change on your own, ask us to describe and defend what we are doing. I *want* you to challenge us all in a new way!"

"If I am good at anything it is questioning. In fact, that is usually how I start a new novel."

"Really?"

"Yes, the open question *'what if?'* usually seeds the concept for a new story."

"That is brilliant! I will set up a meeting with the event managers. In fact, I may hold it here so we can have more Champagne and caviar."

"I am always up for a meeting where Champagne and caviar are readily available! Surely, the combination is *most conducive* for brainstorming new ideas," I said with a sly smile and a wink.

"I agree! There are four leads for the event team. They cover all the main logistical elements for the event, including PR, marketing, finance, and operations, which includes everything from catering to invitations. We also have an overall strategic planning lead that keeps us all on deadline. The trust pays for the event, so we are fine there. I want to make this the largest benefit we have ever had! The arts have never been more important!"

"I agree! Especially coming out of the pandemic. And who exactly are the beneficiaries of the event? Apologies that I did not grasp that last time."

"Dinnae fash yerself!" she said, instantly showing that like Liam, drink only exaggerates her Scottish accent at times. "I am not sure it is all that clear. In fact, consider that yer first piece of feedback."

I laughed for a moment before she continued, "The Cox Trust For The Arts benefits two primary areas in Scotland. First, we supplement the scholastic arts programs in schools across the country—public and private. We want to encourage the education of fine arts through supporting teachers and encouraging new Scottish artistic talent across mediums. The trust is solely focused on painting, sculpting, drawing, photography, and design, including now some computer graphic design. The types of visual arts studied and practiced in our primary and secondary schools. But it does not include literature, music, architecture, or other creative endeavors like theatre or the cinematic arts."

"Understood."

"It is niche to be certain, and we can talk about that construct later. But it is one of the reasons the National Galleries of Scotland is such a valued partner. Like I said, we have found ourselves in the National Portrait Gallery, which is a lovely venue."

"But I assume it has it limits, does it not?"

"Excellent observation! We tried having more people for a few years at larger venues and decided that based on costs, we secured nearly the same amount in donations with a smaller group."

"Makes sense!"

"I would be lying to you if I did not also say that the limited invitation is also something of a draw. People in the ranks of society know who is included and who is not. It becomes a bit of a thing, and I admit, I like the exclusivity of it."

I thought about Sarah not being invited to the last event and could now see Meredith's thinking a little more. I said, "I understand. You would only open it broader if you wanted to expand the brand but if you cannot make the money you need, why pay for a bunch of people to have the best Champagne and hors d'oeuvres with no real gain? You are providing them with a forum to elevate themselves more than the Cox Trust or the benefit."

"Exactly! We have some that come to be seen and may help extend the reach of social media and press, but it is fleeting. They never donate on the night or even after!"

"I think you are right to limit access with an exclusive invitation.. But..."

"You have more thoughts?"

"I do but might wait until I can meet with your team. Tell them I do not need a *'dog and pony show'* of formal presentations or documentation. But I will ask them about numbers from last year. They should be prepared to answer my questions."

"I agree! Let's keep it an informal brainstorming session! Look for my invitation and welcome to the Cox Trust! We will make it official with a press release. Audrey MacKay on my team leads PR and Communications. She will need information from your bio and likely a quote. And of course, you will have the right to edit and approve."

"I will connect her to the PR team at Woodhouse Publishing for everything she needs. Thank you for including me! I am happy to help a charity I believe in. I hope I can offer you what you need, Meredith!"

"I know you will, Corrine! No doubt about it!"

+++

After talking more through our tea service, I finally said, "Meredith, I have an ask of my own, if you don't mind."

"Of course!"

"My next novel is about the lost distilleries in Scotland in the 1920s. Liam thought you could help me here with your extensive knowledge and understanding of Scottish distilleries."

"I do have an *extensive knowledge* of Scottish whisky distilleries," she said with a wink and smile. She was being cheeky with me, and I appreciated her humor.

I said laughing, "I meant no offense."

"None taken! I will say it again... and proudly! Between my own birthright and my marriages, I have an *extensive knowledge* of Scottish distilleries. How can I be of help?"

"I have a few questions. Do you mind if I take notes while we talk?" I asked, already grabbing my Moleskine notebook and pen from my bag before she could answer.

"Not at all! And what I cannot answer, I might be able to point you to someone else who can."

"That would be wonderful! Thank you! Alright, first, my research has told me how much of the Scottish whisky industry is family orientated."

"Aye! It is! Our clan structure and kinship affiliations throughout Scottish history tell you that much! Why wouldn't whisky be born of the same?"

"Why wouldn't it, indeed?" I said smiling at her. "I know through my own research how whisky, especially in the late Eighteenth Century, started locally and often with a laird or clan support for their own use before it was allowed to be sold broadly. And by broadly, I mean likely to a local tavern or a neighboring clan... not like the distribution we think of today!"

"Aye, that is another element that added to the familial designation as whisky was usually a *'home brew'* made for the laird and the clan. It was kept locally. For any sales beyond that the clan must be cautious of the tax man who would certainly follow such an enterprise. Especially if they began to make a name or money for themselves! Admittedly, this was more noticeable in the Lowlands and cities than in the remote Highlands and Islands. The tax man often casually ignored remote Scotland."

"I think I know the reason..."

"Exactly, if a tax man ventured to those areas..."

"He often did not return to England," I said finishing her thought. We both laughed at this, before I continued, "It is not hard to see the future in such an enterprise though. I mean of course that the whisky regions we know of today, started to develop processes and names for themselves for the next century and beyond."

"They did."

"My next novel has to do with more of the 1920s where distilleries were more prolific and established across Scotland and even selling beyond our borders. But in the aftermath of World War One, the resulting Spanish Flu pandemic, and then Prohibition and Temperance movements in other countries including the United States, sales plummeted and many of those family distilleries could not survive."

"That is correct. In fact, the majority closed during the years from the Great War to the end of the Depression."

"Was your family's distillery open during this time?"

"Yes. My father's family began distilling in Speyside soon after the Excise Act of 1823 which ushered in more legality in the UK. Though they had been making their own *'home brew'* for many years before that. There are old stories of how my great-grandfather and his brothers not only dodged the tax man but had an elaborate underground system to brew and distribute their fare. From the stories I heard, it seemed very much like something out of an American gangster movie."

I laughed at this and thought about what lengths people had to go through not to be discovered for their beloved drink.

Meredith continued, "You should explore some of the original distilleries that also ran breweries. While having the two operations of ale and whisky did not necessarily save them from the challenges of the time, many did quite well with the natural combination of the two."

"Yes, I have been researching the MacLeods and Glenammon on Skye a part of my research. They are an excellent example of that as they prospered with both, then struggled, only to close. But they were revived in 2013 and are now a very profitable and popular brand."

"Aye, that is a good one. My own family's distillery was sold to Diageo about twenty years ago and the name is no longer. But my last husband's successful enterprise, *The Caladh,* is on Islay.

"The Caladh?" I asked, trying my best to pronounce it the way she did. I knew it had to be of Gaelic origin but before I could ask what it meant she answered my question.

"Aye! It is Scottish Gaelic and means simply *'the harbor.'* His family were fishers for centuries who found their way into crafting whisky to supplement their income and perhaps keep their workforce happy. The logo and beautiful bottle design reflect the elements of the sea and fishing industry central to the island's history."

"I find this all so fascinating!"

"If you ever want to visit the distillery, I am happy to arrange it. They have a historian on staff that may be of help to you, and they have a grand tasting tour that reflects both the history and the process of whisky making. Because it is a family enterprise and over two hundred years old, my dear husband thought it was important to save, record, and document everything. In fact, the extensive historical archives are what make the tour so captivating."

Whether it was fueled by our Champagne or not, I could see Meredith tear up at the mention of her husband. I felt her emotion. I could not find my words at first but reached out to touch her arm reassuringly as I said, "I would love that! And I am certain I could *easily* convince Liam to take a field trip to Islay for whisky."

Meredith nodded and said finally, "My last husband, Landon Cox was a verra special man. A special soul. He taught me the redemptive power of love. I know that sounds ridiculously romantic, but we spent our time together loving and supporting each other in a way that was so different from what I had experienced with my first husband. We had both been married before and were older. We were only married six years before he passed, but he was the love of my life! All I could see was *forever* when we married and when I lost him, I lost myself for a bit."

There was something about her words and the telling of her love story with Landon that told me her heartbreak was not because he was her last love—he was her *greatest* love. I could tell that she was still in deep sorrow mourning him.

She did not elaborate, and I did not ask. She did not have to explain anything to me. I knew all too well the pain of grief and how it can easily consume you. I knew exactly what she was feeling because I had been there myself. When you fall in love with someone who becomes part of your heart and then passes, you *do* lose a bit of yourself because they take a piece of you with them when they go.

"We have more in common than you might imagine."

Meredith just looked at me as I continued, "A little over five years ago I was engaged to an incredible man, a pediatric surgeon in London. I never thought I would ever marry, but we found each other later in our lives and we fell hard and fast for each other. Before we could marry, he died of a sudden heart attack in his sleep. He was only fifty-four years old."

"*Och Corrine!*" Meredith said shaking her head in disbelief of my words and shared sympathy.

"Losing him devastated me. So, I understand your feelings of immense and sometimes immobilizing grief. While that pain never truly goes away, we are left with some sense of gratitude that we were better to have these amazing men in our lives than not."

Meredith's eyes welled with tears at my words and the confirmation of our new and unfortunate bond with each other. "I am verra sorry for your loss Corrine! We *were* so blessed, weren't we?. As much as it hurt to lose Landon, I agree that it would have hurt more to never had the darlin' man in my life at all. I wouldna change a thing!"

It took me a moment to recover from the emotion of David's story, but I said, "I told myself that I would be content to never have another true love in my life, but my life miraculously brought me to Liam. He is another love I never expected. So, I agree! I *would not* change a thing about loving either of these kind and beautiful men!"

My words were true. As we sat there looking at each other in sympathy for each other's pain, we were indeed grateful for the loves we had. Meredith was correct, we were indeed blessed.

"We should go, lass. It has been a long afternoon and I look forward to speaking with you more about the benefit."

"I hope I can be of service to you and your team."

"I have no doubt that you will!"

We kissed each other on our cheeks before she walked to her car, and I walked straight to Paul's car, where he was holding the door for me.

It had been a long day, and I was ready to go home to my love. I was ready to go home to Liam.

+++

TEN
The Parting Glass

Edinburgh, Scotland
August 2023

Liam and I sat on the garden patio together with a glass of wine. While the air was still quite warm during the day, the fading sunset and shade from the trees ushered in cooler evening air. This offered a chance to light the firepit and connect with each other before Chef Stephan's supper.

"You know that I reached out to Andrew, to help your next novel love…"

Before he could finish his thought, I said, "Yes, and I thank you!"

"I had no response for a bit, but my voicemail was finally returned today by his daughter Abby. Unfortunately, the man is in the hospital."

"What!? Is he alright?"

Liam sighed and said, "Apparently Andrew had a cancerous tumor removed from his liver last month and they discovered that it had metastasized. He now has cancer in his kidneys and lymph nodes. He had multiple rounds of chemo and got so ill that he needed more care than his daughter could handle on her own. He has been there for almost two weeks and may be moved to hospice care at home in the coming days."

Liam was as distraught delivering this news as I was hearing it. With tears in both of our eyes, I said taking his hand in mine, "Oh Liam! Forget books! We *must* see him! We *must* see our friend!"

"Aye! I had no idea about any of this! If I had, I would have gone to see him before now. But Abby and I are now directly connected on mobile, so we will know how he is doing. She has a group text with everyone supporting them.

"This news breaks my heart!"

"She knows that I am here to help them both in any way and even offered my own private doctor if needed. I had Jenny send flowers to her and Andrew from us both. I know this must be hard on her and she told me that she left her family in France. She spends all day at the hospital and then returns to his house alone. She has a young daughter in school and she and her husband agreed to keep her there."

"I cannot imagine! I want you to ask her when we can see him. And Liam, we could have Nate fly her husband and daughter here on the weekends. She needs their love and support to get through this, and they need to see Andrew while he is still here."

"That is an excellent idea, my love," he said squeezing my hand in his. "I did not think of that! I was so lost in the heartbreak if it all, that I did not think past the flowers."

Liam texted Andrew's daughter and we settled on visitation hours on Saturday. I just held Liam's hands tight in my own. We both knew that this sounded dire. This may be one of our last chances to see our dear friend and give him our love and support.

+++

We walked into Andrew's hospital room and found the man sitting upright, talking with his daughter. Dr. Andrew Marshall, a brilliant scholar and historian, was a slight man, in his late seventies, but with the brightest blue eyes I have ever seen. Despite his illness, he sat across from us, with those same bright eyes and a welcoming smile. Everything about the man was warm and inviting.

"It is good to see you, old friend," Liam said walking right in and shaking Andrew's hand. Then he turned to the pretty woman standing by the bed, "You must be Abby."

"I am, Mr. Crichton. It is nice to finally meet you in person."

"Liam, please and this is my partner, Corrine Hunter."

We shook hands as Abby said, "It is a pleasure to meet you, Corrine! My father and I are such fans!"

I looked at Andrew who just winked at me. Then I said, "Well, I thank you! Your father has been an incredible inspiration for my work... especially my last novel.

"Oh yes! Look just here," she said holding up her own copy of *The Old Boys*.

"That is a lovely surprise! I brought signed copies for you both! I can imagine that the days in the hospital are long and thought you might need something to read."

"I mostly read when Dad sleeps or when I go back to my parent's house. I am only on chapter five, but I love it so far."

"I appreciate that, truly."

Andrew said, "Yes, Abby has been raving about it so far. And of course, I thank you for your kind and generous acknowledgement."

"Andrew, you know your gift of inspiration meant so much to me! I hope it is even more clear on the pages of the novel itself."

Andrew then said, "You can both take off your masks. I appreciate you following hospital rules and being so courteous to me, but you can see Abby and I have opted out in this room. What? *Are you all going to kill me?*"

We laughed nervously at his words as Andrew continued, "Honestly, I get it! But realized through the pandemic how much I rely on reading lips to know what is being said. When you get old, my loves, you hit an age where you cannot see and then one day, you cannot hear!"

We both accepted his honest humor but looked to Abby for reassurance. She nodded her head, and we removed our masks. I admit, I realized through the pandemic how much I read lips myself. But I also welcomed his brazen defiance of the rules. The hospital rightly had theirs, but this was Dr. Andrew Marshall's room, and he was in charge here.

"Thank you both for the lovely flowers," Andrew said with a smile. "Everyone has commented on them! They are not only a large bouquet but have such beautiful colors that brightened up this dreary, beige room in an instant!"

"They are still vibrant," I said acknowledging the large bouquet atop the table in front of the window.

"Oh yes and to send me my own flowers at the house was such a kind gesture," Abby said. "Thank you both!"

Liam said, "You are most welcome. Abby, I also wanted to offer the service of my pilot to fly your husband and daughter up next weekend.

He can collect them from Lyon-Bron Airport and have them here in time to have supper with you on Friday. Then he can take them back home on Sunday evening. Your daughter will not miss any school, and you can have the support of your family here with you for a few days."

Abby teared up and when she could finally speak, she said, "That is much too generous, sir! *We could not...*"

Liam interrupted and said, "It is done and the least I can do! My assistant Jenny will coordinate with you tomorrow on the specifics. But know that this is not just a one-time offer. My pilot is available to you as you need."

"*Thank you both!* "she said instantly hugging Liam and then me. *"This is so kind!"*

I could tell we were all emotional with Liam's offer and Abby's reaction. I chimed in and said trying my best to lighten the mood, "How exciting! You will get to see your granddaughter next weekend, Andrew!"

"I would very much like to see her," Andrew said softly. I could tell he was sensitive to his daughter's emotions and perhaps even his own at the prospect of seeing family.

"I will leave you all to talk! Da, I will go on my afternoon walk and see you soon," she said before kissing his cheek sweetly.

"Take your time, love! I am in fine company."

+++

I could tell that Dr. Andrew Marshall was in no mood to be coddled or consoled about his diagnosis before us in this hospital room. We spoke only of how he was feeling today and not about his treatments or prognosis. While we wanted to support him as a friend, Liam and I followed his lead. We let him tell us what he wanted and needed during our visit today.

"Corrine, I understand you are working on a novel about the lost distilleries of Scotland."

"I am, sir! I have been spending a great deal of time at the National Library of Scotland and it has ironically brought me back to my very first novel, *The Ruins of Dunmara*. I focused that novel on the MacLeods of Skye."

Before I could say any more, Andrew said, "Och! Glenammon! That is a fine whisky."

"That is exactly right! It is. And Mrs. Meredith Cox is helping me as well."

"Well, I do not know her personally, but I do know of her connection to whisky. Her late husband Landon Cox made quite a fortune in whisky. Islay, I believe. And he was a generous supporter of the university."

"That is correct, and Meredith said that they have a historian on staff at the distillery that may be of help to my research."

"Well, that will be fine. Corrine, I had Abby bring a book from the house for you. It is just on the table there by the flowers, Liam. Can you hand it to the lass?'

Liam handed me the book titled *Scotch Missed: Scotland's Lost Distilleries* by Brian Townsend.

"Oh Andrew! This is so kind!"

"I was not sure if you had already found the book in your research, but I hope it will be of help to you."

"I have not but can tell just by quickly skimming the back cover, it certainly will! And is in line with the entire premise of my novel. This will be the second time you have given me the gift of inspiration, my friend. Thank you so much!"

"After I got Liam's voicemail, I knew I had just the book for you!"

After a little while of catching up, it was obvious that Andrew was growing weary. Liam and I just looked at each other and silently agreed that it was time for us to go.

"It was good to see you man! Corrine and I should let you rest."

"Aye, thank you both for coming to see me. One of the nurses will be coming in at any moment. They are always checking something every hour on the hour!"

Andrew smiled weakly at us before continuing, "Your visit also gave Abby a break. She has been such a huge help to me, but I know it can be a long and tedious day here in the hospital. Having visitors has become a welcome relief for us both."

"Had we known, we would have come to visit you sooner," I said taking Andrew's hand in mine.

"I didn't tell many people. I think I convinced myself that not talking about it meant that it wasn't real. It is funny how you try to play games with your own mind... despite the stark reality staring you in the face."

"I can understand that line of thinking," Liam said. "But we love you and want to help in any way we can. I will work with Abby to get her family here for the weekend and we will find another time to visit again."

I nodded in agreement as I said, "Hopefully we can see you at home next time. And I will be prepared to speak with you more about this book, once I have had a chance to read it."

Andrew nodded and said softly and slowly, clearly tired from the visit, *"That would be lovely. And thank you again for your generosity, Liam. I would very much like to see my granddaughter again."*

"Of course," Liam said. "It is the least we can do!"

"Rest well, Andrew! We will keep you and your family in our prayers."

"Much appreciated, Corrine!"

"Love you friend!" Liam said hugging Andrew before I followed by squeezing his hand in mine.

"I love you both. *I truly do!*"

+++

We left the hospital in silence and only spoke to each other in the car long enough to decide to stop at The Spence at Gleneagles Townhouse for drinks and supper. I could tell by his pensive silence that today was emotional for Liam. Once we got our drinks, I reached across the table and took his hand in mine.

"Today was a *gift*," I said trying to reassure him with a weak smile.

"Aye."

"It was a gift of inspiration for sure, but it was more than that! It was a gift of *friendship*. I am so glad we could see him. Thank you for offering Nate's services to their family. I know Andrew would have never asked such a thing of you, but I could tell that he was immensely grateful. I am certain he will love seeing his granddaughter, but I mostly think he wants Abby to be able to have the loving support of her family."

"Aye."

I sat silently for a moment waiting to see if he had anything more to say. He did not. I finally squeezed his hand in mine as I whispered to him, *"Liam, are you alright?"*

He looked at me with sorrow in his eyes and confessed softly, *"Today was difficult for me."*

"I know, my love. I know."

I wanted to reassure Liam that everything would be alright, but I could not find the words. The reality was that Andrew's prognosis was terminal. We both knew that unfortunate truth.

"Andrew is not only a good friend, but he has been like a father to me. I love the man! I feel like I did when I lost my own father and seeing the man in the hospital today brought that same pain back to my heart."

I felt the tears well up in my eyes as I said, "I am so sorry! We need to make the time to see Andrew as often as we can. I know things sound grim, and I have no words to reassure you other than we should cherish every bit of the time we have left with him. None of us are guaranteed another day in this life. We should love and support our friends and family when we can. We will see him again. Let's make it a priority!"

"Aye."

We ate quietly and both thought about what a great man and friend Dr. Andrew Marshall is. No matter the length of time we have each known him, he touched both of our lives in such marvelous and impactful ways.

I prayed that my words to Liam would be true and that we would see Andrew again.

+++

Pilot Nate delivered Abby's husband and daughter to Scotland the weekend following our visit. Both Andrew and Abby sent us a lovely bouquet of flowers and a handwritten note to thank us for our generosity. Abby also texted photos of their visit which lifted Liam's spirits, seeing them all so happy together.

Liam visited Andrew two or three times a week and we all met once again after he was sent home to hospice care. He was noticeably more relaxed being home but seemed weak and weary from his fight. I never wanted to see cancer win, but it was clear that the damned thing was. I resented the thought but tried to focus on loving and supporting our friend through this transition. We mostly talked about our books together. His latest, focused on the history of the Battle of Culloden, was just being published. Like all his other books, it was a masterful historical account in his signature storytelling style. He personally walked me through his author proof copy and was ever the teacher and scholar telling me stories of the uprising and battle I had never heard before.

When Liam got the call from Abby that Andrew had passed, he could not even tell me. We were at the house on Loch Leven, and he went straight to the boathouse, took the boat to the middle of the lake, and had a moment to himself.

I did not say anything, but I knew. There would be no other reason for him to leave me without saying a word. I waited for him to finally return and when he did, we sat on the patio and cried together for the loss of our friend.

In a hushed voice, Liam said looking at this phone, *"Corrine, Chef Stephan would like to know what time we want supper."*

"Why don't we tell Chef that we will go to Mythos this evening? I think it would be nice to be in the company of another dear friend and have the house to ourselves in mourning."

"Aye, that would be just fine."

+++

Abby asked Liam to say a few words at Andrew's funeral. He kept his remarks short and to the point. He admitted to me that he did not want to get too emotional, and a long, formal eulogy just opened that door too wide for him.

When it was his turn, Liam stood briefly in the kirk and said stoically before the assembled congregation, "Dr. Andrew Marshall was not only a dear friend for over twenty years, but he also became a surrogate father during that time. After my own parents passed, he and his dear wife Clara nurtured me, cared for me, and even cheered for me when I needed it. In appreciation for the positive impact both had on my life personally and upon the academic world, today I made a gift to The University of Edinburgh establishing the Marshall Prize for students of Scottish History. This gift is in memory of both Dr. Andrew Marshall and Dr. Clara Marshall. They were not only kind people, but acclaimed researchers, inspiring professors, and gifted storytellers. It is my hope that this gift will inspire a new generation of scholars studying and championing the rich history of Scotland while honoring Andrew and Clara's own achievements and legacies for years to come."

The congregation murmured with the announcement and some politely clapped. Liam told Andrew just before his death what he was intending to do, and the man was truly touched.

Abby stood up and hugged Liam as he walked from the pulpit and back to his seat. She was honored that he recognized both of her parents in this manner, and it was clear she was emotional about it. She could not speak, and I watched Liam quietly comfort her. He knew she was appreciative... even without the words.

I just smiled through my tears as he sat down with me again. I took his hand in mine and whispered, *"I am so proud of you! What a lovely speech and gesture."*

"It was the least I could do."

What Liam did not say in the kirk was this bequest was just over £10 million. He would never tout the number, but because it was not an anonymous bequest, the university will send out a press release on the donation next week. The gift was generous and heartfelt in honor of his dear friends.

Abby invited us and a large group to her father's favorite pub after the burial. Liam was keen on attending and had Paul drive us for the day. While tinged with the expected sadness of the occasion, the whisky flowed, and it soon became a festive affair. Along with the Irish, the Scots certainly know how to celebrate a life and send off the dearly departed in a grand manner!

A man I recognized from the band playing a bit throughout the evening stopped by our table and asked, "Will ye sing with us Liam?"

"Aye," Liam said as he stood up and took a large last sip of his whisky.

I asked, "Since when do you *sing*? How did I not know that about you?"

"Love, everyone can sing a pub song! Yer nae Scottish if ye cannae!"

He kissed me quickly, took his place in the back corner with three other men. But it was more than that! One handed him his guitar and took up a fiddle instead. This incredible man never ceases to amaze me! I sat up in my seat in eager anticipation of my love singing *and* playing guitar. Two talents I did not know he had and certainly never expected.

Liam said loudly to silence the room, "In honor of our dear friend Dr. Andrew Marshall, please raise yer glass and sing with us! I am certain ye all know the words. This is *The Parting Glass*."

Some people cheered and others raced to fill their glasses once more. I knew the song was from a traditional Scottish poem and had found itself as a regular Scottish and Irish pub dirge signaling a farewell. That could just be sending a person off with a final glass at the end of the evening but over time it became a song reflecting the *'final parting.'*

Tonight, a dram of Laphroaig whisky was placed on the end of the bar for Andrew, as the man was honored by his family, friends, and colleagues. With the guitar on his knee, Liam started the first verse of the song a cappella, and the other guitarist and fiddle player joined him in playing the tune and singing in harmony at the first chorus to an eager audience ready to sing every word along with them.

"Of all the money that e'er I had
I spent it in good company
And all the harm I've ever done
Alas it was to none but me

And all I've done for want of wit
To mem'ry now I can't recall
So fill to me the parting glass
Good night and joy be to you all

So fill to me the parting glass
And drink a health whate'er befalls
Then gently rise and softly call
Good night and joy be to you all

Of all the comrades that e'er I had
They're sorry for my going away
And all the sweethearts that e'er I had
They'd wish me one more day to stay

But since it fell unto my lot
That I should rise, and you should not
I'll gently rise and softly call
Good night and joy be to you all

Fill to me the parting glass
And drink a health whate'er befalls
Then gently rise and softly call
Good night and joy be to you all

But since it fell unto my lot
That I should rise, and you should not
I'll gently rise and softly call
Good night and joy be to you all

So fill to me the parting glass
And drink a health whate'er befalls
Then gently rise and softly call
Good night and joy be to you all
Good night and joy be to you all"

The Parting Glass, Scottish Traditional Folk

I sang along at the top of my lungs with everyone else in the room. Each chorus became louder than the next as everyone embraced the song and its sentiment. As incredible as Liam was, a piper appeared out of nowhere and sent the audience into a loud and rousing chorus at the end!

When Liam returned to his seat, I kissed him repeatedly on his cheek and whispered in his ear, *"You were wonderful! Wonderful! I learn something new about you every day, and each discovery only makes me love you more."*

"It felt good to send Andrew off with a song and a final whisky."

"It was a fitting tribute. I am so proud to have known him and I admire how you loved and honored your friend and his memory today… in each… and every… way."

"Aye," he said hugging me tight. I could sense his own feelings of loss and sorrow in his embrace.

Dr. Andrew Marshall was a gift of inspiration for me upon our first meeting and instantly became a treasured friend. I know what he meant to Liam's life. The man will be missed, but hopefully, between his own legacy of historical research and books, Liam's donation to The University of Edinburgh, the lives of his daughter and granddaughter, along with my own acknowledgements in my last two historical fiction novels, this incredible man will continue to be honored long after his death.

+++

ELEVEN
Brainstorming At The Balmoral

Edinburgh, Scotland
September 2023

Seated in a large conference room housed in a modern office space near St James Quarter in Edinburgh, I met with the primary leaders of the Cox Trust For The Arts for the first time.

Meredith introduced me to every member of the team and gave me all the details about their responsibilities. Despite my asking not to have formal presentations, the team did a wonderful job with a post-mortem from last year's event. It was quite helpful to hear what they did year-over-year, what worked, and what could be better. The numbers were positive, but the consensus was that they were looking for ways to make some changes. Not change for change's sake. They were intent on preventing the entire operation from becoming stale while exceeding the donation amounts year-over-year and potentially close gaps from the dormant pandemic years.

I could tell they were an eager team and seemed open to trying new things. I took this as an affirmation that my questions and ideas might be welcomed by this team.

Once they finished, Meredith stood up and said, "Thank you team, for everything you have done! You have helped us ground ourselves in the reality of last year's benefit, which was our first return after a pandemic hiatus. I believe it is our turn to hear from Corrine and brainstorm the next event together, but might I suggest that we take the second half of this meeting to The Balmoral? I have found that a brainstorming session is most productive with ample food and drink. I have secured us a table in Bar Prince."

Everyone instantly agreed and gathered their things for the short walk across Princes Street. We might have all eagerly awaited a Champagne, oyster, and caviar-infused meeting, but I appreciated a moment to collect my thoughts and observations from the afternoon on the short walk to the bar.

Meredith held onto my arm as we walked down the street together and said, "I can see your mind working, Corrine!"

I laughed knowing that she probably could because Liam often says the same thing to me. My thoughts do tend to show on my face. I asked anyway, "Can you really?"

"Aye! I can tell you are thinking about everything you heard today! I for one, cannot wait to hear your thoughts and questions! I told you to be disruptive and challenge us. Surely some Champagne will help you do that!"

"You have my commitment! I do not know how organized my thoughts may be the more food and drink we have, but I will do my best."

Once glasses were filled and appetizers delivered, Meredith said, "Corrine, I welcome you again to the team! I would very much like to hear your thoughts from today's meeting. I am certain this entire team would like to hear your thoughts. I must remind you all that this is not a *solution* discussion! It is an *idea* discussion! We do not have to solve anything here today. We all agree that we want to think differently about the future of the Cox Trust For The Arts Benefit and now that we have level-set ourselves on last year, we can talk more about the future together! So, fill your glass and we will keep the food coming. Corrine, you have the floor!"

I nervously chugged the last of my Champagne and was met at once by our server who filled my flute again. I absolutely love that everyone in this bar knows how to take care of me. And they do!

"First, thank you all for welcoming me the way you did today. I told Meredith that this world of trusts and benefits is new for me. Your last event was the first I had ever attended. Your presentation this afternoon helped me see what I did not as an attendee, and I thank you for giving me a much greater understanding. Also, as an author, I am in a creative field that is not supported by the trust so please take my questions and ideas for nothing more than thought starters as you plan..."

"As *we* plan..." Meredith interrupted.

"As *we* plan for next year's event," I said accepting her correction. She was right, as co-chair I could not just passively throw ideas at the team. "I am not here to solve anything for you, but I hope my feedback helps."

"Aye! I asked Corrine to be disruptive, it is up to us as a team to decide what we can and cannot do... what we should or should not do. This is a chance to think about the possibilities and brainstorm together. And what better place to think about possibilities than The Balmoral Hotel?"

Everyone vocally agreed about the venue for this part of our meeting, raised their glasses to the middle of the table, and said in unison, *"Sláinte!"*

Meredith added, "But Corrine, as co-chair, know that you will have a voice in approving the final recommendation with me."

I nodded to Meredith, accepting my new role once again, and said, "The first thing that stood out for me today was just how important this one benefit is to the Cox Trust for the entire year. I also appreciated what you all outlined in learnings year-over-year to try to learn and maximize the impact from your most important annual event."

"Exactly, Corrine! We do not think we have perfected everything but have tried to improve each year."

"That mindset was clear! I have some thoughts if you will allow me."

"That is why you are here, lass! We want *all* your thoughts!" Meredith said, laughing and grabbing another oyster from the silver tray lined with ice. The team laughed along with her.

I can tell everyone at the table is knowledgeable and talented, but they do seem to follow Meredith's lead. In the brief time I have been with them I have seen no one challenge her feedback and direction but I cannot tell if there is a hive-mind mentality based on her position and they all do agree or if they are afraid of her. I will have to observe this lot more to truly uncover the answer.

"It is so easy to gravitate to the names people know or Scottish artists we expect, but what if we *display the future* of Scottish art? The future brought forth by Scotland's *young* talent. The future the Cox Trust is funding and supporting. We could showcase an entire class of unknown and up-and-coming artists either by the country as a whole or by region. We could celebrate teachers and schools dedicated to the arts. The event is prestigious and exclusive, but the wider beneficiaries of the Cox Trust should be the focus! Not just who is in the room on the night making donations."

Half of the table just stared at me, and the other half was frantically taking notes. I continued, "It is a subtle pivot, but could reposition the event and the Trust in a positive way. You could even introduce a Cox Trust set of awards. They could be by age range, or geography, or by medium. The award itself could be a prestigious acknowledgement for an up-and-coming artist in Scotland. Think of something like... and I am making this all up so bear with me... *The 2024 Cox Trust For The Arts Award for Sculpture*' or '*The 2024 Cox Trust For The Arts Young Artist of the Year*' or '*The 2024 Cox Trust For The Arts Teacher of the Year*' or even '*The 2024 Cox Trust For The Arts Scholastic Programme.*'"

"Miss Hunter, do you envision that the benefit would suddenly become an award show?" Audrey in PR asked me directly, and in a slight tone of dismissal. Finally, we are seeing some resistance to an idea versus blind allegiance. I almost welcomed the challenge!

"No, not at all, Audrey! I think you all have genuinely learned that a formal, society benefit works. I am not sure that the attendees are going to willingly sit through an award show. Let me rephrase. Imagine that in whatever venue, your donors can see and appreciate the work submitted, perhaps even meet the artists, and teachers. You could decide that there are no *awards* per se, you just have a collection on display throughout the gallery for artists that met the committee's determined selection requirements to be featured or... perhaps as I said earlier *showcased* is a better word... at the event."

Meredith said to the table, "I like the idea of a *showcase*."

I continued, "That could be a draw unto itself! Imagine an arts teacher or young artist being selected, getting dressed up to attend the exclusive benefit, being featured in Cox Trust media and press, and having the acknowledgement and validation for excellent work from the very same people helping to fund their endeavors. And I can tell you that as an attendee, it would be fulfilling to see the actual manifestation of the inspiration, and the creative talent my donation supports. It makes that donation even more *meaningful*."

"That could be a benefit unto itself!" Meredith said, in agreement. "We could have criteria for each category and feature certain numbers in each and then select one distinguished artist, teacher, or programme to lead each category. Even if we do not call it an award per se."

Everyone just stared at me after my litany of ideas over Champagne and caviar. The silence around the table meant that I kept talking, as I normally do. For some reason I always feel like I alone must fill the void of silence.

"I trust you all to decide what can and should work but I think something like this, as an attendee, makes it so much more tangible than just blindly giving a donation each year out of expectation and obligation in exchange for a night of socializing. Some may do just that and be fine with it. But some of us might like to see first-hand the work we are supporting, celebrate the teachers who inspire, and elevate... even promote... new and unknown artistic talent in Scotland. That aligns with your core mission at the Trust."

Audrey reluctantly agreed and finally said, "It does."

"For the last point, the endorsement and promotion of talent could elevate the prestige of the Cox Trust even more! It could be a designation or recognition that artists and teachers revere and respect. One that they *want* to earn. You have learned that a limited invitation list elevates the event for the donors. Now elevate the beneficiaries. Then you are elevating the Trust. Audrey, imagine the reach and stories you could generate via both traditional and social media with each artist, teacher, or school from the beginning with requests for submissions and throughout the year with those showcased... not just surrounding the single society event?"

Meredith smiled at me, and I smiled back. Whether or not I was fulfilling her request, I knew that by the faces and frantic notetaking around the table, I had at least accomplished one thing and that was to make them think differently. Whether or not any of my thoughts and ideas manifest themselves in the final plan for next year remains to be seen.

Everyone just stared at me, as I said, almost apologetically, "I am sorry! I just rambled my first thoughts and ideas with extraordinarily little to back them up."

My mind was racing with ideas. Meredith smiled broadly at me and said, "I agree completely with Corrine! Our next meeting should be a comprehensive look at what we can do with these ideas. I believe Corrine has given us a great deal to think about and build upon. Starting with, the way I see it, looking at the beneficiaries of the Trust and not just proven and already celebrated Scottish artistic talent, which we have consistently done in the past. I know this is the team to finesse those ideas and make them happen! Should we give you two weeks for a first draft of a recommendation?"

Everyone nodded and declared their agreement to her timeline. I felt a genuine and enthusiastic shift amongst the people before me. Audrey agreed to take the lead on a coordinated recommendation across all teams. Meredith excused herself to the loo for a moment. She nodded her head and with a sly smile left me on my own to defend my suggestions with the team. The minute she did, everyone came to me with a barrage of questions. Instead of staying all night at Bar Prince, I offered to meet with the team next week before their recommendation deadline. When Meredith returned, we both left them to contemplate their next moves as we walked to meet our drivers in front of the hotel.

"Thank you, Meredith! I appreciated today. Have a lovely evening!" I said kissing both of her cheeks.

"The same, lass! You did everything I hoped you would! We will talk in a week or so. Enjoy the rest of your evening and give my love to Liam."

"Miss Hunter, let me get you home," Liam's driver and my friend Paul, said as he rushed ahead of me to prevent me from opening my own door, as he always does.

+++

TWELVE
Plans And Prayers

Edinburgh, Scotland
September 2023

I met with the team at the Cox Trust to hear their first thoughts and ideas after one week building their draft recommendation from our brainstorming session at The Balmoral Hotel. Before leaving, I stopped by Meredith's office to talk about how I thought they were progressing.

I was genuinely impressed by the way they took their own learnings and my feedback to build a new recommendation. I asked simple questions and helped refine positioning but agreed they were more than ready to present to Meredith the following week.

"It is a strong recommendation and not a radical departure," I said. "I believe they were all energized by the discussion and the possibilities to reinvent next year's event with some simple and thoughtful modifications."

"Well then, I cannot wait to hear more next week!" Meredith said in return.

Suddenly, my phone still in my hand started vibrating with a call. The screen showed Ewan's name.

"Excuse me Meredith, I cannot imagine why Liam's son would be calling me. He had a rugby match this afternoon. Perhaps it is a mistake, but I must answer."

"Of course, you should!"

"Hello, Ewan," I said answering my phone. There was no response and I suspected what I told Meredith was true. The lad must have accidentally called my number. That was, until I heard him ask in a weak voice laced with emotion, *"Miss... Corrine?"*

"Yes, Ewan! Can you hear me?"

He said nothing back and every hair on my body stood on end. I left my chair and walked to the window overlooking St James Quarter hoping that it would help our mobile connection if that were the reason for his delay. Something was wrong. I could hear him breathing heavily, "What is it? What is wrong, love?"

"We going to the Royal Infirmary Hospital. You have to come... erm... Da collapsed at my rugby match."

"What?!"

The poor boy beat me to the myriad of questions already forming in my mind as he said instantly, "Mum and I do not know anything. They took him away in an ambulance. *Please come!* Do you know where it is?"

"I don't! But our friend Paul is driving me today and he will certainly know where to go. I will be there shortly, sweetheart. You said you were with your mum?"

"Aye!"

"Everything will be alright. Tell her I am on my way! I am right behind you both!"

I hung up the phone before we could say goodbye to each other and breathed in as deeply as I could. I do not know what made me try to reassure the boy in a way I had no right to. Perhaps I just wanted to reassure myself that Liam was alright.

He *had* to be alright!

Meredith just stared at me. She said nothing but eventually after feeling my emotion at the end of the call, came to me, and put her hand on my arm. When I could finally speak, I left her and ran for my bag under the chair I was sitting in before.

"I have to go!"

"What is it?"

"Liam collapsed at his son's rugby match. Do you know where the Royal Infirmary Hospital is?"

"Christ above! Aye! Get your things, lass!"

She called her own driver instantly on her mobile phone as we walked together arm-in-arm to the elevator. I swear she kept me marching to our destination while instructing her driver and Paul exactly where I needed to go... and quickly! I could not think enough to call Paul myself and appreciated her intervention. Paul sped me through the city straight to the doors to A&E at the hospital.

He said nothing until he helped me out of the car, "You and Mr. Crichton are in my prayers, lass! I will wait for you here in the car park. You call or text the minute you need me, and I will be ready! *I will be ready! You hear?*"

I just squeezed his hand in mine and smiled weakly before running through the automatic emergency doors afraid of what may be waiting for me on the other side.

"Miss Corrine!" Ewan yelled as I ran into the room. He ran straight for me and hugged me tight. We held onto each other, but I could only see Sarah's pained face.

"What happened?" I asked her directly, holding onto her very scared son. I was scared myself and could not let him go. It appears he could not let me go either. Our growing affection had mostly been in words or connections over jigsaw puzzles, or his simple and lovely points of acknowledgement that I existed in his father's life. But now, we were both overcome with emotion and needed each other's support and comfort. I could not let him go.

Sarah said with a sense of regret, "Before the start of the match, Liam said he did not feel well. He looked pale and like he was in pain, but I never asked a word about what he *felt*. I honestly dismissed it in the moment as a hangover or simple headache. You know how men can be *so dramatic* when they do not feel well! Suddenly as the match ended, he fell on the ground, passed out cold!'

"Oh God!"

"I would have asked more questions if I thought it was serious, but the man collapsed on the ground before us all! It was the worst thing I have ever seen!"

Ewan started crying thinking the same, which made me start crying. Liam was a tall man. Surely falling to the ground had to be traumatic for all that saw it. I worried that I was about to relive losing the love of my life, once again. David's sudden death nearly broke me. I am not certain I could survive another loss like that. It would be more than my poor heart could bear. If that is what this moment was, then they might as well take me to the morgue with him.

Sarah continued, "There are always medics on the sidelines for the matches, and they rushed to him instantly. They revived him by sal volatile or smelling salts as you may call it. This was a positive sign that he just fainted, but he was weak and not verbally responsive. He seemed in a daze and clearly still in great pain. We followed the ambulance here and have heard nothing since."

"Where is Eric?"

"He went to a friend's house after school today and has no idea. I should pick him up soon, but we could have Jordaan or Paul pick him up and bring him here, if we need."

"Let me see what I can find out."

Before I could say a word myself, Sarah grabbed my arm, and led me straight to the nurse at the front desk and told him that I was Liam's partner.

I said, "Please tell me who I can speak to about his care, and if I can see him... I am here with his ex-wife and son. We just want to know how he is. His family has not heard anything since he arrived here by ambulance. You *must* tell us something..."

I could not finish the sentence before Sarah said in agreement as she touched my arm, "Aye! Please give us *something*!"

I just looked at her with tears in my eyes and she had the same. Perhaps she loved the man after all if for no other reason than their young son was standing behind her in an absolute broken state after seeing his father collapse. But I believe it was even more than that. I felt like she recognized my love of the man and my position in this *new extended family*.

She propelled me forward so that we could find out what was happening, and I appreciated her for it.

The male nurse at reception said, "Let me see what I can find out for you. Your name?"

"Corrine Hunter."

"The author?"

"The same."

"Aye! Let me see what I can do, Miss Hunter," he said eagerly before walking away.

I don't know if my name helped, and I did not care. The nurse seemed to be helping us and for that I was grateful. Sarah squeezed my arm and said, "You might be the one to finally get us answers! Apparently, an ex-wife, standing here with his son, does not have any kind of influence!"

"You both have a right to know, Sarah," I said weakly and with no real understanding of how medical practices and privacy policies in Scotland or the broader UK accommodated ex-wives or children… or partners.

I could think of nothing but where Liam might be behind the secure double doors before me. And my first thought at that moment was to hug Sarah. I needed to hug her. I needed to hug someone. Ewan was a comfort to me the moment I walked in, but I needed reassurance again. I know she was shocked by my affection, but instantly hugged me back. We were both scared and only had each other at that moment. I appreciated that she and Ewan were both here with me and I was not confronting this uncertainty alone.

After about five agonizing minutes, the nurse came back and said, "Miss Hunter, I need you to put on this mask and I can take you back to

Mr. Crichton through the emergency bay. You can take it off once you are in his private room if you wish. He has been admitted."

We all breathed a sigh of relief that he was alive, and I could see him. But still feared what could have caused him to be admitted. Sarah and I hugged each other again. I touched young Ewan's shoulder as I said to them both before putting the mask over my ears, "I will find out everything I can. Then I will come right back to you. I promise!"

I followed the nurse back through the maze of a corridor of emergency suites surrounding a large nurses bay in the middle before we finally arrived at a series of individual rooms at the end of the hall.

"He is just in this room here," the nurse said as he gently opened the door for me.

Liam was dressed in a hospital gown and propped up in his bed with his eyes shut. He was hooked to an IV drip and heart monitor that softly beeped with his heart rate. A welcome sound that told me, if nothing else, his heart sounded healthy and strong. He did not move upon the opening of the door and must have fallen asleep. I did not want to wake him, but I had to hear his voice. I had to know he was alright. And I wanted him to know I was here with him.

I sat gently on the edge of the bed and placed my hand around his warm, peaceful face. I stroked his cheek and beard gently willing him to wake on my touch. He said in a whisper with his eyes still closed, *"Och, Corrine."*

I instantly started crying, as I said, through my tears, *"Liam, I love you so much!"*

"I know my darlin' and ye know that I love ye more. Please dinnae cry. It will be fine. I will be just fine!"

"I was so scared! You know..." I said through my tears before taking my mask off and kissing him. I could not help but kiss him.

"I know, love. I know. I hate fer ye to see me like this. I know yer thinkin' about what happened to David. I am so verra sorry to worry ye!"

He knew that I was frightened for him and at the possibility of reliving one of the worst moments of my life. He looked pale and was clearly still in pain. The IV drip must have medication in it. He was not slurring his words, but his voice was low and slow. And much like when he drinks, his Scottish accent was more pronounced.

I took his hand in mine, *"Tell me everything."*

"I didna feel well when I went to Ewan's match today. I didna tell ye, but I havena felt well fer several days. I felt feverish and had a growing pain in my belly that moved to my groin. I feared it might be a hernia and tried my best to ignore it. But today the pain was more than I could bear. As soon as the match ended, I took a step and one unexpected jolt shot through me like lightning! I havena felt pain like that in my life! And when it hit me, I fainted dead away. Fer that I am mostly embarrassed."

It was then that I could see the small bruise forming on his slightly swollen and scraped cheek. I touched it gently.

"Aye! I fainted dead away only to land on my face. Thankfully, the pitch is grass. Imagine how I would look if the lad played basketball!"

I laughed at his attempt at humor from a hospital bed and said, "You poor thing! How do you feel now?"

"Sleepy because of whatever they put in this IV but in less pain to be sure. Apparently, I need to have emergency surgery to remove my appendix."

"Oh my!"

"Is Ewan alright? I could hear him call out to me when they put me in the ambulance but was in such a fog of pain and having just fainted that I couldna say the words to reassure the lad myself."

"Like the rest of us he was just so scared. He and Sarah have had no information from the doctors since they arrived. So not knowing what was happening has only added to their fear."

"They collected all my personal belongings when they helped me get undressed. I was instantly put on this IV and could not find my phone to text anyone. How did ye find out?"

"Ewan called me."

"Aye, I am grateful fer that and so glad that yer here with me."

I held his hand tight in mine and smiled. Before I could say anything back to him, the doctor entered the room.

"Mr. Crichton, I am Dr. Matheson and will be your surgeon today."

Doctor Matheson was not only supremely confident, but a gorgeous young woman with brunette hair, bright blue eyes, and a light Scottish accent. I smiled at Liam and tried my best to keep from laughing. I knew we were thinking the same thing. I decided to trade my slight twinge of female jealousy for respect of her position. If she were the one to fix this for us and send him home, I would happily have a beautiful doctor do so with immense gratitude.

Liam said, "It is nice to meet ye Dr. Matheson. This is my partner, Corrine Hunter."

"It is my pleasure to meet you Miss Hunter," she said before turning back to her patient. "Sir, I contacted your personal physician, Dr. Conrad, as requested. He has agreed to the plan for us to continue with surgery. He would not stop it, of course, as this is a medical emergency, but he informed me of your medical history and wanted me to say that he will follow-up with you directly when he returns from Greece."

"That man spends an inordinate amount of *his* time and *my* money in Greece!"

I had no clue who Dr. Conrad was but squeezed Liam's hand in support of his well-medicated humor as Dr. Matheson continued, "Thankfully since the inflamed appendix has not ruptured, we believe we can do laparoscopic surgery to quickly remove it. As with any surgery, if we decide that we need to do more, especially with any signs of greater inflammation or infection, we will."

Liam and I both nodded in agreement to this logical approach.

"If everything remains simple, surgery will take about an hour. Then you will be in recovery for a bit to come out of anesthesia and monitor your vitals. I would personally like your temperature to come down a bit more but believe removing the source of inflammation should help do that in short order. If all goes well, you could be discharged later this evening for home with Doctor's orders for rest and recovery."

"I assure you that I will see to Liam's at-home care, and we will follow all your instructions, Dr. Matheson."

Liam just winked at me. I am not certain if he was already planning a rebellion against Doctor's orders or if he just fancied having a nursemaid at home. Knowing the man as I do, I suspect it was certainly both!

Just then, a nurse and anesthesiologist with the surgical team came in to prepare Liam for surgery. The nurse was carrying a tray with a razor, and I knew this was my cue to leave.

I said to Dr. Matheson directly, "When you are done, you can find me in the A&E waiting room. I need go back there to tell his family what is happening."

"I will see you as soon as surgery is over Miss Hunter and when he is returned to his room, a nurse will bring you back to him. Again, we all hope Mr. Crichton will sleep soundly in his own bed this evening."

I kissed Liam with both hands wrapped around his face and said, "I love you, Liam! *I love you!* I will see you as soon as they let me and hopefully, we will return home shortly after."

"You know that I love ye more. Dinnae worry, Corrine! I am in good hands."

"I have ultimate confidence in both you and Dr. Matheson. I will go out and tell Sarah and Ewan what I have learned. They were so worried... especially young Ewan."

"Give me my phone fer a second. I want to text 'em."

"Mr. Crichton, you may want to give Miss Hunter all your personal belongings instead of leaving here," Dr. Matheson said. "We could certainly keep everything collected once you were admitted in a locker for you when you go into surgery, but since she is here, *that* may be a better plan."

"Aye!" he said in agreement.

After sending his text, Liam handed me his phone and said, "I just told Sarah and Ewan not to worry and that ye would come out in a moment to tell them everything."

He then handed me the small white hospital bag that also held his Rolex watch, wallet, phone, and the key fob to his Range Rover.

"I assume it is still at the school?" I asked holding up the fob.

"Aye! Och! My laptop is on the backseat!"

"Got it! I will ask Paul to deliver it to the house. I am certain he can get one of his friends to help. He is waiting for me outside."

"No. Tell him to deliver the car here and ye can drive me home. There is no need fer the man to stay on call this evening. We dinnae know when we will get out of this place, love. Paul should go home."

"Excellent plan and I agree! I will take care of it and see you soon," I said, kissing him once again and stroking his handsome face.

"*Aye, my love.*"

+++

The air of anxiety had already lifted when I walked back through the doors to the A&E waiting room. I sent Sarah and Ewan home with the peace of mind that Liam was about to have one of the safest surgeries there is, and since the appendix had not ruptured, we hoped to return home this evening. They were equally pleased to have heard from him directly via text and we all hugged each other as they left to collect Eric.

I sent Paul on the errand to retrieve Liam's Range Rover. He was thrilled to have a task and to be of service to us both. He was picked up by one of his fellow chauffeur friends to retrieve the car and returned it to the hospital in no time. He told me where the car was parked before leaving me for the evening with not only the key fob, but more loving support and prayers. More than anything, I appreciated that navigating the task helped make time go by faster through Liam's surgery.

I was still nervous but kept my focus on hope and gratitude that we were only worried about an unruptured appendix and not something more serious. I just silently prayed, sent texts to friends to let them know what was happening, and watched the minutes slowly tick away one-by-one on the large clock hanging on the back wall over the A&E reception desk.

"Miss Hunter?" Dr. Matheson asked, walking into the waiting room, and taking off her surgical mask. I instantly stood before her as she said, "Everything went exactly to plan. We removed Mr. Crichton's appendix. I must say, we are so thankful that, while severely inflamed, it remained intact. I am not sure he had much time to spare to be honest, but this made surgery all the easier. Fortunately, we saw nothing that caused us any added concern. He is awake in recovery and once he is moved back to his room, a nurse will come and collect you. We will continue to monitor his vitals for a period before the on-call doctor agrees to his discharge. Again, it is my hope that he will sleep soundly in his own bed at home this evening."

"*Thank you*, Dr. Matheson!" I said with all the emotion I felt showing on my face. I stood before her with hot tears streaming down my face and I could barely say the words. I was so relieved that Liam was well and was immensely grateful for Dr. Matheson and her entire surgical team.

She placed her hand reassuringly on my shoulder and said with a smile, "I have no idea how the man will be as a patient at home, but I believe you will both be fine! He seems to have a *very good* sense of humor."

"That he does!" I said laughing through my tears. "And whatever you put in his IV only enhanced it!"

"He should start to feel relief from the removal of the appendix, but it will be replaced by the pain of his incision and surgery. You should know that most patients feel so well that they are often over-confident after surgery because they still have anesthesia and pain medication in their system. The nurse will send you home with instructions, so you both know what to do or *not* do. You will have the expected post-surgery rules like no heavy lifting or exertion for a time along with wound care. But it will also include symptoms to watch for that would signal he needs to see his doctor or return to us at once. Some patients find that the third day after surgery is generally the worst when everything wears off in their system. We will send you home with some pain medication, but Mr. Crichton may decide that he needs little more than what he can get over the counter now that the primary source of pain has been removed."

"I understand. Thank you again!"

"You are most welcome, Miss Hunter."

Not even ten minutes later, the nurse brought me back to Liam's room. He was awake, but clearly out of it. He said nothing. His eyes were glassy, and he had a cheeky grin on his face as he watched me walk toward him. I wanted to laugh but could not. For God's sake! The poor man just had emergency surgery!

"How do you feel?"

Liam just looked at me with narrowed eyes as if he were processing both the question and his answer in slow motion. Finally, he said, "My head's mince... but I am alive. How do *ye feel, lass?*"

I kissed him quickly and said caressing his beard with both of my hands, "Not as high as you but relieved. Please rest. Paul delivered the car and as soon as they let us, we will go *home*."

"Home," Liam whispered the word still in a fog of anesthesia and drugs as he fell asleep with his hands holding mine.

I just held his hands, kissed each of them, and whispered almost in prayer in return, *"I want nothing more than to take you home, my love."*

+++

They did not discharge Liam until nearly ten o'clock after his temperature came down to an acceptable level. Removing the inflamed appendix finally showed in all his vitals and the on-call doctor released him to my care with our detailed list of post-surgery instructions and medications.

Liam was completely on another planet as we drove home. He had little to say to me as I helped him gingerly step up into the passenger seat of his Range Rover. When he finally spoke, he told me that I was not a particularly good driver. I let it go the first time, but finally after the sixth mention told him that he was perhaps not the best judge of my driving since he could not see straight. He laughed considerably at his own drugged state and agreed. He was in no condition to judge my driving this night!

The minute we walked into the house I said, "I want you to get into your pajamas now, love."

"Aye! My trousers are *too tight*! They filled my belly with too much gas! I feel like I *cannot even stand up straight*!"

"Alright, alright! You will feel so much better in a moment. Come with me."

I led him to our bedroom. If he had not been through so much today, he would have made me laugh again. I told him once that my former fiancé David Bryant was goofball funny, but a highly medicated Liam Crichton was also goofball funny! I tried so hard not to laugh due to the seriousness of the situation, but tonight this man seemed intent on making me do so!

I helped him get undressed and into his loose pajamas to protect the dressing over his incision and lessen the tightness his trouser waistband had on his slightly swollen, post-surgery belly.

"Do ye know they had to shave me?"

I did know this as I saw the razor the nurse had on a tray when she entered his hospital room, but just asked innocently in reply, "Did they?"

"Aye! I lost an appendix *but* gained half of a manscape!"

"Liam! My God! Do not make me laugh!"

"Ye never know, ye might prefer it! We could do the other side, if ye want."

I could not help myself! I laughed at his clearly loopy state and his statement so much that I could barely get his slippers on his feet and had to sit on the floor trying to stifle my giggles. Of course, he was oblivious to the humor of what he said but seemed pleased with himself that he made me laugh. His silly grin told me that much.

"I can feel the incision," he whispered to me like he was sharing a deep, dark secret.

"No, you can't, love! I am confident that you can't feel much of *anything!*"

He just looked at me and said with all seriousness, "They had to cut me open to get to the appendix, Corrine."

"I know. Are you in any pain? They sent us home with instructions and medication if you needed anything."

"No. I just wanted to tell ye... *I can feel it!*"

"Got it! Chef Stephan left us chicken orzo soup and fresh baked bread in the kitchen. I am not certain you have had anything but your toast and tea this morning. Even if you aren't hungry, it may be comforting and nourishing for you to have a warm meal. And with all the drugs, it would probably be good to have something more in your stomach tonight. I can bring it to you. Do you want to sit over here in the chair by the fireplace, or would you prefer supper in bed?"

"No." I just looked at him with narrowed eyes as he continued, "I mean, I dinnae want it in here. I will come to the kitchen with ye."

"Alright, then!"

I helped Liam up from the edge of the bed and walked with him slowly to the kitchen so I could prepare his late and soothing supper. While simple, it looked and smelled comforting after a long day at the hospital. I am not sure that I had anything since my own breakfast toast and suddenly felt famished.

While the soup and bread were warming, I said, "I know it is late, but I promised that we would call Sarah to tell her when you were home and to reassure the boys. Especially, Ewan. He was distraught, love. He needs to hear your voice tonight."

"Aye, give me my phone."

I retrieved his phone from my bag, and he called Sarah on speaker so we could both hear the conversation.

"Tell me how you are, Liam!" Sarah said instantly when she answered the phone.

"I am home but still in a fog of anesthesia and drugs. *Lots... and lots... and lots... and lots... of incredible drugs!*"

She said laughing, "I cannot tell that *at all*! Let me put you on speaker to speak to the lads quickly so you can rest. Corrine, we want to stop by tomorrow, but I will text you first to ensure we are not disrupting the recovering patient's rest and recovery."

"I know the boys will want to see their father, especially Ewan. He absolutely broke my heart today! We will make it happen, but I will let you know how Liam is feeling in the morning. I am sure you can tell he is still quite out of it. So, I expect he will sleep it off!"

"Aye! We should probably count on being after school anyway, so hopefully that will give him a slow start," she said. "I am putting you both on speaker. I let the lads stay up until we heard from you. It is your Da, my loves."

"*Da!? Da?* Are you home?" the twins asked in unison.

"Aye, lads! Dinnae worry. I am home with Corrine who is makin' me chicken soup."

I spoke up and said jokingly, "You mean, Miss Corrine is *warming up* chicken soup courtesy of Chef Stephan!"

I heard Ewan laugh and then Eric asked, "Are you in pain?"

"No, love. I still have drugs in my system from surgery, so I mostly feel sleepy. Ewan?"

"Aye?"

"I am verra sorry ye had to see me faint and I am sorry I was in such pain that I couldna reassure ye. Everything is fine, son! I am home safe and sound."

I could hear Ewan crying and he could not speak. This sweet boy broke my heart once again. I put my hand to my mouth to try to remain quiet. Liam looked at me with tears in his own eyes. I finally said for both of us when I realized Liam could not respond to his son himself, "We will see you all tomorrow."

Sarah said instantly to help end this call and offer her own comfort to her sons, "Thank you for calling and letting us all know you are home. Sleep well and feel better, Liam!"

I hung up the phone for him as Liam was overcome with his son's emotion. The drugs in his system along with what he had gone through today made his own response even more overwhelming.

"*It is just fine,*" I said hugging Liam as he held me tight. "Ewan will be fine, my love. He was scared. Getting your text had to be a relief! Now talking to you even more. But seeing you tomorrow will mean everything to him. He will have the reassurance he needs!"

I made us both bowls of soup with bread on the side. We ate together in silence before I could finally take Liam back to the bathroom and tuck him into bed. It was such a sweet relief to see my loving man resting before me.

Liam was quiet, but I could tell he was not only still quite drugged but exhausted from the unfortunate events and emotions of the day. I know he had to be physically and mentally exhausted. Finally, he said in a weary whisper into the dark when I joined him in bed, "*I love ye, Corrine.*"

"*My darling man, you know that I love you more. Sleep well!*"

I waited for him to drift off to sleep and thought about nothing more than I was so glad that he was here with me. I listened to his soft breathing and was reassured by every constant breath.

The day unfolded in a way that brought me nothing but fear and pain at the start because it resurrected the memories of David's unexpected death. And I could not bear the pain of young Ewan crying before me. After his apology, the lad started to become a close ally but today, my heart broke with his in a way I had never felt before. Through his honest show of emotion, I felt genuine *love* for the boy. I like to think that with the way he thought of calling me straight away and embracing me at the hospital, he felt the same.

I was overcome with my own emotions and left our bed for a moment. Sitting on the stool before my makeup mirror in the bathroom, I finally broke down and sobbed tears of relief and gratitude into my tissues.

Suddenly, I felt two strong arms around my shoulders. I looked back into the mirror at the man I loved and said, "Oh, Liam! *I am so sorry!* I did not mean to wake you!"

"I know, love. Please dinnae cry."

"I just needed a moment. My emotions caught up with me. I am so relieved you are not only home safe and sound, but healthy."

"Do ye know that I met ye a year ago today, Corrine?"

I turned around instantly, looked up at him, and asked as I took his hand in mine, *"Today!?"*

"Aye!"

"I am so sorry that the events of the day made me forget, but I give you total props for remembering that when you are drugged out of your mind!"

We laughed together as he said lovingly before pulling me up and kissing me, "I couldna forget the day that I met the love of my life."

"Oh Liam..."

"Come back to bed, my love."

+++

"You did not have to do this," I said to Sarah who walked into the house with two huge bouquets of flowers.

"Only one is ours, you have five or six bouquets and gift baskets outside."

"Oh, my! We gave Mrs. Clarke the day off. And I admit that I turned the doorbell off because I knew that Liam would sleep in after our late-night return. I did not even think to turn it back on until about an hour ago and clearly did not look at the cameras when I did."

"Not to worry! I told the lads to bring them all in for you."

"Thank you!"

Aside from Sarah's own bouquet we had flowers and gift baskets from Tom and Elaine, Meredith Cox, Kate and Luke, Colin and Mark, and James and Diana MacLaughlin. Our lovely driver, Paul texted me regularly for updates and left a sweet card and small tin of his wife's delicious homemade Scottish Whisky Tablet at the door.

Chef Dan sent word to me and Chef Stephan via text that he was sending food from his restaurant, Mythos, for this evening. Chef Stephan said that he would deliver the food himself, along with his regular restocking but he would ensure we both had what we needed before leaving us alone while Liam recovered. News traveled fast through our circle of friends with the few texts I sent from the hospital waiting room, and I appreciated all of them for loving and caring for us so.

With the last deliveries from the front placed on the kitchen island, Ewan asked me, "Where is Da?"

"He is sitting there in the back garden with his tea. Go to him, love."

Ewan smiled at me and ran with his brother to the patio doors. Sarah and I watched their reunion from the back of the kitchen island. The boys hugged their father tight, and he hugged them back while kissing them both on the tops of their heads.

I bit my lip, but when I could finally speak, I said, "Through everything... all the changes... one thing is certain. These young men love their father, and he loves them."

"Aye, it is as simple as that," Sarah said staring at the emotional scene before us on the still brightly lit patio garden.

Love and family, whatever form that takes in life, are the most important things. I relished seeing it manifested before me, and I thanked

Liam for bringing me into his family. As uncertain as I was at the start about ex-wives and children, I now appreciated my new *extended family*, and I could honestly say that I loved them all.

Without question, it was as simple as that.

+++

THIRTEEN
An Honorable Name

**Mayfair, London, England
September 2023**

Pilot Nate flew me to London for the day to see my dearest friends and their newborn baby girl. Liam's London driver delivered me to their gorgeous townhouse on Berkeley Square. I wished more than anything that Liam could have joined me on this trip, but he was still recovering from his appendectomy and did not need to travel. While I missed him, I welcomed the opportunity to support my friends just weeks after they became new parents.

"Look at this sweet angel," I whispered as we all stood over the wee babe sleeping soundly in her bassinette. Her room, designed by proud Uncle Colin, was fit for a princess. It was in all manner of white and grays, with a subtle mix of supporting floral and plaid patterns. Despite the distinct animal theme featuring baby lambs and rabbits, this room could easily be a fine guest room and not a nursery. It was calm and sophisticated. With

the number of unopened gifts scattered around the room, it was clear this lass was already cherished and adored.

Kate whispered as she put her hand on my back, *"She will be up soon. Let's sit and talk for a minute in the kitchen while we can, my darling."*

Once we were back at the kitchen island, Luke met me instantly with a glass of wine with ice and Kate a sparkling water. I said, "She is gorgeous! But tell me how you are Mum and Dad!"

Luke took a sip of his own drink and asked while laughing, "You cannot see the weariness in our eyes, Corrie my girl?"

"To be honest, that is to be expected with a newborn, love!"

Kate responded instantly to me saying, "It is! But my God! I told Luke that we were too old and set in our ways for this disruption! However, I must admit that as I say those words to you, I only have to look at her sweet face, and my weary complaints disappear in an instant."

"I have such new love in my heart for both my wife and now my daughter, that I cannot put into words!" Luke teared up for a moment and said kissing Kate on her cheek. "I just look at my two girls in amazement and wonder! How did I get so blessed?"

"And you all are healthy?"

Kate said, "Yes. She is thriving. I had a little postpartum but think some of it was not just hormones in my system but a natural fear as a new parent that I did not know what to do with this little life, now under my care! Oh yes! There are a million books, but no one *really* tells you what to do! Corrie, you literally leave the hospital, get in the car, and realize that you are on your own! You must keep this child alive, and it is *fucking* paralyzing at the beginning! Not to mention you must deal with another soul that has their own personality and expectations communicated only in coos and cries that you must learn to decipher."

Luke laughed as he said, "You have never been calmer, darling!"

"Then this child has *truly* changed you all!" I said laughing with Luke.

They both smiled and nodded in agreement. In my brief time in this house, I could see that this baby girl had not only changed them both in very positive ways but brought them closer as a couple. I sat in amazement before my dearest friends and honored their new family.

"Have you decided on a name?"

Kate and Luke looked at each other before he said, "We have. We were intentional about not providing the baby a name before birth..."

Before he could finish, Kate interrupted him saying, "You know that I was so scared that I was too old for this and feared it could end at any moment, so I could not bear to connect to the baby that way. I had to keep some distance between my head and my heart."

Kate teared up on these words and it was so beautiful to see her in such a softened state. Kate Woodhouse was a lovely person and a caring friend, but she certainly had sharp edges. Edges that had served her both personally and professionally. Now I could see that some of those edges were rounded and smoothed by motherhood. This sweet baby girl may be the best thing to ever happen to her.

"I understand that... I do! You told me the same many times and that is why we did not have a baby shower for you."

Kate continued, "That is right! My own fears also kept us from finding out whether it was a boy or a girl."

"Oh, my loves," I said.

"We had a running list of possible names, but agreed to wait until the babe was here. She was unnamed for the birth certificate until last week."

"*Really?*"

Just then, the loud cries of a newborn resonated on the baby monitor sitting atop the kitchen counter.

Luke instantly set about warming a bottle as Kate said almost apologetically, "I was not particularly successful at breastfeeding. We bonded but she wasn't quite eating enough. She wants to be with me, and I am still pumping, but she is a heartier eater during feedings with a bottle."

"I make no judgments! She tells you what she wants and needs! Go for it, Mum!"

"We will be right back," Luke said handing Kate a bottle before handing me my own. "Here is the Sancerre, Corrie my girl! You know where the ice and soda are. Help yourself!"

"Thank you, love!"

Both left me alone in the kitchen as they went to the nursery. I could hear it all on the baby monitor they left on the kitchen island. I smiled watching as these dear friends of mine were so loving and attentive in the changing and feeding of their daughter. I do not think I expected anything different but have never been so proud witnessing the genuine love displayed before me on the tiny black and white monitor.

I thought for a moment about not having children of my own and questioned whether I felt any regret. I never thought it was in the cards for me, but wondered if like Kate, it could also change me if it happened. I shook my head and decided that I could not lament a life that was not meant to be. I was learning to be softened in new ways with Liam's sons.

Just then, Kate carried a barely awake, milk-drunk beauty to me. The instant she placed her in my arms, I started crying.

Once I could finally speak, I asked through tears, *"Isn't she the most precious thing?"*

Luke said proudly, "You asked about her name earlier. We would like to introduce you to *Bryant... Elise... Woodhouse... Matthews.* Bryant is in tribute to David."

Luke did not have to explain the name to me. I knew the second he said it. I cried even more above this sweet girl, though I tried not to wake her now that she was peacefully asleep in my arms.

I could not speak, so Kate did, saying through her own tears and taking Luke's hand, "I adore her name because it is in honor of an incredible man whom we all loved but I must admit that I also adore it because it is so unique. My daughter has the most unique name, and it makes me so happy! I want her to have everything, and her name tells me that she is *deserving* of everything!"

"Bryant?" I asked when I was finally able to speak. They just nodded as I continued, "Oh friends, this touches my heart so! She is so beautiful and peaceful."

They both laughed as I am not certain there is such a thing as a peaceful newborn, but Luke admitted, "We held off on naming her. We had an idea of course! We wanted to honor David and create a name that this sweet girl could embrace and eventually understand, but we also believed that she should tell us who she was. We wanted her to almost agree that the name was right for her."

"Absolutely!" I said sweetly in her ear, *"You tell Mum and Dad who you are my sweet darling!"*

Kate continues, "And she *does!*"

Luke agreed instantly, "She *does!* This babe has shown us her own preferences—and even humor—from the very start!"

I teared up again as that epitomized David Bryant to a tee. He was a skillful pediatric surgeon, and parts of his life were structured and deliberate... almost rigid at times. But outside the hospital he was so funny and appreciated a laugh more than anyone I have ever met. To see this baby girl before me, bearing his name, made me proud. David and I had no children of our own, so it was truly a blessing that in some way his spirit, even just his name, could live on. It was a continuation of a life that we all cherished and loved.

I whispered to her as I kissed the top of her head, *"Oh my darling! I cannot wait to tell you all about him!"*

Luke said, putting his arms around my shoulders lovingly and looking at his daughter, *"We all will!"*

Kate added, "Bryant worked for both! If it had been a boy, it likely would have been Bryant David."

Before I could react at the notion, she continued, "Corrie, we would like to ask you to be godmother to our daughter."

I smiled at Luke and Kate and said through my tears, "Thank you both for this honor. For carrying David's name forward and for making me godmother. I will love and support this precious girl for the rest of my life!"

"We know, my darling! That is why there was no other choice!" Kate said. "We made both Colin and Mark godfathers with you. You will now have to return to London for the christening."

"There is no question about that! Absolutely!"

"We booked it early, love. It is on the second of October. I wanted to use my leave to the maximum to bond with her and Luke overlapped his paternity leave from the hospital. So, we are going to travel a bit to see family, but mostly we wanted to insulate our new family and just be with each other at the start."

"I understand completely! Liam and I will be there to honor her in every way, regardless of my newly gained responsibility! I have never been a godmother before!" I said gently kissing the sleeping baby once again on top of her head before handing her gently back to her mother.

I meant my words. I would love and care for this sweet girl for the rest of my life. I would do this on my own, of course, but I was even more committed out of respect for David's name and in honor of his memory.

+++

Kate came back to the kitchen after putting Bryant down and said, "Corrie, my darling, before you leave, I have more good news to share! I wanted to let you know that you made *The New York Times* Bestsellers List for next week."

"*What!? Are you serious?*"

"Congratulations, Corrie my girl!" Luke said clinking his wine glass with mine. "That is excellent news! Well done!"

I said, still in disbelief and with tears in my eyes, "And so fast!"

"Yes, but you know from the weekly reports Gemma sends us, sales including the pre-orders are strong. In fact, better than any novel you have ever published at this stage. And each new positive review has only boosted sales even more across all formats in the United States, Canada, and the UK. You will debut at fifteen. All book covers printed from here on out will reflect that designation. We will also move forward with new market translations to expand your reach. I will need you to approve the art for the covers of the French, Spanish, and German versions. Gemma will send the proofs to your email early next week."

"Oh my God! I am so surprised by this! I can't wait to tell Liam!"

"There is more, my darling."

I just looked at her and narrowed my eyes, uncertain what could be better than this incredible news. News that every author dreams of hearing.

"We had a preliminary inquiry from a well-known American television production company about possibly optioning the book for a series. You know that historical Scottish stories have a loyal fanbase and they believe this novel has legs."

"Legs enough for a series?"

"Yes! They think they can expand on what you have written. They love the history, the characters, and the story."

"Oh my! We have *never* had that kind of inquiry before!"

My head was now swimming with possibilities and pride. I knew this novel would do everything I wanted. It would honor the old boys of Aberlour, and it would restore my reputation as an author. *The New York Times* Bestseller List and now the possibility of a television series were unexpected bonuses.

"It is incredible, my darling!" Kate said. "Despite my parental leave, I have informed my assistant that I will stay on top of this development. I encourage you to alert your own attorney. We would likely want this to move quickly."

Luke said, "I am so proud of you both!"

"Thank you! I do not know what to say," I said softly, still stunned by Kate's words.

I left Luke, Kate, and Bryant and rode to the airport in the car with a heart overflowing with love. Love for my first goddaughter, my dearest friends, and that *The Old Boys* was doing so well. My heart was full!

There was only one person I wanted to speak with. I wanted to tell my own love everything about today! I started a text. I started a call. But I decided not to complete either task. I would be home shortly and this news I wanted to tell Liam in person. I wanted to hug and kiss him when I did so, and I wanted nothing but the same from him when he heard the wonderful news.

I stepped off the plane in Edinburgh and Paul asked out of courtesy, "Where to Miss Hunter? Home? Or do you and Mr. Crichton have supper plans elsewhere in the city?"

"Home please, Paul," I said as I smiled to myself.

Yes, home to my love please!

+++

Liam and I changed clothes briefly on the plane before takeoff. My blush pink Jenny Packham dress was complimented by a custom Philip Treacy hat and Liam was in a navy suit and tie. Both felt too formal and restrictive for our short flight home. When we emerged from the back bedroom, in much more casual and comfortable clothing, I was seated before a bottle of Dom Perignon and two Champagne flutes.

"Are we continuing the christening celebration on our short trip?"

"Of course, we celebrate Bryant this day, but also your birthday, my love," Liam said before kissing me.

"Oh Liam! You remembered!"

Today was in fact my birthday. I said my words in both respect for his remembering the date and in some part still lamenting not knowing his own birthday in July. A day I will now *never* forget! Only Kate mentioned my birthday at some point in the photoshoot and of course, my dearest friends wished me well on the side. We clearly had only one focus today... and that was our sweet baby girl, Bryant.

"I did! And I wanted to celebrate you with the same bottle we shared on the night we met."

"And while we did not share it together, you also provided the same for my fiftieth birthday in London last year."

"Aye."

Liam popped the cork himself and poured our glasses before saying again, "Happy Birthday, my love."

"We had a rapid succession of birthdays and events in the last month, haven't we? How are you feeling Liam?"

"Aye, we have! I feel much better. I would say I am back to normal, one hundred percent. But how is it that I now have two fifteen-year-old lads? That fact alone makes me feel old and tired!"

"They are handsome boys, just like their father," I said smiling at him sweetly and thinking that Liam not only recovered from his emergency appendectomy but seemed to take on a new, life-affirming energy. He was as handsome as ever and made me blush with his lingering stare across his own glass.

We kissed each other quickly before he wrapped his free hand around my waist and whispered in my ear, *"It was lovely to see you with the baby today."*

I leaned back and looked up at him with tears forming in my eyes and asked, "Do you regret not having another child? A girl perhaps?"

I did not necessarily fear his answer, but I still wondered how I felt about not having a child of my own. My question was not just for him. It was one I kept asking myself over and over. Since Bryant's birth, I have thought about it more. A lot more. I seem to vacillate between thoughts of regret of the unknown life I could have had and an acceptance and appreciation of the beautiful life I had.

I wanted nothing more than to land on acceptance, but sweet Bryant made that difficult today. She is absolutely the most beautiful child I have ever seen! Holding the blonde, blue-eyed darling in my arms brought me an intense level of love and emotion that I had not felt before. I think I cried most of the day in church and then again at our private lunch.

First, I was thankful that my lashes stayed on. Second, I appreciated that my former fashion model of a friend had hair and makeup on standby for all of us. She wanted beautiful photos and with her chosen Glam Squad support and her brilliant photographer today likely got them!

In our photos today, the perfect darling made both me and her godfathers look beautiful. She is a natural beauty like her mother and a ham before the camera like her namesake. Bryant never cried once. She got fussy for half a second before Mum realized it was time for a feeding, but after that she presented herself perfectly before cameras and when she was no longer needed, slept peacefully either in her mother's arms or in her pram.

I do not know how to describe my new emotions. It is not the same love I feel for Liam, or felt for David before, but it is just as deep in my heart and soul. This precious little girl will be another forever love in my life. I know that for a fact!

"No, love. I am blessed to have the lads that I do. I just want them to be happy and healthy and I do not need another. Why are you lamenting this?"

"I don't know. Bryant has just brought up so many emotions in me," I said starting to tear up again. "I mean, despite the honor of her name, I think I am just working through acceptance that I will never have children of my own. But I did worry that if you wanted more children, I could not offer that to you."

"I told you once before that I did not want to be nearly sixty years older than a wee babe. And I don't!"

"I understand that. Even if it were a physical possibility, I do not think I would want to be a mother at fifty-one myself. More power to those that choose that path if they can, but I don't think I could."

"You do not have to be a *biological* mother to be a mother to someone."

I just looked at him with narrowed eyes as he continued, "My love, you can be an incredible *godmother* to Bryant, and eventually a *stepmother* to my own sons. You know how Clara Marshall was a mother figure to me later in my life after losing my own. Corrine, you can be an incredible inspiration and loving support to children that are not your own and that is a noble and beautiful thing."

I wrenched my mouth and bit my lower lip, trying my best to keep my tears at bay. I wanted them to stay in my eyes, versus crying before him again. I feel like I cry before Liam too often. I told myself that it was because *my Scot* makes me feel safe and loved, but I do believe when he opened my heart back up after the loss of David, every emotion and feeling I had suppressed for years became magnified.

"That is a lovely thought. Thank you for reassuring me. I have just been thinking about it so much lately. I want you to have *everything*, Liam."

"Och, Corrine! I do! I do have *everything*, but so do you, my love! You just need to see it!"

I nodded in agreement. I needed the reminder and appreciated Liam's honest delivery of it. I do have everything I am supposed to, and I need to be grateful for every bit of it.

Changing the subject, Liam said, "I decided at the last minute to take the lads to the Rugby World Cup in Paris this coming weekend. Fancy coming with?"

"Of course! Who doesn't fancy a trip to Paris?" I said back to him while thinking to myself that his question was ridiculous. I mean, seriously! *Who doesn't want to go to Paris?*

"I have Jenny on it and thought we could see Scotland play Ireland on Saturday the seventh at the Stade de France. We will arrive on Friday and return on Monday. Sarah approved the boys missing two days of school and they are chuffed to bits."

"To go to the match or to miss two days of school?" I asked laughing over my glass.

"Och, both! We will have only the best and you should shop and spa however you want."

"Well, that sounds fine, but if I go, I want to go to the match with you all. This is a point for me to learn and continue to connect with you and the boys. Is that possible?"

"Of course! I love you even more for wanting to attend the match with us."

"You can get me a ticket as well?"

"Of course, I can! And we will likely be in a private Skybox suite. Jenny should have confirmation of it all tomorrow."

"Will you help me know what to wear?"

He laughed at me but said nothing.

"I am serious, Liam! I want to support Scotland. It isn't about being fashionable for Paris. I can handle that part on my own! But I have nothing in my wardrobe representing Scotland other than beautiful wool sweaters and all manner of Harris Tweed and plaid... certainly not Scottish Rugby."

"Aye love! We will kit you out!"

+++

FOURTEEN
The Suite Life In Paris

Four Seasons Hotel George V
Paris, France
October 2023

Pilot Nate delivered us to Paris where we were met by a driver who took us straight to the Four Seasons George V hotel. We had the stunning Royal Suite configured with two bedrooms. I always gravitated to a fine hotel but have never stayed in anything this grand. The hotel welcomed Liam straight away and did everything to ensure we were all comfortable and wanted for nothing. We were treated like royalty the minute we stepped out of the chauffeured car!

The living space between our bedrooms included a marble fireplace, a dining area seating up to eight guests, and a huge private terrace. The décor and art were sublime in all manner of ivory, soft green, and peach. But the marble bathrooms, walk-in closets, and dressing areas were beyond anything I had ever seen before. There were also fresh flowers throughout the suite, making it even more beautiful and welcoming. It felt like a home and not a hotel.

Etienne, our own dedicated concierge for our stay, toured the suite with us, ensuring we knew every fine feature, as members of the housekeeping staff unpacked our bags and ensured fresh towels were warmed in each bathroom.

"Da! There was a note for you left on the bar," Eric said handing his father an envelope.

Once opened, Liam just confirmed as he handed the note on hotel stationery to me, "Chef Stephan wishes us a good visit and a win for Scotland. He personally saw to the custom drinks in the bar and has arranged for our breakfasts to be delivered to the pantry each morning at eight o'clock. We just need to instruct Etienne if we want it served at the table at another time."

"That is lovely! I can see he has plenty of my Sancerre and sparkling water stocked in the bar with your whisky."

"Etienne can get us anything else we want."

"You are correct, sir," Etienne said in his mesmerizing French accent. "You know how to contact me on mobile or on the direct line on the phone. We can get anything else you want for the bar, your coffee and tea service, or adjust breakfast timing and delivery to suit your schedule on the day."

Upon his words there was a ring at the bell. Etienne answered the door for us and returned to the dining room pushing a white cloth covered cart with a large silver iced bucket holding two bottles of Champagne, cut glass flutes, salmon and caviar blinis, and a beautiful cheeseboard adorned with grapes and assorted fresh fruit.

Etienne said as he entered the room, "Monsieur Crichton, on behalf of The Hotel George V let me welcome you and your family once again to Paris. Would you like me to set up on the dining table, bar, or on the terrace for you, perhaps?"

"It is a beautiful day, Corrine. What do you think about the terrace?"

"It *is* a beautiful day, and the terrace sounds fine. But perhaps we have it all set up in here and that way we don't have to bring it back in."

Liam and Etienne both looked at me in a manner that told me that *we* wouldn't have to bring *anything* back in... *ever*! I knew that I had made a mistake—albeit a minor one—in grand hotel living. This kind of hotel experience with a concierge at our disposal was not something I was used to, but I hoped they would both forgive my slightly awkward entry into the suite life at Hotel George V in Paris.

"Mais oui, Madame Crichton. I will set it all up here at the bar. Then let me pour you both a glass. Which do you prefer? Rosé or Brut?"

After a quick smile and wink from Liam at Etienne either making his wife or confusing me with his ex-wife briefly, I answered in French, "Rosé, s'il vous plait!"

Liam said, "That sounds fine to me, as well. I did not know that you spoke French, love."

"Well, I am certain Etienne will tell you that my French is barely adequate. However, as a Canadian, there is an expectation that you can speak and understand some basic French. My mother was also French-Canadian from Montreal, so it helped that I heard it spoken at home."

"Your French is just fine, Madame," Etienne said as he handed me an expertly filled flute.

"Merci, Etienne!"

"De rein," he said, smiling at me before he handed Liam his own glass.

"Before I leave you, may I take any clothes to be pressed or shoes to be shined for this evening?"

"Oui," I said. "I could use some pressing."

Liam and I walked back to the dressing room with Etienne, and each pointed out the items already expertly unpacked earlier and hanging on the racks for him to take.

"I have this dress, jumpsuit, and blazer that just probably need a bit of steam to remove the few wrinkles gained from our short flight here."

"I have a suit and shirt I would like pressed as well," Liam said. "The lads also have blazers and shirts that likely need to be pressed. We can check in their closet if their shoes need shining. I would wager that they do."

Once Liam looked in the boys' closet, he realized his assumption was correct and sent their suits and shoes away with the man.

"I will return these items within the next two hours, if not less, so that you have for dinner."

"We will go out for a bit of a stroll after our Champagne, no rush. Our reservation at Le George is late. I think eight-thirty. Is that correct, Corrine?"

Remembering the itinerary Jenny provided us, I said, "It is. Exactly."

"Madame, do you need anything from the spa? We can happily send up anyone to do hair and makeup for you if you do not have your own already planned… along with any other services you require, of course."

I suddenly felt nervous that I had not planned any hair or makeup and answered, honestly, "No sir but thank you! I may visit the spa on Sunday, but let's see how Scotland fares on Saturday first!"

Etienne left us just as the boys joined us on the terrace with their own Champagne flutes filled with Ginger Ale. We all stood on the patio in the warm glare of an autumn sun and overlooking the historic art deco fountain of The Three Graces.

"Now that we all have our glasses filled, should we make a toast, Liam?" I asked, smiling at him and then his sons.

"We should,' Ewan said in agreement before his father could answer me. We just smiled at each other in anticipation of his father's words.

Liam thought for a moment and finally said over his glass, "To my dearest loves here with me in Paris and to a rousing Scottish victory tomorrow! Sláinte!"

"*Sláinte! To victory!*" Eric and Ewan yelled in unison, raising their own glasses to ours.

I nodded in agreement and said, "To victory! I am so happy to share this experience with you all!"

"This is so much fun!" Ewan said excitedly and almost bouncing on his toes, as he does. "Miss Corrine, are you excited about the match with Ireland tomorrow?"

"I am! And thank you for helping me have all the right clothes to wear. I am counting on you Ewan to help me learn more about rugby this weekend. I did watch the very first match between France and New Zealand. It was so much fun!"

"Aye! France did well in that match!"

"Home field advantage, I suppose!" I said as the boy just looked at me. "I was sorry to hear that your favorite player decided to retire earlier than expected."

"I know! I was gutted Stuart Hogg retired but he will be a commentor on telly so he will still be here! Scotland has so many talented players. You are going to *love* it!"

"I appreciated you texting me the results of how Scotland has fared in the tournament so far and that they lost their first match." After losing their opening game to South Africa in a hard-fought, defensive struggle, Scotland bounced back against Tonga and Romania, dominating the opposing team in both games. "I used to watch the Six Nations with friends at the pub when I was in London, but I have never attended a live match in person. This is an exciting adventure for me!"

"You should come to one of my matches sometime," Ewan said with an inviting smile.

I smiled back at him and then at Liam as I said, "I would love that, sweetheart!"

I could tell Liam was a proud father that his son was continuing to welcome me into his life with this invitation. We both took note of his honest ask and continued acceptance of me in his life. I sincerely hoped to see young Ewan play a rugby match one day.

+++

After an afternoon exploring Paris and randomly meeting many other Scots in town for the match on our journey, we returned to the hotel in time to get ready for dinner. Once we were all dressed in our finest, we were set to meet in the living room.

Liam had on a black suit, with a black tie and a light lavender shirt with the cufflinks I gave him for Christmas. I had on a beautiful and voluminous black dress with puffy sleeves from Scottish designer Olivia Rose, high heels, and all the diamond jewelry Liam had gifted me.

"You look stunning, love. I will be right back," Liam said as he poured me another glass of Champagne and kissed me quickly. He took his own glass into the other room to see how the boys were faring and returned with two smartly dressed lads in their freshly pressed Thom Browne navy suits, checked blue and white shirts, and newly shined loafers with no socks typical of the designer's unique style.

"Now here is a handsome trio!" I said pulling my phone from my evening bag as the three tall Crichton men walked into the room. "Stand in front of the fireplace and I will take your photo together."

After a few shots of Liam and his sons, Ewan, ever the charmer, said, "You look bonnie, Miss Corrine, you should take a photo with us."

Liam said with a smile, "Give me your phone, love and I will take it."

I stood between the handsome lads as Liam took our photo. He said handing me my phone back, "We should get one of all four of us. We all look so smartly dressed for our dinner together this evening. Perhaps we can get someone in the restaurant to take it for us."

"No, Da!" Eric exclaimed. "That would be *embarrassing*! I can set it up here on the table and take it."

Eric expertly set my phone to take our photo on a timer and the images came out great. As I forwarded the photos to the boys and Liam, I realized this was the first time the four of us had been photographed together. These were the first images of our *new extended family,* and I cherished them. Liam could sense my grateful energy and squeezed my elbow as he smiled at me. I wanted to believe he cherished this quiet relationship milestone as much as I did.

Liam asked taking the last of his Champagne, "Shall we go to the restaurant, my loves?"

We all followed him willingly through the hotel and were seated together at a round table in the lovely, contemporary Le George restaurant. I read the menu and realized the fare was Italian-

Mediterranean. I said instantly to Liam, "Oh! Chef Dan should come here!"

"Love, Dan used to work here."

"Did he *really*?"

"Aye!"

"That's incredible! Is this where you stole him from?"

"No. I told you that I stole him from a Michelin-starred restaurant in Edinburgh, but he worked here first."

"Then the man has had an incredible culinary career."

"Aye he has! I think Dan has only worked at Michelin-starred restaurants and that is why he so driven to secure the designation for Mythos."

"I have no doubt he will!"

Liam ordered us a glass of Champagne and the boys some sparkling water as we all discussed what we might be interested in for supper. He suggested that we all get the tasting menu, noting that most of our initial selections were on the list and that the chef would give us other treats to try only adding to the experience. We all agreed, and our spectacular dinner consisted of:

> *Tomato Bell Pepper And Strawberry Gazpacho, Burrata*
> *Saffron Arancini, Tomato Tartare*
> *Sea Bass Crudo, Caviar, Yuzu*
> *Tuna Crudo, Eggplant, Balsamic*
>
> *Chef's Carbonara Tortellini*
>
> *Pan-Fried Sea Bass, Clams, Tomatoes and Marjoram—*
> *Or—36 Hours' Goat With Vegetable Crust*
>
> *The Chef's Scarpetta*

Semi Fredo Al Pistachio, Herbs From The Garden, Citrus Sorbet

We all chose the sea bass main, and I had everything but clams. Liam was correct. The chef gave us additional assorted tasters, mid-course palate cleansers, and special treats throughout the service. We also had a fine cheese plate with our frozen dessert triumph. Everyone seemed pleased with the options presented and each course was more impressive than the last.

The boys were well behaved and seemed unphased by the grand, formal surroundings or the sophisticated menu. I could tell they wanted more food, but they knew well enough that we still had the remnants of what Etienne delivered earlier and that there would certainly be additional sweet treats with turndown service. I was impressed that they did so well. Their manners were impeccable, and they showed confidence and respect when interacting when the servers or the chef came to our table. I should have expected nothing less from them as along with their parents' expectations to be kind and respectful, this was the only life they had ever known.

Our conversations remained light and on the surface about the food, the room, or other diners. Liam held my hand often during dinner and made me feel loved and included. I think he could sense that I was slightly intimidated by the grand hotel and the attention we received since our arrival. His loving kindness reassured me and by extension, restored my unsteady confidence before his sons.

Despite Eric's continued lack of apology, the atmosphere when we were all together was generally positive. My growing relationship with Ewan took some of the sting out of Eric's indifference and made our interactions more cordial and natural than when we started. I can only hope Eric would start to accept me in some way... if for no other reason than I had no intention of going anywhere.

As we finished the last of the wine and Liam signed the bill, he asked, "Does everyone know what time we leave the hotel tomorrow?"

"Aye, Da!" his sons said together in an exasperated teenage way.

"Aye, Da!" I said in solidarity as all three Crichton men smiled at me.

"We will have breakfast at eight and then spend some more time exploring the city. We will return to the hotel and our driver will pick us up at six o'clock to take us to the stadium. We will be early for the game at nine, but I figured we would all want to shop a little and enjoy the festive atmosphere.

"I definitely want a new Scotland jersey with the Rugby World Cup logo!" Ewan declared instantly.

"We have a private Skybox suite at the stadium with food and drink throughout the match.

"We do?!" Ewan yelled across the table.

"Aye! We are just above midfield. The suite entitles us to a tour of the pitch and stadium before the game as well. We must be there early to do that so that we do not disrupt any training or broadcast efforts before the match."

"That is *awesome!*" Ewan said leaning back in his chair and folding his arms across his chest. He was clearly thrilled to not only be at the game but have such fine accommodations. Part of me wondered how he did not expect such a grand set up considering where we were staying and who his father was, but the lad was genuinely thrilled at the prospect of private box seating. "Do you think we will get to meet any players? Will I get to meet Stuart Hogg, Da?"

"I do not know," Liam said honestly. "I guess if someone comes out early or Stuart is broadcasting before the game, you *could*."

"Oh my God!! I need a silver Sharpie pen just in case! Can we buy one tomorrow? Any of the players we meet can sign my new Scotland jersey. And if they do, it will go right on the wall in my room at the new house."

I just smiled at the eager lad and hoped that he could meet some of his favorite players tomorrow. I could tell that Eric was excited but seemingly more so for his brother than himself. I think he may have been the lad that wanted to miss two days of school more than to see the match.

"Eric, if I may," I said hearing my own voice shake as I spoke to him across the dinner table. Why this boy makes me nervous confounds me! It *irritates* me! We both still seem unsure of each other, and we should be past that by now. Or at least I wish were past that by now.

Irritate is the wrong word. I just hate the notion of a fifteen-year-old boy making me unsure of myself. His resistance to the loving relationship I have with his father makes me feel insecure and tentative. While his brother has become kind and open to me, Eric cannot find it in himself to do the same.

"I am not sure if you know that I am a co-chair of the annual Cox Trust For The Arts benefit next year."

He said nothing but nodded his head. I could not tell if he knew this fact or just accepted my words. His silence meant that naturally I kept talking, "They are changing the structure of benefit this year to feature emerging artists, arts programs, and teachers across Scotland. Well... I think you should submit some of your paintings for consideration."

"Me?"

"Yes. I think you fit the brief fully, love. Your talent is remarkable but also uniquely celebrates Scotland. You are a young Scottish artist, and you deserve to have your work shown in the exhibit. I believe you would do well. Will you consider it?"

"Aye, Miss Corrine."

"I am not part of the selection committee but would feel like I failed you by not telling you about it. I will say it again... I think you could do *well*. Really well." The lad said nothing, as I continued, "I will send you and your parents everything you need to submit your work for consideration, and I can help you in any way you need. The deadline is November first."

"Erm... do I have to *give* them my paintings?"

"That is an excellent question! For submission, you will just provide photos of the paintings you want the selection committee to evaluate. If any are selected for the showcase, then yes, you will give them the actual paintings for the exhibit, but you will get them back right after."

"Thank you, Miss Corrine!" Eric said, sitting even more upright in his chair. Liam took my hand in his and squeezed it.

I believed Eric's words. I could see in his face that he was honored to be asked to submit his work. I could see that he was thrilled to be seen as an emerging Scottish artist. And I could also see that he was perhaps still a tad uncertain about *me* trying to help him.

+++

FIFTEEN
The Rugby World Cup

Paris, France
October 2023

Once we returned to our hotel suite, Liam poured us each another glass of Champagne and placed the large tray of sweets left at turndown service in the center of the coffee table. He and I sat before this bounty and watched both Eric and Ewan instantly grab two large handfuls of macarons to take to their bedroom.

"Goodnight, Da and Miss Corrine!" Ewan yelled as he walked away from us with his mouth filled with sweet treats.

"Faites de beaux rêves!" I yelled back in return, slightly laughing at them both.

Liam and the boys just looked at me as I translated, "Sweet dreams!"

"I am most impressed with your French," Liam said putting his arm around me.

"Merci beaucoup!" I said kicking off my shoes, sitting up on my knees, and kissing him sweetly on the sofa. I stroked his beard and said, "I have wanted to do that all evening. You look so handsome!"

"Then perhaps you should do it again."

I followed his instruction and smiled sweetly through my kiss as he pulled me to him and turned my entire body to cradle me in his arms. I said with my arms around his neck, "I am not sure you want your sons catching you making out with your *girlfriend* on the sofa!"

He laughed and said plainly, "Well, if Da's still got it, *he's got it!*"

Now I was the one laughing. I said, popping a strawberry flavored macaron in his mouth before kissing him again, "I think Da's still got it, clearly!"

"Then, this old man thanks you! What would you like to do tomorrow, my love?"

"I would like to shop a little, but you boys don't need to join me for that. I have been to Paris many times so I do not feel the need to visit any tourist or cultural sites, but I will happily join if you want to. Now that we have taken our first photo of the four of us, I do think we need our obligatory Parisian photo together with the Eiffel Tower behind us. But that is it."

"I agree. As you can imagine teenage lads don't love museums all that much," he said laughing at the admission. "We have been here many times and I suspect that they would both say they have seen them once and do not need to see them again."

"I can understand that! But I honestly think they are singularly focused on the match with Ireland and little else in Paris could be as appealing for them on this trip."

"I don't know if you heard the side conversation at the table, but the lads requested time at the hotel gym and pool. Otherwise, I have nothing else planned."

"Well since the match is late, why don't we make it a slow start tomorrow? We can tell Etienne we prefer a later breakfast and enjoy this beautiful suite. I can shop while you boys are at the gym and pool. Then we can have a late lunch or snack together before we go to the stadium."

"I will text Etienne now. What do you think? Ten o'clock for breakfast?"

"I think that would be fine. We have everything we need for tea or coffee if we get up earlier. And we know the boys will *not* be up early."

"Etienne is going to ask me if you want a driver for your shopping."

"Oh no! That is just too much! All the shops I want to visit are close to the hotel. I can manage the short walk. But I think a relaxing start to the day could be welcome since we will return here late in the evening."

"Aye! A slow start might be the best plan. We may not return to the hotel until well after midnight. Let me go tell the lads so they know what to expect before they fall asleep," he said kissing me again and emptying his glass of Champagne. "Pour me a whisky, will ye?"

+++

I sat on the stool in front of my dressing table and watched Liam in the mirror as he started to undress and began to put on his pajamas behind me. I smiled thinking about my handsome man and how we were faring on our first extended family trip.

I am in Paris with the man I love and his sons, who I am also starting to love. Liam asked me to see what I had in front of me, and I do feel grateful. Like him, I have everything. I just needed to see it. I walked to him, wrapped my arms around his waist and kissed his bare shoulder.

"*Och Corrine,*" he whispered putting his hands over mine.

"*I love you, Liam. I just had to tell you that and I wanted to thank you again for bringing me to Paris.*"

"*You must know that I love you more,*" he said, turning to kiss my lips and then my neck. "*I am happy you are here with us.*"

At some point, he looked at me with a sly smile and continued in my ear as he ran his hand underneath my nightgown to my lower back, "*We just have to be quick and quiet.*"

"*I know we can do the first, I am not so certain about the second.*"

He picked me up and carried me to the bedroom as he said in a thick French accent laced with his own charming Scottish accent, "*What exactly are you accusing me of Madame Crichton?*"

I laughed stroking his beard as I whispered breathlessly in his ear, "*Nothing that I am not accusing myself of Monsieur Crichton!*"

+++

"*I cannot believe it! I cannot believe it! Can you believe it?*" a young Ewan Crichton said bouncing on his toes as we walked into our spacious Skybox suite overlooking the bright green pitch at the Place de Stade.

Ewan was not only thrilled to be in such comfortable accommodations but had just met his favorite player, Stuart Hogg, on the sidelines during our tour of the pitch. Ewan had enough time to show his hero that his gallery wall at home was centered around Stuart's signed jersey. The confession, photographic evidence, and pure reverence made

Stuart more than happy to sign Ewan's newly acquired Scottish Rugby World Cup jersey... *and* take a selfie or two. The boy was over the moon!

As the game started the fever pitch in the Crichton suite only escalated with the audience below. Both teams lined up for the anthems, I admitted, "I just realized, I do not know the words to the *Flower of Scotland*."

Liam took my hand and said, "It is alright, love! The lads and I will sing it loudly for this family."

And they did! Along with every other navy-shirted Scot in the stadium they sang every word of this unofficial anthem with passion and conviction for their country and their team.

> *"O flower of Scotland*
> *When will we see your like again*
> *That fought and died for*
> *Your wee bit hill and glen*
> *And stood against him*
> *Proud Edward's army*
> *And sent him homeward*
> *Tae think again*
>
> *The hills are bare now*
> *And autumn leaves lie thick and still*
> *O'er land that is lost now*
> *Which those so dearly held*
> *And stood against him*
> *Proud Edward's army*
> *And sent him homeward*
> *Tae think again*

Those days are passed now
And in the past, they must remain
But we can still rise now
And be the nation again
That stood against him
Proud Edward's army
And sent him homeward
Tae think again"

The Flower Of Scotland, Roy Williamson

Ireland dominated Scotland from the very start and went into the half with a score of 26-0. Ewan and Liam sat together and animatedly strategized the next steps and adjustments the team must make in the second half to stay alive in the tournament. Eric and I found each other more interested in the food available in the back of the suite during the break in play and began chatting amongst ourselves.

"I know the score isn't all that encouraging so far, but are you having fun, Eric?"

"Aye! Well… I mean…"

I just looked at him as he tried to find his words. Finally, he said, "I don't love rugby as much as Ewan does. I don't love any sports to be honest, but it makes me happy that my brother is happy. So, aye, that makes it fun for me."

He took another pause and said with enthusiastic conviction answering my original question, "I *am* having fun!"

"That is sweet," I said thinking more about his words. "I am the same. I do not know much about Scottish rugby, but I am having fun being here with you all and learning. I suppose it helps me connect with you more."

"I would feel left out if I did not do sporty things with Da and Ewan."

"I admire that. I mean, I admire that you try to connect with them on their terms, but I hope they do the same for you. I hope they are also supportive of you and your interests."

"Aye! They support me but you know them well enough that neither is all that suited to painting and art."

I laughed as I looked over at the animated father and son duo still plotting Scotland's victorious second-half comeback.

"You have me there! I cannot disagree with you on that point!"

We both ate some of our food in silence, before I said again, "You know Eric… perhaps this is another reason for you to submit your art to the Cox Trust. While those two may not be interested in artistic expression themselves, I know that they appreciate your talent. They will want to support you, I *know* it!"

"Aye," he said. "We are different in many ways, but I know that they support me. I do."

"They do, love," I said feeling like for the first time, I had a real, honest, and genuine conversation with Eric Crichton. As he walked away from me, I just smiled at the thought. I caught Liam's eye and we smiled briefly at each other. I know he did not hear the words himself, but this was a positive moment and we both recognized it at the same time.

+++

"That try was scored by Ewan Ashman!" Ewan exclaimed to us all before explaining more to me directly, "He's also originally from Canada, Miss Corrine but plays for Scotland."

"Well done for him! How fitting that the first Scottish points are by another Ewan!?"

"Aye!" he said with a sweet smile. "Thank you, Miss Corrine!"

The Crichton suite was energized with points finally on the board for their beloved Scotland. I watched all of them celebrate animatedly with each other. Sadly, the final score was Ireland 36—Scotland 14. Pool B was tough and had a bitter end for Scotland as their run at the 2023 Rugby World Cup ended that night.

"I am sorry, loves," I said as we all put on our coats and prepared to leave. The pitch below us still had remnants of the Irish team celebrating and a few Scots commiserating.

Ewan said instantly, "I'm not all that bothered with a loss, to be honest! I *love* rugby, met my favorite player, and saw my first World Cup match in person tonight! What could be better? It only makes me want to play rugby *even more*... and I hope one day to play for **Scotland**!"

I smiled at young Ewan and then Liam as he said placing his hand in his son's hair, "I know you will, lad! And we cannot wait to watch you!"

Despite the loss to Ireland and their elimination from the Rugby World Cup, which might have been seen as devastating, this contingent of Crichton men seemed on top of the world. They had fun at the match together. We were a triumphant quartet marching through the halls of the Place de Stade in Paris to our waiting driver.

Young Ewan, who is such a massive fan of the sport, took every bit of his experience tonight in the most positive way—and that was as a devoted player and fan. Win or lose, he still loved the sport, his favorite team, and his country. I hope that one day we do get to see Ewan's dream come true and we will get to watch the lad play the sport he dearly loves for Scotland.

+++

We finally returned to the hotel and were such a weary bunch that we said little to each other as we found our way to our beds. It had been a long and emotional day, and everyone was clearly exhausted.

I whispered to Liam across the pillow, *"I feel like we have turned a corner. Do you feel the same?"*

"I do. Tonight especially. While he still has not said the words I expect, I was happy to see Eric speaking with you alone at the match."

"I know you did not hear what you wanted but the boy was kind and confided that he was less interested in rugby but loved it for Ewan. I told him that I appreciated his point of view. He was there with nothing but enthusiastic support for his own brother as much as his country. He touched my heart the way he said the words! It meant a lot that he felt comfortable sharing his honest emotions and feelings with me."

"Aye! I know the lad is not especially fond of sports... never has been. At least not the way Ewan has. But it does say something that he supports his brother so and he still sees sport as part of their connection."

"Exactly! And it was not some grand *'sacrifice'* he was making for Ewan. He genuinely loves spending this time with him… and with you!"

"Aye," Liam said, pensively. Perhaps he was thinking about the connections between all three Crichton men.

"You and I are both only children, so it is a new dynamic to see the incredible bond of brotherhood, but also of friendship. I don't know if that is normal for siblings…. never having any of my own. I can only say that in my opinion, they are blessed to have each other."

"Aye! Twins have an incredible bond! Sarah has three older sisters, so she helped me think more about how siblings connect. But twins are unique. We always said that we were happy that they loved each other, and it was obvious from the start. As wee babes, they used to hold each other's hands constantly. They had to be connected. As they got older, Ewan used to also cradle Eric's head lovingly, especially if the lad cried or was upset. The scans showed the same nurturing behaviors even before they were born."

"How sweet is that?"

"From the earliest age as toddlers, when they fought, they could not stay mad at each other for long. Their love... their bond of brotherhood... as you said, *always* triumphed in the end."

We remained silent for a bit before I finally whispered wrapping my hand around Liam's waist bringing him closer to me, *"Il était une fois..."*

He pulled back and looked at me with narrowed eyes across our pillows.

I translated, *"Once upon a time..."*

Liam stroked my cheek as I continued, *"Once upon a time...* there was a young boy that hated me, and I think that after tonight, he no longer does. He may not *love* me. But I do not think he *hates* me."

"Och, Corrine!"

"I will say it again, Liam. *Thank you!* Thank you for bringing me to Paris with your sons. It has been a special trip for me."

"My love, it has been a special trip for us all. The only thing that could have made it better would have been a Scottish victory on the pitch tonight."

+++

SIXTEEN
Our First Christmas Together

Crichton House
Edinburgh, Scotland
December 2023

Liam promised we would spend our next Christmas holiday together and true to his word, one year into our relationship, here we were. According to the agreed schedule, his sons were with their mother for Christmas Day, but Sarah delivered them to the house in the late evening as she, Jordaan and Polly were heading out early the next morning to see his family near Aberdeen with the hopes of getting ahead of an impending winter storm. I welcomed Liam all to myself for the day, but we all agreed to save our holiday gifts for Boxing Day.

When I woke up that morning, I found a large basket of gifts and a bouquet of flowers on my bedside table and smiled. It was made even more special that Liam woke up to the same. This sweet man somehow knew that I would create a special gift for him that was not placed under the tree, and he waited until I had delivered mine while he was asleep and then did the same. I could only turn over and kiss his cheek until he woke.

"You darling man!" I whispered in his ear, through repeated kisses.

"I thank you but can see that I am not the only darlin' in this room."

"Should we open together before the boys come downstairs?"

"We should!"

After cleaning ourselves up a bit and donning our robes, Liam brought us tea from the kitchen. We both sat opposite each other on the bed and set about opening our gift baskets. We smiled and kissed after unwrapping each thoughtful and significant item including sweet treats, whisky, and... pajamas. Oh, how we both love comfortable pajamas! Liam, of course, gave me lacy lingerie that I loved instantly, though I think he loved more. I gave him a new Breitling watch, but I had an extra special treat with a photo book of our trip to the Rugby World Cup in Paris. It was a wonderful trip, but it was made even more memorable because that was when we all finally came together. It was our first trip with just the four of us and things had only improved with the lads, especially Eric, since then. It was a special trip for me, and I had to commemorate it with our photo memories.

"This is so thoughtful and creative, Corrine!" he said flipping through each page. "I knew you took photos during the trip but never expected to see this. I cannot wait to show it to the lads!"

"They will each find the same book under the tree, my love. I made it for all three of you."

He kissed me again and whispered in my ear, *"That trip was so special, wasn't it?"*

"It finally felt like everything was right for our new family. No. I should stop saying that. Not *new*. Our *extended* family."

Liam whispered again, *"You have not found the most important gift in your collection, my love."*

I looked confused and started tearing through what remained of my basket. Buried deep, under two more boxes of chocolates, was another large box. This time instead of Cartier red, it was Tiffany blue.

"Liam!" I said as I untied the red holiday ribbon around the box. "What jewelry magic have you conjured again?"

"You will see."

Inside the large box was a stunning two-strand pearl necklace with an ornate diamond clasp, matching bracelet, and diamond and pearl earrings.

"Oh Liam! They are so beautiful," I said immediately putting the earrings in.

"You always wear pearl earrings during the day, and when I saw them, I thought of you. I wanted you to have these. Then I could not pass on the full set. You deserve them *all*."

"I love them! They are gorgeous!" I said before kissing him again.

Just then, we heard the boys running down the stairs. Oh, how they do *love* to run! The good news is there was no mistaking their approach in the house. I am convinced no Crichton lad could ever truly sneak up on you!

"Prepare yourself, love. Christmas has arrived at Crichton House and there is no telling what wonders are under the tree for us all!"

+++

Chef Stephan left us with a breakfast frittata of ham, asparagus, and Gruyere cheese along with homemade cinnamon rolls to place in the oven when we were ready. Liam set about making us all tea or pouring juice for those that asked for it. Every one of us enjoyed the sweet and savory bounty. Then the boys miraculously helped with clearing all the plates, and not just their own. They did so willingly and without being told.

I said, "Thank you for helping with breakfast, lads! Chef Stephan told me he will return this afternoon with a Christmas turkey and all the trimmings. And he said that he was making a sticky toffee pudding just for you."

Ewan threw his head back and yelled, "That is my *favorite*!"

"Och, I wanted cranachan!" Eric said, folding his arms before his chest in a disappointed huff.

I said instantly, "Well, you just might have both! Chef Stephan taught me how to make cranachan last week and secured some beautiful fresh raspberries for us. I will work on it for you after gifts."

"Thank you, Miss Corrine!" Eric said, sitting himself upright in his chair, clearly satisfied that he would get the dessert he preferred. I should have asked him if he wanted to help me, but I could not. While things have been much improved since Paris, we still do not have that kind of relationship. Liam was right, a shared task of cooking or completing a jigsaw puzzle was not going to bring us together enough for Eric to deliver the apology his father had expected for many months.

Liam asked the lads, "Should we see what wonders Father Christmas left under the tree?"

"Aye, Da!" the boys yelled in unison and instantly ran for the festive Christmas tree between the patio doors and the fireplace. They sat on the floor while Liam and I sat together on the couch with our tea.

There was no shortage of gifts. Clearly both Father Christmas and Liam Crichton still understood the concept of divorce guilt. I am certain the boys, now fifteen, no longer believe in Father Christmas, but we all enjoyed the gifts he left for us. He took care of us all! Big or small, the gifts were meaningful and thoughtful. I silently thanked Liam, Sarah, and maybe even Liam's assistant Jenny, for the bounty that energized our morning and our interactions. We all smiled and laughed through the entire exercise. It felt festive and fun. It was another sign that our extended family was becoming more relaxed and open.

The boys seemed happy. At the end I handed out my own gifts for them. They both got a wool cashmere sweater and button up shirt from Campbell's of Beauly in the colors I had learned over time that they each gravitate to—blue for Ewan and green for Eric. For my last gift, I watched each of them open the photo book of our visit together to Paris and the Rugby World Cup.

They excitedly looked through the pages of their books and remembered our fun trip together. I wanted to speak, but I could not. I suddenly felt emotional. Liam took my hand in support. He could tell by my words this morning that the trip and the book meant so much to me. I wanted them to cherish our captured memories as much as I did.

Finally, I collected myself and said, "I was so thankful for the time we all spent together in Paris, learning more about each other, learning more about rugby, and cheering on Scotland. I took so many photos, but as you will see, many here in the book are the ones that you or your father sent to me, and well... I wanted to commemorate the time we spent together. I gave a copy of the book to your Da this morning and I hope you both enjoy it as well."

Ewan came to me first and said hugging me, "I love it, Miss Corrine! It was a fun trip, wasn't it?"

"It *was* a lot of fun!"

Eric said, "Aye, thank you Miss Corrine! That was a great trip! And our thinking was the same!"

Just then the lad retrieved a small box from under the tree and eagerly handed it to me with a smile. The gift tag read *To Miss Corrine From Eric and Ewan'* and I almost started tearing up again.

"What is this?"

I genuinely did not expect a gift from either of them. The boys stood before me and smiled at me with the same sweet smile I see from their father. They eagerly nodded to me to open the gift to discover the answer myself. Inside I found two beautiful silver picture frames. The first with the photo of the four of us dressed in our dinner finery from the Hotel George V suite on our first night in Paris. The second was from our Skybox suite overlooking Place de Stade at the Rugby World Cup match between Ireland and Scotland. These sweet lads also saw this trip as a turning point in our relationship and I absolutely loved them for it!

I said though my tears. "I will cherish this forever! Not only the moments we shared together in Paris, but that you both thought to give to me those precious memories in such beautiful frames! Thank you!"

Ewan said, "We love you, Miss Corrine!"

I could not stop the tears as Liam stroked my back. I know he was looking with pride as his sons, together, finally letting me in. And maybe he was looking proudly at me finally taking my rightful place within our new extended family and in the lives of his young sons.

Finally, the boy that had been the slowest to accept me as part of his father's life, came to me and hugged me tightly. He now saw this *new family* was not a replacement for the old but an expansion... and finally, I was fully accepted as part of that expansion.

"We have one more gift, Miss Corrine," Eric said as he walked to the tree and pulled out a large package from behind. "This is for you."

"Oh my!" I said as I started to open the package before me. Liam kept his hand on my back for support. I looked at him for reassurance and silently asked him if he knew about this gift. He shook his head slightly. I could tell that he wanted to see what his sons had done as much as I did. While the gift was for me, this was clearly meant to be a Christmas surprise for us both.

Under the festive wrapping and large bow was a gold framed painting. The signed, original Eric Crichton watercolor was a beautiful depiction of the back garden at our new house here in Stockbridge. It was in full summer bloom and the colors were bright and beautiful! The back stone wall and double patio were expertly painted.

Ewan, proudly beaming for his brother's artistic talent and the surprise gift said excitedly, "Can you tell where it is? *Can you?*" Before I could find my words, he exclaimed, "It's the back garden!"

Eric then said proudly, "I painted it of course, but Ewan and I used our allowance to have it framed. We hope you like it."

I recognized the blooming garden and back of our beautiful home immediately, but it took me a moment to realize that the painting also showed me sitting outside of my study on the patio. I was seated at the table, shaded by the red sun umbrella, with my computer in my lap and my feet propped up on another garden chair.

"*Is that me?*"

"Aye Miss Corrine!" Eric said proudly.

I could not speak because I was so overcome with emotion. Liam said, speaking for me and rubbing my back for support, "Lads, it is beautiful!"

"It is stunning, my loves! Thank you both for this beautiful gift! I will hang it proudly in my study," I said through tears as I stood up, hugged each boy, and kissed them on top of their heads. *"This is such a thoughtful gift! Thank you! I love it! I absolutely love it!"*

"This is not a gift, but I also wanted to show you this," Eric said he pulled an opened, folded envelope from his pajama pants pocket and handed it to me.

I sat back down and gave him a look of uncertainty. But as soon as I unfolded the envelope, I could see that it was sent from the Cox Trust For The Arts.

I smiled up at him and asked, "Is this what I think it is?"

Once the letter was unfolded, I held it in front of Liam so that he could read it with me. As we read in silence together, I couldn't help but smile. The lad had all three of his submitted paintings accepted to be part of the artist showcase. He would be featured as one of Scotland's emerging young artists. A designation that not only included his work being exhibited under his name in the Scottish National Portrait Gallery but supported by additional social marketing and PR via the Cox Trust. Support that would serve as a foundation to a well-deserved career as an artist.

"Oh Eric! All three were accepted for the showcase! I am so proud of you! *So proud!* What an honor!"

Liam said as we both stood up to hug Eric, "Aye, lad! We are both *proud* of you! Congratulations!"

"I have to write a biography and Mum said you could help me, Miss Corrine."

"Absolutely! We can write it together."

Liam was emotional and kept kissing the top of his son's head as he said, *"Well done, lad! Well done!"*

I told Liam once before that perhaps his boys showed their sensitivity and emotions in different ways. As I have gotten to know them, Eric and Ewan have proved me right time and again. But more than that, they proved that there are many paths to acceptance of change. Just like there are many stages of grief, each of us processes the changes happening around us in our own time and in our own way.

Finally, this sweet lad apologized to me in a way neither I nor his father expected. Eric Crichton chose his own path to redemption. He did it on his own terms. He did it when he was emotionally ready and when he felt not only comfortable with the change happening around him but also safe in our *extended family*. He did it in a way he could best communicate his feelings and acceptance. That was through his art and actions... not his words.

I not only loved the boy for it, but I must admit, I respected him for it.

+++

SEVENTEEN
Playing For Keeps

Edinburgh, Scotland
December 2023

I must admit that the time alone since Christmas had been good for me and Liam. I love this man and how he loves me. What was once a new relationship was becoming a comfortable one. But it never lacked the passionate connection we shared from the start. My love with Liam became deeper because of the improved relationships with his sons and admittedly, even his ex-wife.

One evening before the fireplace at Crichton House on Loch Leven I said, "Back to Hogmanay planning, love. Jenny has been helping me with arrangements, and we need to make some final decisions. Do you want to go to Gleneagles or The Balmoral Hotel?"

"Balmoral."

He was definitive in his answer, and I said, "Alright. Balmoral it is! We have reservations for dinner at Number One. I expect you to be in formal attire."

"You mean a formal kilt?"

"I *do* mean a formal kilt, sir! And while it may be cold, it has been a while since I have seen those knees! I will be in cocktail attire myself. Would you like anyone else to join us on the night?"

"No. I just want to be with you."

"Just us," I said kissing him again through my smile. "Sorted and done! I will confirm everything with Jenny."

+++

"Is this a new kilt?"

"Aye, you told me to be in a kilt! Why wouldn't I be in a *new* one? You are in a gorgeous *new* cocktail gown yourself!"

"This is just a tartan plaid I have not seen before."

"Is it just the *new* tartan that you fancy?"

Liam's new kilt was largely charcoal gray with thin lines of ivory, and red. Somehow it seemed darker than the ones he had worn before and almost festive for the season.

"No. No sir, it is not just the tartan," I said in agreement and with a smile. He knows me well enough that I do have a thing for his bare knees peeking out from a kilt. I always have and I always will. I walked to him and kissed him before I said, "You know I fancy you in a kilt."

"It is custom. I had it made at Stewart Christie. They are doing the same for the lads. Perhaps we can get you a sash or skirt to match."

"I would love that! I would be pleased to match like we did for Mark and Colin's wedding. I would have happily added something to my dress tonight."

My dress was all manner of black lace and silk. The skirt hit me just below my own knees but had a small slit that made it sexy. I wore my hair up and displayed the diamond earrings and bracelet Liam had given me.

"Let me kiss you before I put on my lipstick."

Once I put on the deep red shade he said, "Och love, you look stunning! Though I would expect nothing less! Paul is outside for us when we are ready."

"Let's go, my love!"

+++

Our dinner at Number One was one culinary triumph after another. We had the seven-course, holiday tasting menu which they thoughtfully and lovingly modified for my shellfish allergy. But I can tell you that as gorgeous as my meal was, I was especially envious of Liam's scallops and langoustine courses. The full Scottish larder was on display, and we devoured every delicious bite.

We laughed together throughout the entire meal. I am certain our wine pairing with each course increasingly fueled our lighthearted humor. I was especially glad to have a glamorous date night with my handsome Scot in such a fine and festive place.

At the end of the dessert course, I said, "I have a gift for you."

"Do ye now?"

I have always loved how drink enhances his Scottish accent. It is truly one of the most charming things. I kissed him through my smile quickly across the table before I handed him a small, wrapped box pulled from my evening bag and said, "Yes, I do! This arrived yesterday and I brought it with me tonight."

He opened the small package and found a piece of paper folded inside. He looked at me with narrowed eyes and asked, "What is this?"

"Open it."

He unfolded the paper and began reading, "Och love! You have a television show?"

I nodded and said, "It is official! *The Old Boys* has been optioned for a series on an American cable and streaming network! I wanted you to be the first to know!"

He stood up and came to sit next to me kissing my cheek over and over. "My love! What an incredible thing! I am so proud of you!"

"The deal is lucrative, and I get the chance to be both a contributing writer and an executive producer. They did not just purchase the rights to the book; they have brought me in as a producer and a writer. But the best part is that it will be filmed here in Scotland. Liam, this is all so overwhelming and new, but I am thrilled to bits! Kate and I have never had this happen before, so we both have a lot to learn. You and Andrew made it all possible for me!"

"No love! No. Ye did this on your own! Yer an incredible talent!"

"I could not have redeemed myself as an author with this book without Andrew's gift of inspiration and your love. This announcement is in celebration of the role you *both* had in this novel! I love you both for what you did for me! *Thank you!*"

"How can I or my attorneys help? You know I would do whatever you need."

"I know that I asked for our business lives to remain separate, but I do think your attorneys and mine need to chat. Like I said, all of this is so new and having additional legal advice may be helpful."

He kissed me on the cheek and said softly in my ear, *"Consider it done! With this good news, should we have one more celebratory drink at Bar Prince before Paul takes us home?"*

"Of course! If they can squeeze us in, that is," I whispered back. *"It is New Year's Eve."*

"I am certain they can, love."

"It is not yet midnight. Perhaps we can stay and then watch the fireworks over Edinburgh Castle! I would love that, Liam. Can we stay?"

"Aye, my love!"

He nodded in agreement, signed the bill, stood up, and put his hand out to escort me upstairs to the bar. I wanted to go home with him but for some reason did not want our festive and celebratory night to end just yet.

+++

We sat across from each other and smiled. Our eyes were dreamy with love and drink as we watched each other sip from our glasses. Without saying a word, Liam looked across his whisky and I looked at him back across my white wine spritzer. Both drinks were delivered at lightning speed upon being seated in the very same booth where we met each other for the first time. While Hogmanay, it felt like the celebratory evening in the room was just for us! We were celebrating our first year together, the success of my novel, and the progress made as an extended family in that brief time.

I asked, "This is the booth I met you in, is it not? I am slightly surprised it was available when we walked in on such a busy night at the hotel."

"I believe it is," he said with a smile. "I met ye right here and ye won me in an instant with talk of the *heart* missing from your novel and I believe of... *hearing voices*."

"Liam! Don't make me laugh! You said that last part just as I sipped my spritzer! The bubbles almost went up my nose!"

Suddenly, this man seemed to be on a mission. I looked at him suspiciously and with narrowed eyes over my glass before taking another slow sip. I stared at him until he finally said, "If you *laugh*, then you *lose*!"

"Oh no! You are not seriously going to play *the game* against me *again*!"

"If you laugh, Corrine Hunter, you have to buy the bottle of Champagne I am about to order."

Before I could say anything back to him about how much drink we already had for the evening, he stopped the server and said, "Sir, we would like a bottle of Cristal for the table."

"Aye Mr. Crichton! Right away!"

"So much for restraint," I said, mocking him for his expensive choice. At £500 a bottle, this man will be a fierce competitor. Perhaps he also knew that with his audacious selection, I have absolutely no intention of losing. I will *also* be a fierce competitor tonight! The server immediately presented us with the bottle and poured two glasses before placing it in the silver ice bucket stand next to the table.

I said, teasing him, "I believe we are one for one on the score for this *ridiculous* game."

"Aye. We are. Though some of us paid more than others."

I laughed instantly. While the score was technically even; I was ahead on spend. "Oh, I get it! Is this your chance for some sort of redemption? Your competitive male pride needs me to pay for a bottle of Cristal, now?"

"Perhaps."

"If you are looking for an easy win because it is a holiday, you should know that I give you no grace this night, sir! I am *incredibly competitive*!"

"Aye! I do know that and expect nothing less from you, my love. *But I plan on winning tonight.*"

"*Good luck, Liam Crichton!*"

I smiled at his recognition that I was ahead in our games but wanted to challenge him slightly. Perhaps my own pride got in the way, but I loved this silly, juvenile game and how it bonded us. I have absolutely no intention of losing tonight! This was my chance to up the ante and increase my winning percentage. That means the man before me *must* buy another bottle of Cristal tonight!

"To our future!" Liam said, raising his glass to mine as we sipped our beautiful bubbles, staring at each other intently. Just as I had before, I reached my hand up and stroked his cheek and beard before he lovingly took my hand to kiss the inside of my wrist.

"When is the game over?" I asked.

"When I say it is!" We both yelled at the same time mimicking his original instructions.

"Och no, Corrine! The game tonight is *mine*," Liam said in a determined way and preempting my own attempt to hijack the game. "I started it. That is the rule!"

"Ah! Here you go again! Making up the *rules* as you go!"

He just smiled at me, and I finally nodded my head in understanding and reluctant acceptance that he managed the rules of the game he started tonight.

Despite not having a nosy neighbor to watch us, it was still fun, and we are playing this simple game perfectly. We sipped in silence and stared at each other until he took a small white envelope out of his waistcoat pocket and placed it on the table in front of my glass.

"What is this?" I asked.

"Open it."

The server stopped by the end of the table and topped off our glasses. I waited for the lad to leave before I carefully opened the envelope and pulled out a small card that read simply in Liam's own steady handwriting:

Marry Me.

Before I could react, he reached his hand out for mine across the table. I took his hand and squeezed it as I felt every happy tear land on my cheeks.

"In this verra room, ye said I changed yer heart, but Corrine Hunter ye changed *mine*. My love, ye have changed my *entire* family! My lads! My own relationship with my ex-wife. I love ye, Corrine. I will love ye forever! *Marry me!*"

Before I could collect myself and utter a single word in response he stood up and knelt before me with a red Cartier box pulled from his sporran. Once opened, he revealed three beautiful platinum and diamond eternity bands with each ring consisting of approximately five carats of brilliant cut diamonds. The trio of rings stacked together were stunning!

"I knew ye preferred a band versus a solitaire, and when I saw it, I couldn't let ye have just one. One fer us. One fer our extended family. And one fer our future. What do ye say, my darlin'?"

I laughed as I pulled him up from the floor, kissed him, and said, "*Yes! Yes*, Liam, my love! I will marry you!"

Liam put the three sparkling rings on the ring finger of my left hand and kissed me again. With tears in both of our eyes, we looked at each other and smiled throughout the entire thing.

Everyone in the bar started cheering for us. Alessandro, the bar manager, and a team of bartenders were instantly mobilized delivering another bottle of Cristal, a tray of chocolate truffles, and a beautiful bouquet of white roses.

"Congratulations, Miss Hunter, and Mr. Crichton! We are all so happy for you both on this special occasion!" Alessandro said before refreshing our flutes himself.

"Who knew Bar Prince at The Balmoral was so romantic?" I said laughing through my tears and taking the bouquet in one hand and my refreshed flute in the other.

Despite his genuine show of emotion, Liam looked down at me and said through his own tears and a triumphant grin, "You laughed, so you *lose*. You just bought yourself a bottle of Champagne, madam!"

"Tonight, I am not playing for pride or for Champagne, I am *playing for keeps*! You are mine and I am yours! Forever!"

Liam kissed me and asked, "Playing for keeps?"

"Yes. The definition is simple! It is to play a game not just for fun but to play to win without holding back. You give it your all because the wagers are kept by the winner at the end. This is not just *fun and games*, I bet on you from the start Liam Crichton, and I can think of nothing more serious than marriage. You think I lost tonight but I won, love! *I won!*"

"Aye! Forever, my love! With that definition, we are *both* playing for keeps and we *both* won."

"I bought a bottle of Champagne, and got a fiancé on the side," I said laughing again as I took Liam's hand in my own. I smiled from ear to ear as I looked down at the three sparkling diamond Cartier bands now permanently on the ring finger of my left hand.

+++

EIGHTEEN
The Cox Trust For The Arts

The Scottish National Portrait Gallery
Edinburgh, Scotland
February 2024

One of the recommendations made by the planning committee that Meredith and I accepted instantly, was to hold a two-day event this year. Day one would be dedicated to the artists, teachers, and their families highlighted by the Cox Trust. The participants could attend a small early evening reception, see the exhibition gallery, and celebrate their inclusion in the prestigious showcase.

The venue of the National Portrait Gallery had occupancy limits that made it impossible to host showcase members and the society event on the same evening. The good news was the extra event allowed us to invite the press in early and give the PR and social marketing teams additional time to secure photographs and interviews with those recognized by the

Trust within the gallery hall itself. Day two would be the expected formal society fundraising benefit, hosted by me and Meredith.

We met Eric, Ewan, Sarah, and her new love inside the doors of the gallery. Liam and I were both nervous to meet Jordaan for the first time, but having been through what we had ourselves, wanted to give the man some grace. Or at least I did.

Neither of us knew him and did not know what to expect. Add that his affair with Sarah was one of the catalysts for the divorce, only made today's meeting an awkward moment for all involved.

We never heard from Sarah about how the first introductory meeting went and heard little to no mention of Jordaan from Eric and Ewan. Liam and I agreed that we would wait for her or the boys to tell us what they wanted us to know. From the lack of feedback, we assumed that she might have encountered some of the same resistance from her sons that we did at the start.

Liam hugged his sons together and then kissed Sarah respectfully on her cheek. I did the same before the boys left us in our adult awkwardness to explore the sweet treats counter set up for the reception. We stood in silence before Sarah finally said, "Liam and Corrine, please let me introduce you to Jordaan."

"Jordaan…?" Liam asked, reaching out his hand while apparently waiting for a surname.

Somewhat annoyed at both the question and the answer, Sarah said, "Jordaan… *Lau*."

Jordaan instantly replied, seemingly annoyed himself at Liam's response, "I only use my first name professionally…. and it is Jordaan with *two* As."

Jordaan politely shook my hand after his clarification, but I could tell, if for no other reason than the number of times he pulled at his shirt collar, that he was supremely uncomfortable. Whether that discomfort was being in a suit and tie, being in this environment, or just being in our company, I could not tell. I suspect it was a combination of all three. It was apparent that Jordaan with two As did not want to be here.

Like Liam, Jordaan was tall, but he was much thinner. He looked exactly as you would expect a yoga instructor to look. Long and lean. He had his long brown hair tied back into a man bun. His dark eyes were rimmed by long dark lashes and made his serious, lingering stare even more intense.

Liam shook Jordaan's hand as a gentleman. He told me that he wanted to be open to a man who loved Sarah, but he mostly needed to feel comfortable with the man who was living with his sons. It was a fair expectation for a father. Not knowing anything about the man and the fact that Sarah invited him and his young daughter to live with her made him uncomfortable. I believe he wished Sarah had offered him the same courtesy of an introductory meeting so that he could accept the man living in his old house with his children. He believed this first meeting was regrettably late.

I tried to put Jordaan at ease and said, "It is a pleasure to meet you Jordaan! We have only heard good things about you and young Polly."

"Aye, thank ye! She is the forever love in my life! Erm...along with Sarah, of course!" Everyone stared at him as he tried to correct himself again, "I mean... I mean... I am just a verra proud girl dad!"

Jordaan clearly seemed enamored with and at least slightly deferential to Sarah. Outside of that, he just seemed painfully nervous. It was clear that he was out of his depth.

Changing the subject Jordaan said, "I believe congratulations are in order..."

Sarah interrupted and said, "Aye! Congratulations to you both on your engagement! How exciting! The rings are stunning, Corrine! And the lads are chuffed to bits. They were so happy that you let them know first, Liam. *Really* happy!"

Liam just nodded but said nothing.

I could not tell fully, but I did feel genuine support from Sarah at that moment. Our engagement was another mark of progressive change for us all, but I said simply, "Thank you! That means a lot."

No one said anything else on the topic so I could not help but ask, "Have the boys embraced Miss Polly, Sarah? I can imagine having a young girl in the house had to be quite an adjustment for them!"

"They have! Polly won them over in an instant! Just as she did me! They do have moments of apprehension with a young child in the house... a wee lass... but she loves them as much as they love and protect her."

"Then we are very happy for you both!" I said as Liam squeezed my hand in his. I could not tell in the moment if he was asking me to reign in the compliments or if he was still uncertain of the man standing before us. I decided instantly that I needed to stop talking. I just barely got into this extended family myself and did not need to push it. For some reason, I felt the need to help Jordaan do the same if I could, but realized instantly that it was not my place to do so. I truly did not know this man or if he deserved such an enthusiastic welcome and blind support.

"Eric Crichton and family?" Audrey from the Cox Trust called across the entrance hall.

"Aye," Eric said upon his return and raising his hand slightly.

"Och! Hello, Corrine!"

"Good to see you," I said shaking her hand while pulling her toward our complex and awkward group. "Audrey, let me introduce you to my fiancé and Eric's father, Liam Crichton. Liam, Audrey leads PR and Communications for the Cox Trust, and she is one of the team members I have worked closely with on this year's benefit."

"It is a pleasure to meet you, Audrey!" Liam said shaking her hand warmly.

I continued full introductions to our entire party before she said, "It is a pleasure to meet you all! I am your dedicated host today for the Cox Trust Showcase. Eric, lad, I am ready to take you and your family to where your artwork is exhibited. We will want to secure some photos and quick videos for social media. If you agree, we will just need each of you to sign a waiver. And if any of you would prefer not to be photographed or mentioned, we will absolutely respect your wishes. We will take a family photograph for you to mark the occasion of your visit to the exhibition hall. The Cox Trust will never use the image in any way. It is our gift to you."

Everyone nodded in understanding as Audrey continued as a true PR professional, "Eric, since you are not of age, only your parents will receive the image. How you use and share is up to you and your family. Of course, if you choose to make the photo public, we will ensure you have all the Cox Trust handles and hashtags to extend your reach. And once public, if we are recognized by name on a public account, we will obviously acknowledge and extend it on social media ourselves. All the information is here in this waiver."

She brought up a standard legal waiver for the use of our names and likeness in images for use by marketing and PR for the Trust on her iPad. We all signed our names willingly, understanding and agreeing to the terms as individuals and as an extended family group. Sarah and Liam co-signed on their son's forms based on their age as minors. The only exception to this agreement was Jordaan. I could see the suspicion in Liam's eyes as we both silently wondered why the man would be here but decline any photographic evidence of that fact.

We followed Audrey and our young artist to where his paintings were prominently displayed on a special exhibition wall constructed on the ground floor of the Great Hall. Under the painted astrological sky on the ceiling and the large stained-glass windows, the temporary exhibits were remarkably constructed and curated. Audrey explained that we had the benefit of the gallery experts in the design and construction of the exhibits around their own. Once completed, the Scottish National Portrait Gallery asked to keep the impressive exhibits up for an entire month. This only added to the additional exposure of the Cox Trust for the Arts and the artists included in the showcase.

"Oh, my!" I exclaimed upon seeing Eric's three paintings under the banner of *'Emerging Young Scottish Artists'* on the display. "This is impressive, isn't it?"

Audrey said, "Eric, you should know that your work is featured first here in the *Emerging Young Scottish Artist Showcase* because in this age group, which includes artists all under the age of eighteen, you were also chosen by the selection committee as the very first recipient of the *Cox Trust Emerging Young Scottish Artist of the Year Award*. This designation includes primary placement here in your category exhibit, a crystal plaque with your name engraved, a cash award of £500, and a gift basket worth £150 of assorted art supplies from some of our corporate partners. Congratulations, lad! Well done and well deserved!"

"I had no idea! I don't know what to say but *thank you*," Eric said humbly accepting the award and prizes handed to him before turning to his parents and eagerly hugging them both. We all stared down at his custom glass sculpture engraved with his name, award, and the year.

This was the first time that Liam and I saw his submitted works. Eric's three submissions consisted of two large acrylic paintings. The first was of a rain-soaked New Town Edinburgh looking from Princes Street Gardens with the iconic clock tower at The Balmoral Hotel visible in the distance. The second was of a sun-drenched Loch Leven Castle ruins on the island in the middle of the loch near their country house. The third was a dramatic and moody watercolor painting of the ruins of Castle Dunnottar near Stonehaven overlooking a turbulent North Sea below. It retained some visible pencil sketches underneath his masterful brushstrokes and looked unfinished at first, but I would not change a thing! It showed the artist's craft and talent capturing the light and dark.

Audrey said, "Eric you must also know that you are the youngest artist to have *three* submissions accepted by the Cox Trust selection committee. That was another factor in your award. In fact, I can tell you that only one other adult painter and one adult sculptor had three submissions accepted."

"Well done, love," his mother said instantly. I could feel Liam's emotion when he took my hand in his again. He agreed but could not yet say the words. I knew he was proud and much like me, could not speak when emotional. He needed a moment to collect himself. I stroked his hand held tight in mine hoping to reassure him.

Eric's art was displayed beautifully in the Gallery with his name and photo on a display stand that read:

Cox Trust For The Arts
Emerging Young Scottish Artist Showcase 2024

Eric Crichton
Fifteen Years Old
Edinburgh

Emerging Young Scottish Artist of the Year

Eric Crichton's creative point of view is evident in his submitted acrylic and watercolor works. His admiration for Scotland's history, architecture, climate, and landscapes not only set him apart from other artists in this category but give a glimpse of a level of artistic talent well beyond his years.

Liam said hugging him tight around his shoulders and kissing the top of his head, "I am *so* proud of you, son!"

I smiled at him and said with my hand on his shoulder, "Well done, Eric! This is incredible! Absolutely incredible! What an honor!"

"Thank you, Da and Miss Corrine! I *never* expected this! Never in a *million years!*"

He received the same praise from his mother, brother, and Jordaan. I know that his surname had to help, but standing before these paintings and thinking about the one he gifted me at Christmas along with the others proudly hanging in our home, it was clear Eric Crichton *deserved* this accolade. His talent was advanced for his age and the thought that he was largely self-taught only added to my favorable opinion. I was proud he could display his gift and talent to others in such a prestigious forum. There were second and third place honorees in the category, but in this display, Eric Crichton's work clearly stood apart from the others. He *deserved* to be the first Cox Trust Emerging Young Scottish Artist of the Year.

We celebrated Eric and his accomplishments together as we all stood in the gallery entry hall now with Champagne, sodas, and sweet or savory treats passed around on silver trays with the others featured in the showcase. The entire evening was festive! I made the rounds as one of the hosts before returning to my extended family on the side of the room. At some point, Sarah and I found ourselves standing together with our glasses in hand.

"Sarah, I know you will attend the benefit tomorrow and wondered if you would like to have Paul coordinate with your driver, so we arrive at the same time? I mean, with Eric's showing and award, I thought we could show a unified front in support of your son," I said while instantly sensing her apprehension upon my words. I tried to correct myself and continued, "But… perhaps that is not how *this* works."

"I appreciate you saying that, Corrine. *I really do!* You are being kind, but Jordaan will not attend the formal event with me tomorrow evening. So, I don't think you want Liam arriving with both his ex-wife *and* new fiancée on his arm. I understand and appreciate the desire to show support for Eric, but you need to think more about the appearance in society. We do not have to hate each other, but it might be best to keep everything separate… at least for the time being."

"Oh really? I mean… about Jordaan. I agree with your point on Liam and society. I thought it might be the four of us. I am just so new to all of this, and I wanted to show our united support of your son together."

"Aye! I understand and appreciate you looking out for Eric. It is my first time back at this event and we will all celebrate the lad together. We just don't have to do it on the red carpet."

"I understand completely."

"Jordaan has no one to care for wee Polly, so he will not be here with me. Erm... and... well, he doesn't feel like this is a world he wants to be part of."

"It takes some getting used to, that is a fact! I am still learning about Edinburgh and Scottish society myself... as you can clearly tell."

"Yet here you are as co-chair after only one year in Edinburgh," she said. I could hear the slightest tinge of jealousy in her tone at my own rapid ascension in Edinburgh society, but I chose to think that she mostly wanted to lament that I was a more willing participant than Jordaan.

"If it is a world you want to be part of, Sarah, will you both not have to find a compromise on occasion?"

"I think he wants me to have what I want in my life; he just isn't sure he needs to be part of certain areas of it. And this is one of those areas."

Every couple should have some parts of their lives—whether that be hobbies and interests, friends, or work—that are their own. But her words and her tone told me it was possibly more than that. I could tell by Jordaan's demeanor and actions this evening he had no intention of embracing this world or sharing it with Sarah, even out of obligatory support. I am not sure how she convinced him to be here at all, to be honest!

But if Sarah has what she needs, and Jordaan does as well... who am I to judge? I cannot understand what a motherless three-year-old adds to the mix and Jordaan's decision in support of his daughter may very well be the right one. But I did question the excuse slightly. Certainly, with Sarah's money, they could afford a nanny to care for the lass—even for just one evening. In fact, someone was staying with the child tonight. Why couldn't they stay with her tomorrow? It appears Jordaan has a legitimate excuse for a well-timed absence when he needs it.

Sarah said changing the subject, "I can tell my lads have grown to love you, Corrine. I thank you for accepting them and making them feel comfortable with you. I believe you are a good woman. You are a woman I respect."

I could tell by her words and her tone that she was still lamenting her own situation. I said, "Thank you for saying that. It has been a process to be sure! I *do* love your sons. You and Liam have done—*are doing*—a wonderful job raising two fine young men!"

Answering the question, I did not ask, she freely confessed, "I told you that the lads were quick to embrace wee Polly. The sweet lass is a blessing to be sure, but they have not been as welcoming to Jordaan. They want absolutely *nothing* to do with him! On a good day, they just tolerate him being in the house. On bad days, if he says too much to them, they either ignore him outright or argue... and I mean *defiantly* argue. It has made our house... erm... *uncomfortable* at times."

"I do not know Jordaan, but if he is kind and respectful to you and to your sons, I would say simply... give it some time. It will just take time."

"Aye!" I could hear the resignation in her voice as she continued, "I believe he is a good man, but he lives in what the lads see as their father's house. They have been unbearably cold to him. Almost to a point of painful shame to me as their mother. Now, I understand what you felt in the beginning."

I continued trying to reassure her, "We had a little bit of a head start. That is true. It was not easy, and it was not equal. Both lads had to find their own point of acceptance in their own time. You know that Ewan was more accepting of me than Eric at first, but I appreciate where we all are today!"

"Aye," she said as a small tear fell onto her cheek.

I touched her arm as I said, "I love your sons, Sarah! You and Liam are loving parents. And they are loving boys. Just give them some time."

"Aye, thank you," she said as tears welled up in her eyes. "It has all been much *more difficult* than I expected."

"Remember what Liam told me when I met Ewan and Eric that first night… he said we did not have to all be best friends from the start. I will offer you the same advice and I will say again, give them time. Give yourself some time… and I must say, some grace. We are all learning."

Sarah and I are not equals, but we have found a way to communicate based on two important points of respect. First her respect for my genuine love for Liam and her sons and second, my respect for her role in their lives. A role she will always have. The lads have accepted me, albeit reluctantly at first, and I believe she finally has as well.

Perhaps everything Elaine told me about Sarah was a result of her own anger toward the Prestons because of their resistance to her marriage to Liam at the very start. Or perhaps it was just the outward manifestation of a gradually disintegrating marriage. Our confrontation in the middle of Boots now seemed like a distant memory—a moment in time—between the two of us. From what I could see on my own, Sarah wanted all the men in her life to be happy. She just wanted to be happy as well… and standing before her now, I am not certain that she is.

Liam came to collect me and said that Paul was out front with our car. We all had another round of celebratory hugs and kisses to our emerging young Scottish artist.

I said touching Sarah's arm briefly and then reaching my hand out to Jordaan, "We will see you at the benefit tomorrow night, Sarah! It was so nice to meet you Jordaan. Have a wonderful evening!"

Jordaan nodded to me silently as he shook my hand. I could tell he still felt out of place but genuinely accepted my words. He said politely, "It was my pleasure to meet you both."

Liam shook his hand and nodded in agreement but said nothing back to the man. I put my hand on Liam's back for reassurance. I know this afternoon brought up emotions he did not expect. Just like he says about me, I could feel his energy shift the minute we met Jordaan, and it has been off ever since.

I said, "Eric, love, congratulations again for this well-deserved honor! I am so proud of you and your work! So proud! Mum, Da, and I will celebrate your accomplishments tomorrow night!"

Eric hugged me and then his father as he said, "Thank you! I love you, Da!"

I reached for Ewan and hugged him, "Good to see you, sweetheart!"

Liam followed suit and the boy said in his father's arms, "I love you *both*! Night!"

+++

Liam and I rode together in the back of the car in silence. We held hands but said nothing to each other or to Paul. Our friend dropped us off in front of the Stockbridge house with the most polite and professional of farewells. I suspect he knew that not everything went to plan this evening.

"I will pick you both up tomorrow at seven o'clock, Mr. Crichton."

Liam said nothing more than, "Aye! Thank you."

He walked to open the door to the house, and I turned to Paul, took his hand, and smiled weakly before saying, "We will see you tomorrow. Goodnight, sir!"

"Goodnight, lass!"

We walked into the house and were met instantly by a welcome and hearty seafood Carbonara pasta dinner from Chef Stephan. We ate together in silence apart from the occasional mention of how good the homemade pasta and the chilled white wine were.

We got ready for bed in silence. Liam walked out of the bedroom, and I followed him slowly to the living room bar, where he poured both of us a whisky.

"*Sláinte*," he said as he clinked his glass with my own.

"*Sláinte*," I said in return. He just looked at me. Finally, I said, touching his arm, "Come sit with me, my love."

He followed me to the sofa and remained silent. I felt his energy was not completely negative, but he was clearly struggling with his thoughts and emotions.

"*Talk to me,*" I whispered taking his free hand in mine.

"*I am conflicted,*" he replied with a weary sigh.

"*How so?*"

"*This afternoon was...*"

He could not finish his thought and just looked at me. One trait Liam and I share is we cannot speak until we can control our emotions. I needed to give him a moment and just squeezed his hand in mine and smiled at him supportively.

When he still said nothing, I tried to help him by asking, "Awkward?"

He took another sip of his whisky before saying, "Aye! I could not be prouder of Eric. It was emotional to see the lad achieve such an honor...

and I cannot wait to brag about him to everyone in the room tomorrow night. I will be the unofficial Cox Trust tour guide to celebrate everything my son has achieved!"

I laughed as I said, "He deserves this honor!"

"Aye, but despite my genuine pride for my son this evening, it was difficult to meet Jordaan."

I just sipped my glass, hoping he would elaborate. I admit that I selfishly wondered if he was jealous of the man. If he confessed such a thing to me tonight, I am not sure what I would think myself.

Finally, he said, "Ewan told me that they *hate* him."

"You know that your sons hated me at the beginning, as well. So much so that they excluded me from your birthday supper and..."

"*Love,*" Liam said shaking his head. He needed me to listen to him. I had to ignore my own path to knowing and loving his sons and listen to what the man was trying to tell me about Jordaan.

"You are right! I will not defend a man I met for the first time tonight myself. Tell me what Ewan said."

"He said that when Sarah is not in the house he yells at the lads. He tries to tell them what to do... and that usually involves *serving* him?"

"I'm sorry... what do you mean?"

Suddenly I was afraid of the term and what he meant. Liam, clarified instantly, "That was a poor choice of words. I meant that he expects them to bring him food and drink, clean up his own plates, or care for his daughter. He treats them like they are servants in their own home."

"Of course! What teenager wants to be told what to do?" I asked flippantly. Liam's face told me it was more than expected teenage rebellion. He seemed slightly annoyed by my indifference and sarcasm.

I corrected myself again and asked, "What are you not telling me, Liam? I feel like there is more to this story..."

"Jordaan tells the lads constantly that they are nothing but the entitled brats of a rich man. Corrine... erm... Ewan said that he believes he is *abusive* to Sarah... *and* wee Polly."

"What do you mean by *abusive*?"

Every horrible possibility ran through my mind with the words Liam was choosing to use tonight. He just looked at me.

I clarified my question, "Know that when you and Ewan say *abusive* it is a broad accusation and definitely not something I want to hear in relation to the treatment of women or children."

"I agree and I pressed the lad on it. I made him describe it to me and give me examples. He said that he treats everyone in the house like they work for him and are nothing. But in the process, yells at all of them and even curses at them, while making his demands. He yells at his daughter when she cries. I hate to say it but believe on my son's words the man seems to be relishing in Sarah's money and lifestyle but doesn't respect her or anyone else in the house, including his own wee daughter."

"Could this be why the boys embraced the young girl so quickly?"

"Aye! They feel like he is not kind to her, so they are protective of a young lass that cannot defend herself. For that, I am proud of my sons."

"I am so confused! Sarah has talked of nothing but adoring this young girl and painting the picture of Jordaan as a loving, doting father. In fact, tonight, she told me that Jordaan would not attend the benefit tomorrow because he did not feel comfortable and had no one to care for Polly. His staying home was a rejection of this world and Scottish society... but somehow still *honorable* in caring for his young daughter. The contradiction in what you are saying here is apparent."

"Aye," Liam said taking our glasses back to the bar for a refresher. Once he handed me a refilled glass he continued, "I do not believe Ewan would lie to me. Eric, as you know, remains to himself when his own emotions get in the way. Ewan tells his truth honestly. I think Sarah is making excuses."

"For Jordaan or for herself?"

"Both, perhaps. I think she is compensating her own choices and for the wee lass."

"I do not doubt for a second that Sarah loves Polly."

"I agree! Like you said, she has been clear on that from the beginning. But Jordaan and his daughter should not be in that house. If he is verbally abusive to Sarah, my sons, and his own daughter... I *do not want* him there!"

Liam was clearly distraught over what Ewan said to him and I loved him for his words and his genuine protectiveness. Liam is an honorable man and would not only protect his own sons but any child. He would absolutely protect Sarah and I respected him for it.

He finally asked, "What did you make of him refusing to sign the waiver and being photographed?"

"I looked at you instantly and knew we thought the same thing... it was odd. He can live with them but does not want to be photographed? He also chose not to be part of the family photograph that would not be published in any way."

"*Aye,*" Liam sighed.

We sat silently for a moment before I asked the expected and dreaded question, "Do you think he has something to hide?"

"Aye, I do! I mean, why come to the gallery reception in support of my ex-wife and son only to reject every bit of it in the end? I tell you that everything about *Jordaan with two As* is a falsehood!"

"You need to know that I tried to counsel Sarah tonight and told her to give it some time but what you are saying is more than I knew from her. She said nothing more than the boys had not accepted Jordaan. I confess, I simply took it as the same resistance I had at the start."

"You did the right thing, love. I appreciate your continued attempts to connect with Sarah. I must accept how much is different now. But I will not have a man treating my sons, my ex-wife, or even his own daughter poorly."

"What can I do?"

"Remain a support to the lads. If they tell you more, I want to know about it. Tomorrow we will see Sarah at the benefit. Perhaps she will tell us more on her own... when *he* is not there with her... *and* she has a glass or two."

"I'm sorry."

"Why are you sorry?"

"I'm just sorry for Sarah and the boys, but I am mostly sorry we could not all find happiness."

"Darlin' we *will all* find happiness! It just may not happen for us at the same time. You and I got a head start!"

I took his face in my hands before I kissed him and said, "*We did*, my love! We did!'

+++

"You look so beautiful," Liam said as I put my shoes on in front of the mirror of the walk-in closet before checking my hair. I put it up tonight. My navy evening gown with a square neck and long, A-line skirt was a perfect choice so that I could wear the new diamond and pearl jewelry that Liam gave me at Christmas.

"I am so proud of Eric and all of the work for the Cox Trust but suddenly feel *nervous*," I said to him over my shoulder as he zipped up the back of my gown.

"Why?"

"Many reasons. This is the first benefit where I am co-chair and still feel out of my depth in Edinburgh society. I know we have a lot to uncover, but I can understand why Jordaan felt out of place to the point he could not attend. I sometimes feel the same insecurity."

"You will be fine, my love! And your thinking is *nothing* like Jordaan's!"

I knew that he was protecting me but also still resented Jordaan. He did not appreciate the comparison I should not have made.

"Meredith expects me to be an equal host with her tonight and as an introvert, will take some effort for me... to be *on*. I mean, it will take a great deal of my energy tonight. I hope you understand."

I wanted him to know that without the specific words, I would give everything to the arts benefit and the Cox Trust tonight and would likely have little left for him. Add to it all the emotions of what may be happening with Sarah, I was uncertain of how this evening might go for us.

He kissed me again and said, "I understand completely! Tell me how I can be of help to you. When you need me, I will be there. Even if it is just refreshing your glass!"

"Well, that is a start and *definitely* a sign of true love!"

He kissed me again as I whispered into his ear, *"I cannot seem to stop worrying."*

"I will say it again... you will be *just fine*, my love!"

+++

Paul dropped us off in in front of the Scottish National Portrait Gallery on Queen Street. We ran the obligatory gauntlet of press photographers straight into the front door and were instantly met by Meredith and a young man holding a tray of filled Champagne flutes.

"This is a welcome sight on both counts!" Liam said as we kissed Meredith on each of her cheeks and secured our own glasses.

"I saw ye arrive and thought we could celebrate this evening together before we are joined by the masses."

We all clinked our flutes together as Meredith said, "Liam, Corrine has been a blessing and an inspiration to the Cox Trust!"

"Aye, I am very proud of her!"

"Congratulations are in order, I believe," Meredith said raising her glass to us both. "Emerging Young Artist of the Year *and* an engagement!"

"Thank you, Meredith," Liam said. "Our focus tonight is only on the benefit and my son. My sincere thanks to you and the selection committee for honoring Eric's work."

I added, "We are so proud!"

"Aye! The lad is talented to be sure," she said over her glass. "I sincerely wish ye all the best for a verra long and happy marriage."

"Thank you," I said looking at my Scot.

"I know Sarah will be here tonight. Are ye in a good place?"

I looked at Liam and we both knew that as much as we loved Meredith this question was a tad cheeky, but we wrote it off because of the Champagne. It was evident this was not her first glass as her Scottish accent was quite strong.

Liam asked with a wink to me, "Are you worried about a brawl between exes in the middle of the Scottish National Portrait Gallery, Meredith?"

"Och no!" she said, seemingly shocked by Liam's response. "I just wanted ye to be comfortable tonight, love."

I said instantly before taking Liam's hand in mine, "We will all be just fine!"

+++

Based on my new responsibilities as co-host, Liam and I found ourselves on opposite sides of the room for most of the evening. After retrieving a new glass at the bar, I went looking for the man. I found him standing alone in front of the exhibition wall and his son's beautiful paintings.

I walked up and put my hand on his back and exclaimed cheerfully upon finding him, "Here you are!"

He just looked at me and I could see the tears in his eyes.

"My love! What is this?"

"I never thought I could love you more, Corrine! What you did for Eric and by extension Sarah and Ewan, makes me so happy. *Thank you!*"

"Liam, I did nothing but encourage the lad to submit his work for consideration. I am just co-chair of the event, and you know that I had nothing to do with the arts council or their selections. You can see it before you on this wall! Your son is a talented artist, and he earned this honor on his own!"

"I know but..."

"Stop. You are breaking my heart with your tears. I do not have a handkerchief or tissue in my handbag."

I just wiped his tears from his cheeks with my thumbs.

"You helped encourage him and it makes me happy that that he listened to you! It feels like we are becoming more of an extended family every day. It fills my heart with such joy and gratitude! *Thank you, my love!*"

I hugged him tight and whispered in his ear, *"No. Thank you!"*

I pulled back and looked him in his eyes as I continued, "I was defensive about Sarah. I admit it! She intimidated me. And it wasn't just the confrontation in Boots. It was her role. She would always be here. Then I tried to be perfect for your sons and there is no such thing! I was so afraid of children and ex-wives that *I forgot who I was* for a moment."

We laughed together before I continued, "You told me to look at all that was around me and be grateful for it. Only when I started doing that and being myself did I realize that it was enough. How they see me… like me, or don't… it was *enough*. Once I gave that to the boys and Sarah, I took a lot of pressure off myself. I like to believe that simple acceptance also took pressure off *all* of us."

"I have so loved watching you. You lamented not having children of your own, but I want you to know that *you do*! You know that wee Bryant will adore you her entire life and now I think you have two teenage lads that love and respect you as well."

I thought about how things progressed so quickly with David and now Liam. I was so convinced that I did not want or deserve this kind of love that I ignored the possibility of it completely. When it finally happened to me, it happened in an instant. Now, two times over. I could not be more blessed with the incredible men brought into my life. That blessing now includes two more young men, and yes, even their mother.

+++

NINETEEN
The Old Boys

Prestonfield House
Edinburgh, Scotland
May 2024

This time the camera flashes were in celebration of the just-announced television series, *The Old Boys*. But all I could see was Liam's welcome hand reaching into the car for my own.

"It was good to see you, Paul. Once again, I decided to leave my wrap here for the short walk in. One of these days I am going to learn that I do not need a wrap for these events! They never seem to make it past the back seat of the car!"

"Aye, Miss Hunter," he said laughing with me. "Ye or Mr. Crichton can text me when yer ready, and I will meet ye both right back here! I am *so* proud of ye, lass! Congratulations!"

"That means a lot to me! Thank you!"

Our beloved driver Paul was not just delivering us to an event but had in fact been contracted by the production company to handle my personal delivery to locations and studios across Scotland this past week and again once filming starts later next year. So, in addition to working for Liam, this contract meant Paul would basically be fully dedicated to the two of us all year.

He was as proud as any father could be and told me that he bragged to his friends that he knew me from the beginning. I was truly comforted knowing Paul would be by my side during this new adventure.

I had to attend a press event earlier in the day where we announced the executive producers, writers, showrunners, and initial casting. We still have a long way to go, but it has all started to become real. Tonight, was a modest, celebratory party at the old stone stables at Prestonfield House in Edinburgh. It was a lovely location, and they converted the venue into a festive party that had a distinctive look and feel of the early Twentieth century befitting the time of the novel. The band even wore military uniforms of the time. I have a feeling the wardrobe department was getting a head start by testing some things out tonight, and it made me smile.

I was treated like royalty all week at the large Wardpark Studios in Cumbernauld, North Lanarkshire. I was surrounded by actors, screenwriters, and producers who were genuinely interested in what I had to say about the characters, story, and history behind the book. I was given presentations with initial production and costume designs and a rough draft of planned filming locations across beautiful Scotland.

It is an emotional and validating experience to see your work come to life before your eyes. As an author, you see it all in your head as you craft characters, places and stories, but the reality is that you only get to manifest a book. You hope that with your descriptions the reader can see everything with you. Seeing the initial planning and designs for the production made it even more real for me.

I took Liam's hand and stood tall next to him as we walked before the cameras at the step and repeat backdrop showing the name the new series we were announcing. Liam and I dutifully smiled and listened to the expected litany of provocative questions from the photographers on our way into the event.

"How long have you been together now?"
"Did you think you would last this long as a couple?"
"Are you engaged to be married yet?"
"Do your sons approve of this relationship, Liam?"

Despite everything, that last one caught me off-guard the most, but I tried to keep my face calm and stoic. We have played this game before, and I am not giving any indication of a response. Children should be off-limits and there was not one single question about my novel, the story, or the fact that it was becoming a television series. Not one.

Once we got inside, Liam immediately tried to calm me. He could feel my energy turn negative on the short walk inside.

"The bastards!" I said, seething with anger and frustration, and still blinded by the flashes.

"Love, you had to know the questions were coming."

"How are you so calm? *Your sons!* I am almost in tears over it! And I *cannot* see you!"

"All I can think in the moment is this has nothing to do with me. This is for you, Corrine. This is your night. I want you to enjoy every minute of it!"

"Yet not one question about the show or the book! *I am livid!*"

"Let this nonsense go."

I nodded to him. He was correct. This *was* my night, and we should enjoy it together. I could not help myself as I said in a whisper, *"It hurt me."*

"I know and that is why I adore you," he said before he kissed me passionately. "I love that you love my lads the way you do."

"I do love them."

"And they love you! That is all that matters!"

"Perhaps if they pay attention to their photos, the cheeky bastards will notice the stunning rings on my left hand and realize they got the answer to at least one of their questions!"

Liam kissed my left hand and the rings he so lovingly gave me as he said, "Aye! Let them discover the answers on their own. We owe them nothing! Now, where is the Champagne?"

+++

"I wish Andrew could be here with us," I said once we commandeered our Champagne flutes from the bar.

"I was just thinking the same thing," Liam said softly. He raised his glass to mine and said, "To Andrew! And to you, my love!"

We clinked our glasses together and smiled thinking of the dear friend that we both loved and missed, how he influenced this story, and perhaps brought Liam and I closer in the earliest days of our relationship.

Soon we were joined at the bar by Kate and Luke. As we all kissed each other and shook hands, Kate said, "Congratulations, my darling! This is so exciting, isn't it?"

"It is! It is also insanely overwhelming! I am still trying to take it all in. Each day has been an adventure. It is all so new!"

"Well, by the looks of it, you are off to an incredible start, Corrie my girl!" Luke said, placing his hand reassuringly on my back in support.

"Thank you, love! How is my darling girl?"

Kate said showing us photos on her phone, "Bryant is growing too fast! Nine months old last week. Can you believe it?"

"No, I can't!" I said shaking my head. It *has* gone by too fast. I also missed my sweet goddaughter. I realized how quickly daily life can get in your own way. I needed to get down to London to see her.

"We had Sunday roast with our parents to mark the day, but I think her first birthday will be a grand affair! Prepare yourselves for a party in September!"

"Aye!" Liam said. "We did the same with my sons! You want to celebrate the milestone, but the wee babes are *so confused*! On their first birthday, Eric cried... no... the lad *screamed* through the singing of the Birthday Song and Ewan just put his hands in the cake repeatedly and giggled. It was an absolute disaster! Sarah and I were on our own and just drank wine through the entire thing!"

"Exactly, Liam!" Kate agreed and clearly appreciated the support. "I expect the same, and confess, this party may be more for her parents than sweet Bryant herself. Wine will be included!"

Luke said, "Surely we will have earned a party after surviving the first year!"

Before I could say anything, Kate said grabbing my left hand, "Now! Let me see the gorgeous rings that are blinding me! Oh, Corrie my darling! They are stunning! Well done, Liam! *Well done!*"

"Congratulations to you both again!" Luke said before patting Liam's shoulder and kissing my cheek once more.

"Do you have a date?" Kate asked.

"We have been so busy with all of this of late, that we haven't settled on anything just yet. We have agreed, however, to keep it small."

"Aye! We agreed to keep it small and intimate."

I continued explaining for us both, "As you know, Liam has been married before, and I have never had grand designs on a large wedding. So, I may convince him to go to the Registrar's Office and just have a small reception."

Liam took my hand and smiled at me. In our discussions, I knew he wanted me to have everything and would not agree to a small wedding without a *grand* reception. But we would not argue this continued point of disagreement here this evening in front of our friends. Kate also knew what I went through planning a wedding with David and respectfully avoided asking anything more on the subject.

"Liam said he wants Colin to help me plan," I said squeezing his hand in mine.

Kate said, "I agree! He did such an amazing job for his own wedding! I would hire the man in a second! I am not sure he saw his interior design company turning into a wedding planning enterprise, but he is an expert in grand events! *Christ!* I may need to see how the man feels about planning a birthday party for his goddaughter's first birthday!"

"You should, darling! Colin and Mark's wedding and reception was perfect, wasn't it?" Luke said, agreeing with his wife. We all nodded in agreement with them both. Luke changed the subject and asked looking about the suddenly filled room, "Corrie my girl, do you know everyone here?"

"I met a lot of the people in this room this week, but our interactions were fleeting. I did some press with the producers and showrunners over the last few days, but I doubt I could tell you their names. It was all just too much!"

Kate said, "Gemma will send us a report at the end of the week, but I can tell you that the American book tour last month and the limited press for the series that hit this week has resulted in a huge spike in sales. We expect to see you move back up the *New York Times* Bestsellers List next week."

Liam said, "That is wonderful news!"

Kate said to Liam, "Much to her chagrin, we added tour dates in the UK and Western Europe along with some remote press next month."

"Normally, I *would* be averse, but it has been fun and will only help book sales and the series. I can't complain, Kate. You all have made it easy for me and I thank you."

Just then one of the executive producers came by and said, "Welcome to the party, Corrine! It has been an exciting week, hasn't it?"

"It has! Thank you, Nancy! Please, let me introduce you. This is my fiancé Liam Crichton, my publisher Kate Woodhouse, and her husband Dr. Luke Matthews." I continued with introductions and said to my party, "Nancy Wagner is one of the executive producers of the television series and has been a help for me from the very beginning."

Nancy was one of the first people I met when we signed the deal. She is an Emmy Award winning producer from the United States, and a seasoned veteran of the television industry. She embraced me and the story instantly. I expected to learn a great deal from her and despite her tough, non-nonsense exterior, she had gone out of her way to guide me through the process of creating an adapted television series.

Nancy shook hands with everyone and said, "It is a pleasure to meet you all! We are so glad to take on this exciting project and work with Corrine to continue this story! It is a story we all believe in!"

Kate said, "We are so proud to be part of this project! I knew this was a special novel the minute I read it, and the thought of a series is an honor and a testament to Corrine's immense talent!"

"It is!" Nancy said in agreement. "I hope you will enjoy yourselves tonight and be sure to meet as many people as you can. We will be working a long time together on this project! And if I can help make any introductions, do not hesitate to seek me out."

"Thank you so much, Nancy!" I said as we clinked our Champagne flutes together.

Once Nancy walked away, the four of us smiled at each other. This novel has changed all our lives, and I could tell that each of us could not wait to see what the television series would do!

+++

I ran to the loo at some point and walked back in to survey the bustling room from the side. It was a happy and celebratory party in a beautiful venue. I saw Liam talking with Luke, Kate, and a group of actors on the opposite side of the room. I smiled to myself that we could share this event, this moment in time, together. Soon I was joined by a man holding a Martini glass filled with olives.

"I heard your talk yesterday in the Writer's Room," the man said simply and without emotion. He was dressed in all manner of brown, wore glasses, and looked a bit disheveled. I knew he looked familiar, and that I had met him once, but I could not think of his name. In usual fashion, I never remember a name, but rarely forget a face.

"That was a lot of fun for me! Thank you for including me in the session. Please remind me of your name again."

"Ben Gordon, Head Writer."

"It is nice to meet you again, Ben. I apologize. It has been a busy week and I have met so many people. I am trying hard to keep everyone's names and responsibilities straight. I know it will eventually come together for me."

He gulped his Martini and said without emotion, "You have a lot to learn."

At first, I thought he was sympathizing with me and the navigation through the sea of new names and faces encountered this week. That was until he continued, "Your *little* story has a lot of work ahead of it to actually make it onto the screen."

His contempt was now suddenly palpable. I tried not to be offended as I said in the most positive voice I could, "I understand my novel was not written with a television series in mind. But the way I see it... we have an opportunity to make a remarkable story even better! A series will not only bring this story to life but take it even further than the novel did itself."

Before I could say anymore, he said dismissively with a large sigh and as if he were talking to himself, "I do not relish having to deal with another *traditional author* who has no understanding about writing for the television screen and is going to be overly protective of their *own* words and *precious* characters."

I could not help myself and said instantly, "You know nothing about me or what I understand or expect. Should you not see this as an opportunity as Head Writer to collaborate with the original creator of the story and even help them learn?"

He scoffed at this and said, "I am not paid to train anyone. I have been forced to work with *your kind* many times before. It *never* goes well!"

"*My kind?* Are we not both writers?"

"We are *not* the same."

"Then I wonder what the common denominator is in that *miserable* equation?"

"*What?*" he said, finally looking at me.

Before I could answer his question, Liam walked up with a new glass of Champagne for me and said, "I thought ye could use a refresh. Is all well fer ye, love?"

My darling man could feel my energy shift from across the room and walked straight into this unfortunate and unnecessary conflict. I loved him for saving me by being here himself and with a new glass. Both would surely calm me. I could feel the blood rising on my cheeks and my anger steadily growing.

"Thank you," I said taking the flute he offered. "I am fine, love."

I took Liam's free hand in mine and finally answered Ben's question, "I was just thinking that you seem to have an extremely negative opinion of traditional authors and that has impacted your ability to have a positive working relationship with them. Have you ever considered that perhaps *you* are the problem?"

He looked at me sharply and I smiled triumphantly and continued, "Manifest whatever negativity you need to feel better about yourself, but tonight is a triumph! It is a celebration of my novel that will become a television series and that series has given you a job. *You are welcome!*"

Liam squeezed my hand in his. I should not have said the last part, but I was incensed by the man's rude dismissal of me as an author. I was also unnerved by his negativity when I had been so welcomed by everyone else associated with this project during the week.

I continued, "I admit that I have a lot to learn in this new world of translating books onto the small screen and writing for that screen. But I am *willing* to learn. If you have no patience for that, no interest in collaborating with *my kind*, then I am not certain this partnership will work. The choice is yours!"

He stood before us both with his mouth half-open and did not say another word. As rude and arrogant as he was, he either did not expect my rebuttal or did not have the courage to speak to me in the manner and tone he did with Liam standing by my side. I ended this conversation by saying, "I wish you a good evening, Ben! I hope you enjoy the rest of the party."

Liam led me directly to the furthest corner of the room with his hand holding mine. He knew that I needed to collect myself and temper my emotions from the very personal confrontation he walked into.

"*Are ye alright?*" he asked in a whisper in my ear.

"*No, I am not!* But I will not give him the satisfaction of destroying my evening. *Please* do not comfort me in front of him. I love you for it, but I do not want him to think he made me emotional. I can feel his eyes still on me. I would like a new glass, love. Please," I said as I immediately downed the glass in my hand and handed the empty vessel back to him with a weak smile.

Liam took my empty glass and left me standing alone at a high-top table. He soon returned with newly filled glasses for us both. I explained who Ben was and what he said before he arrived to rescue me.

As much as I wished I could stand by my own words of defiance, I eventually whispered over my newly acquired Champagne flute, "*Liam...*"

I felt myself become more emotional just saying his name. He is my heart. It could have been the confrontation with Ben that just happened or the amount of drink I have had so far tonight myself, but I knew that I was done. Despite my words at the start, I was no longer in a celebratory mood. I no longer felt rebellious against Ben's judgment. I no longer wanted to be in this room. I only wanted to be with my man. And I wanted to be with him *anywhere* but here.

"*Aye, love. Tell me.*"

"*I want to go home.*"

"*Corrine...look at me!*"

I did as he asked, as I felt the tears well up in my eyes. I just breathed in deep as he said, "This night is for ye, love! Are you sure ye want that arse to ruin yer celebration? He is nothing! He is absolutely *fucking* nothing! And I am certain the man speaking to ye was quite drunk. I could smell every one of the Gin Martinis he had this evening as soon as I walked up to ye both."

Liam was right. The man was drunk, but I felt all the Champagne I had tonight hit me as well. I could not find my words as I did not want to speak to another person. I was done for the evening.

I was done.

"I just want to go, and I do not want a grand farewell. Saying goodnight to everyone will just keep us here even longer. I will text Kate later and explain. We are supposed to meet her and Luke for lunch tomorrow at The Balmoral before they head back to London."

As much as I hated it, this unfortunate confrontation *did* destroy my evening. It might have destroyed any confidence I had walking into this room. At this point, I had to go. I *wanted* to go! I did not want to be here anymore. I could not pretend I was celebrating anything. I just wanted to be in the safe comfort of home.

I said nothing else but looked at Liam and shook my head. He watched each tear fall one-by-one onto my cheeks before he finally said putting his arms lovingly and protectively around me, "I understand, my love. It will be fine. It will be just fine! Let me text Paul now."

+++

We rode home in silence, but Liam held my hand the entire way. I just looked out the window at the passing lights of cars and said nothing. I stewed over the conversation with Ben and willed my tears to stay in my eyes. Liam talked to Paul occasionally about the event or traffic across town to keep me from having to engage.

Once inside the house, I walked straight to our room and got ready for bed. I decided I needed water and found Liam at the kitchen island with his whisky.

He just watched me before he finally asked, "Do ye want to talk about it?"

I did not really want to talk but appreciated him asking me the question. I finally said in a whisper, *"I am angry."*

"I dinnae blame ye one bit! Tell me."

"I am *angry* that this man—drunk or not—insulted me. I am *angry* at myself that I insulted him right back! I am *angry* that I let one unfortunate conversation ruin my evening. And I am *angry* that the person I will have to work closest with on this project has such a low opinion of authors like me. If there is no resolution, he will not have just ruined my time at a party, Liam! He could make the entire experience working on the series miserable for me! This week... this evening... was such a triumph and he ruined it all. He ruined my *confidence* in an instant! *And that makes me so angry!*"

"First, what I heard from ye wasna an insult but an honest response to the man's own offensive opinion and words. Ye should never feel like ye cannae defend yerself. Ye know that too often women shy away from saying what they should because they don't want to *cause a scene*, or they feel like they will be cast as a *bitch*. I dinnae want ye to ever let someone speak to ye the way that man did! And if I had heard what he said myself, he woulda had more to deal with than an *insult!*"

I smiled weakly because I knew how Liam was defending and reassuring me. I only wanted to be with him surrounded and protected by his love. I knew he would make me feel better... and he did. I walked over to his stool, and he put his arms lovingly around my waist and whispered in my ear, *"I love ye Corrine."*

I kissed him quickly and ran my fingers through his hair and then over his beard as I said softly in return, *"You must know that I love you more. Come to bed, Liam."*

+++

"Miss Corrine?"

"Good afternoon Mrs. Clarke! Come on in, please!"

"I wanted to bring you this bouquet of flowers that arrived while you and Mr. Crichton were at lunch with your friends."

"Oh my! They are beautiful, aren't they?"

"Verra! I replaced the water for you and put an aspirin tablet in to preserve them. Where would you like them sat?"

"I think the corner of my desk should be fine," I said as I took the card from the bouquet.

Once I opened it, it read simply,

I am <u>willing</u> to learn.
With sincere apologies,

Ben

I went to find Liam as I wanted his advice and perhaps some reassurance. I was not sure what to think about Ben's apologetic gesture as anger still lingered on the surface from the previous night. When I found him on the garden patio, I handed him the card and said, "This came with a large bouquet this afternoon. What do you think?"

"I think it is a start," he said with little emotion before handing the card back to me.

"But..."

"He needs to prove it and not just declare it on a florist's card."

I looked at Liam as he clarified his thinking, "Like I said, this is a fine start. But it is a passive start. His actions going forward and treatment of you and will prove whether these simple words are genuine."

I nodded my head in understanding. He was right. It was a start, but a start in words only.

Liam continued, "Let's be clear, love. I have no intention of granting this Ben Gordon the same latitude I gave my own sons in making it right!"

I could tell that Liam was acting as my protector and I loved him for it. But he was right. It was easy for Ben to be contrite either in the face of embarrassment for his drunken words to me or simply in trying to preserve his job and position, having insulted not only the author of the book influencing the television show he was employed for, but also an executive producer.

"I agree. We will start working remotely over email while I am on the UK book tour. Perhaps some distance from last night will help."

"I appreciate your positivity, and hope for a fresh start. I do."

I could tell that Liam was still uncertain of Ben Gordon and his simple apology on a florist's card. I chose to lean into the positive if for no other reason than I hoped this professional collaboration and my first experience in writing for television could be salvaged.

+++

TWENTY
My Scot, The Husband

Crichton House
Loch Leven, Scotland
July 2024

Liam's sons wrapped up another school term and booked sleep-away camps for the first two weeks in July. Eric was in an art camp near Inverness and Ewan had been accepted in an under-sixteen Scottish rugby-sponsored sports camp near Aberdeen. We fully accepted the schedule change for them to pursue their passions and will spend most of August together at Crichton House on Loch Leven once they return.

Leaning across Liam's bare chest early one morning, I said, "Someone has a birthday coming up at the end of this month!"

"Who exactly?"

"Stop it! You know that I would never be able to live with myself if I missed another Liam Crichton birthday!"

"You were *so* distraught!" he said laughing while twirling my curls around his fingers.

"I was! But look how far we have come since then!"

"Aye! My sons love you. And Christ above! I believe my ex-wife loves you!"

"Do not make fun, Liam! I cherish these relationships and our extended family! I am so grateful! However, I am sorry that Jordaan and wee Polly did not work out for Sarah."

"You had to see it coming... despite her love for the lass and admiration for a single father... or his... erm..."

"Do *not* say the words, man!" I said instantly sitting up and pointing my finger at him while laughing. He just smiled at me and said nothing more. I knew he wanted to say that she was being satisfied by Jordaan in other ways, but I did not want to think about it, let alone hear the words from his mouth.

"At least I no longer have to worry about a man who had no respect for my sons in their own house!"

"I understand that! It takes some pressure and uncertainty off for sure! But do you know that the boys never said a word to me about him? Nothing! I did not ask, of course! But nothing. It was like the man did not exist."

"Ewan told me that he has not been in the house regularly for some time... but would leave his lass there for days on end!"

"Poor girl!"

"I believe he found someone else but had no problem letting Sarah tend to the care of his daughter! Ewan said that the grandmother stopped helping, as well. It was all left to Sarah."

"She loved the child but shouldn't be taken advantage of."

"I agree."

We sat silently for a moment before he said, "I am changing the subject, but you know that with everything for the novel and series, we have made little progress on wedding planning."

"I know! I am sorry, love!" I said before kissing him quickly.

"Do not be sorry! I just want to talk about where you are in your thinking. It has been a while since we last broached the subject… and when we did, we were not in complete agreement."

The disagreement was largely mine and he was being polite about it. I took a moment before I finally said, "You know that I have never been married, but I do know that I do not want the *show* of it. It is not just my age. I never saw myself in a long white dress and veil. Perhaps we just do the basics, legally, together, and then we have a grand reception with our friends. What do you think?"

"I disagree. You have never been married and I want you to have a wedding with your dearest friends. It doesn't have to be grand. We can keep it small and short. But they should be with you. You know that Mark and Colin were already married but still had a small ceremony at their reception. With everything they have done to care for you and love you, they along with Kate and Luke deserve to be with you at this moment in your life."

"*Liam, love,*" I said through a sigh laced with emotion.

Liam was not trying to challenge me; he was honoring my friends. By extension, he was honoring David's memory once again. I *loved* him for it. I loved *everything* about his intentions.

But I was still hesitant.

Perhaps I did not want to plan something that I feared I would never see. I did that with David, and it only added to my grief when I lost him. We planned something neither of us wanted or needed. We just wanted to be married to each other but the formality and tradition of it all got in the way of that happening. It was all ended by his untimely death. I tried to explain my thoughts so that my beloved could understand my continued resistance. A legitimate resistance that had nothing to do with him but everything to do with me. I had to find the words to explain.

"We planned everything, Liam," I said fighting back my tears. "We had to because we had to honor his patients and schedule with the hospital for him to even take the time off for a wedding and a honeymoon. Also, his mother was insistent on a large ceremony and had *a lot* of say in planning. *A lot!* I did not fight her because she was to be my mother-in-law and she seemed to have a great interest in the event. So much so that she booked The Savoy in London for the wedding and reception before David or I could say a word. The Bryants also had more family, friends, and business associates to invite than I did. My own parents were already passed so I willingly let her lead."

"You're afraid."

"Perhaps I am!. No... not perhaps. *I am!* I am afraid because I don't want to make the same mistake twice." I could no longer hold back the tears and just held my face in my hands.

"Love..."

"It was an absolute waste of time and money, Liam! I feel like I lost so much time *planning* with the poor man before he died. Those are some of the last memories I have of a man I loved, and they are worthless and superficial! We were talking about who got invitations, where they sat, or the *fucking* tablescapes and wine list! I *just* want to be with *you*. I want to be married to *you*. I don't need anything else. I don't need the show of it."

Liam just nodded his head as I continued, "I know! *I know!* I say the words aloud, and it sounds... it feels... *irrational*. Maybe even *dismissive* of this important event in our lives, traditions, or of those that should celebrate and support us. That is not my intention, but I *don't* want a big wedding. I just want to marry you. *That's it!* And then when it is done, we can celebrate in a grand manner with our dearest friends and family."

I knew he was listening to me, but his silence meant that I kept talking as I normally do. I kept explaining through the tears that suddenly overtook me, "Could we do more? *Yes! Absolutely!* You could afford to deliver everyone we have ever known here to a castle in Scotland or rent out a fine hotel for a week with a series of fancy dinners and countryside events before and after our wedding, but I do not *need* that. I do not *want* it! I just want to be with you, Liam!"

"I hear you love, and I understand more about your resistance to a grand wedding," he said finally. "It makes sense. And to be honest, I agree on some level. Sarah and I did the formal Scottish wedding, and the planning caused more stress and aggravation than the ceremony and reception deserved." I laughed at this as he continued, "I just want to give you everything, love."

"*You are* my everything and that is all I need."

"So, no honeymoon then?"

"If you want to consider something in Scotland, I am open. But I am happy to go to the house on Loch Leven."

"We have to do more than *that*!"

"What if we go to Skye together?"

"That is an option, but with your thoughts of Scotland, I immediately thought about the North Coast 500. What if we have Jenny look at a possible itinerary? We can drive together and stay at incredible places like The Torridon, and self-catering along the way... including Skye."

"I think that would be lovely! I had so much fun when you drove us to Aberlour and Inverness. I haven't been to some of the areas north of Inverness other than on my driving route to Skye through Ullapool. And I would like to see the isles of Harris and Lewis… the Outer Hebrides. It would all be new for me."

"I have taken note. In the interim, why don't we have a dinner party here at the house? It can be a belated engagement party or at least a chance to host our friends again. It has been a while since our last party."

"Why don't we make it a birthday party for you, love?"

"I can agree to that! Let's work with Jenny to see what is possible on short notice."

+++

We were still planning wedding dates and a possible Scottish honeymoon but confirmed a large summer dinner party in the back of the house on Loch Leven for Liam's birthday. His birthday was on a Wednesday this year, so we settled on Saturday, July 27th as the date for the party. This time, we invited more people and agreed to have a small band. Chef Dan was on point to lead the summertime Mediterranean feast from his restaurant and Jenny and I planned everything else.

Liam surprised me on the day with a full Glam Squad for hair and makeup and representatives from my favorite fashion house, Alexander McQueen. After trying on several dresses, I settled on an ivory crepe and satin striped, wide-legged tuxedo pantsuit with a lace waistcoat. It looked modern and I felt powerful in it. More than that, as the least restrictive of the options, I felt comfortable. I also liked the idea of wearing the pearl and diamond earrings and bracelet Liam gave me at Christmas.

As the team put the finishing touches on my makeup, Liam said looking at his phone, "Love, we have an *issue*. The lads have apparently left home and are on the train to St Andrews as we speak."

"*What!?* Why would they do such a thing?"

"I have no idea! Perhaps they heard we were having a party for my birthday. We have some time, but we must go get them and either bring them here or send them back to Edinburgh on the train."

"I know they are smart boys, but I do not like them being on the train alone, Liam."

"Nor do I."

"But we have guests arriving in the next hour and a half. Surely, we cannot both be gone from the house."

"I trust Jenny and we have Chef Dan here tonight as well. They can manage it to start. Most will just want food and drink when they arrive, and we have that in abundance. I would like you to come with me because you will keep me from losing my temper with these lads for this irresponsible nonsense! Sarah is beside herself that they are traveling alone!"

"Alright, alright," I said. "Tell Sarah we will handle it. We can do this!"

"Aye."

We left the house with instructions for Jenny, Chef Dan, and Chef Stephan should people start to arrive before we return. The long dinner table outside looked lovely. They were already setting up the band at the end of the dock and finishing the many hanging lights and placement of candles and lanterns. Menus and place settings were complete. We had confidence that any early guests would be met with our planned hors d'oeuvres and drinks from the bar on the patio until we could return to Crichton House.

We rode together in worried silence along the winding roads to St Andrews. I could tell Liam was annoyed with his sons and as much as I did not want to admit it, I was as well. This act of rebellion, while expected for teenagers, now felt coordinated to be on today of all days. They were suddenly pitting themselves between Liam and Sarah to be here today and for that I was disappointed. Things had been so positive as of late and I did not appreciate this unexpected distraction.

"This does not look like a train station," I said as Liam parked in front of a non-descript stone building in St Andrews.

Liam said simply looking at his phone, "This is where Eric said they were. Perhaps they walked down from the station to get a bite to eat."

When we walked in the front door, I heard the voice of Ewan Crichton echo off the gray marble walls, *"Miss Corrine!"*

Suddenly I saw Ewan and Eric Crichton in front of me in formal kilts matching their fathers. I turned back to Liam and said sarcastically, "Apparently these two lads think they are attending a party tonight!"

Liam smiled and said as he put his arm around my waist, "They are, my love. But they need to be the best men at their Da's wedding first."

I breathed in as the tears instantly formed in my eyes and whispered, *"What?!"*

"Aye, Corrine. We are at the Registrar's Office. I made special arrangements for them to be here for us on a Saturday."

Just then I heard the sweet squeal of a baby as Luke, Kate and Bryant came around the corner to join our wedding party.

Kate said loudly, "Corrie my darling, Liam said that you needed a flower girl this afternoon!"

I instantly put my hand to my mouth and started crying. To see my dearest loves before me and to realize that this entire day had been a plan

Liam concocted on his own made me emotional. The entire marble hall was filled with love, and I could barely breathe under the weight of it all. My heart was so full it was about to burst.

"Is this *really* happening?" I finally asked, smiling up at Liam.

"It is," he said, kissing me quickly once more and putting his hand to my back.

"Come here my sweet girl," I said taking Bryant in my arms and kissing her over and over on her cheek as she giggled and cooed in my ear. I absolutely adore this darling lass! I held onto her as I looked at the faces of my gorgeous wedding party.

"Look at you in your pretty dress, Bryant," I said in awe of my gorgeous goddaughter.

"Are you surprised Miss Corrine!" Ewan asked excitedly, and almost bouncing on his toes as he usually does. This boy has more energy than anyone I have ever known. I wish I could bottle it because there are some days, I wish I had it myself!

I put my arm around him and then kissed the side of his head. I did the same for his brother and smiled thinking that they have both grown so tall in the last year, that I can no longer kiss them on the tops of their head like Liam can.

"Very surprised, sweethearts! I had no idea! I was so upset about you boys being on the train alone. You look so handsome in your kilts! And when did you both get so tall?"

Eric said laughing with his arm still around me, "Och, no train! There is no direct train to St Andrews from Edinburgh."

"I did not know that!" I said looking at all three Crichton men in disbelief. They took a gamble that with my affinity for driving myself through Scotland or my repeated use of a car service, I wouldn't know much about train routes and stations. Their gamble at my ignorance certainly paid off.

"Da sent us up with Paul. But we will ride back with you to the house! Mum will be there waiting for us."

"I will just say that you will pay for this clever deception, but I love you both. Are you ready to have a stepmother, lads?"

Eric said as both boys nodded their heads in the affirmative, "Aye! We have a friend at school, Geordie Marks and his Da just got remarried this year but he says he does not have a stepmother, he has a *bonus* mother. I think Ewan and I have the same."

"Oh, my darling boys!" I said hugging each of them again. "I love that! I am so happy to have you here for this special moment!"

"We all love you, Corrie my girl!" Luke said, as Kate handed me the small bouquet of white flowers, tied with the same tartan as the custom Crichton kilts, and took back her beautiful daughter in exchange.

She said instantly, "Stop crying, my darling! Save those lashes for the photos. I do not have anyone here to help you with your makeup."

We laughed together at the thought. It was then that I saw the photographer in the distance silently recording these precious moments for us all.

Kate continued as she walked away from me with a smile, "Luke will escort you down the aisle and we will all see you at the end."

I said taking Luke's arm, as I looked at my bridegroom, "Well then, should we be married, Mr. Crichton?"

"We should, my love!"

+++

Before Luke and I entered the room, he whispered to me as we both stared at the door before us, *"Corrie, my girl, you know that since David died, we have all tried to protect and care for you. It was our way of honoring our dearest friend."*

"I know and I love you, Kate, Mark, and Colin for it. I do! I would not be here without your love and support... that is a fact!"

"I could not hand you to a man that I thought was undeserving to take that responsibility from us. You are marrying a good man, love."

"Oh Luke! Dammit you are going to make me cry again! And I can hear your wife in my ears telling me to save my makeup and lashes!" I said as I dramatically tipped my head back willing the tears to stay in my eyes.

"She would be most unhappy with me if I ruined your photographs. Are you ready?"

We laughed together as I said squeezing his arm, *"I love you. And yes, I think I am ready to finally be married."*

Luke walked me down the short aisle before taking position with his wife and daughter at my side. Liam's sons waited with him at his side. The ceremony was brief and basic in its legal requirements so that we could all sign the required documents, and the staff could return to their weekend plans.

Once we got to the exchanging of rings, I exclaimed interrupting the officiant, "Oh Liam, I do not have a ring for you!"

"Not to worry, love! I have both rings here in my sporran."

And he did. He handed me his simple Cartier Platinum band. I placed it on his ring finger and said with a smile, "With this ring, I thee wed."

He did the same, with another gorgeous Cartier eternity band. The difference was that this one had alternating diamonds and sapphires. It looked striking in the stack with my three diamond engagement bands.

Liam's sons were so happy for their father. Bryant was a perfect darling, as always. I am convinced this child not only has the innate grace of her mother but an uncanny sense of when cameras are around.

Kate introduced me to the only two loves I have ever had in my life and her husband, their baby girl, and Liam's twin boys were a bonus. While I missed Colin and Mark, this was exactly who should be here to support us both at this moment!

We were pronounced husband and wife. It was done. As Liam kissed me at the end, he then whispered in my ear, *"Let's go home and feel all the love we have surrounding us. The party tonight is a celebration."*

"Does everyone know what I did not?" I asked, looking up at him in newlywed bliss and taking his hand tight in mine.

"Not everyone. Jenny, Dan, and Stephan knew of course! And I told Sarah to have the lads here on an off weekend."

Kate continued, "Liam called Mark and Colin and explained the rouse and goal to keep things at the ceremony small.

Luke said in support, "He was incredibly considerate of them both."

"Oh, my loves!" I said shaking my head and squeezing Liam's hand tight. "I agree on keeping this small and will hug and kiss them both the minute we arrive at the house."

Liam continued, "Everyone else believes it is the garden party you organized for my birthday and will be surprised when they discover they are at a wedding reception. Jenny will tell them just before our arrival. I just have to text when we are on the way back. I admit I like the surprise of the whole thing!"

I laughed at his continued excitement at the rouse and asked, "Where is everyone staying?"

"For those not here locally, I put up at The Balmoral but arranged drivers for them all."

"Oh, love," I said overwhelmed again with emotion and in awe of the planning behind the scenes of which I was unaware. I just kissed his cheek over and over.

Kate said, "It is such a blessing, Liam! And we thank you for the adjoining rooms! We have our nanny with us and will send Bryant back to the hotel before dinner so we can dance the night away with you both."

"Then let's go home and celebrate with our friends!" I said squeezing my new husband's hand in mine.

"Aye, Mrs. Crichton!" Liam said kissing my hand. "Let's go home!"

+++

We walked into the house and were instantly met by the Glam Squad who ushered us all back into our bedroom. They knew that Kate and I would both need lashes and makeup touched up after our emotional surprise ceremony… and we did!

Despite everything Jenny and I planned for Liam's birthday party on the lake, she and Liam had been planning our wedding and reception all along. I could not stop smiling and would have to have words with Jenny for her uncanny ability to serve us both. The woman was not only a pro party planner, but she also never let on for one second in our own discussions that there were other motives at play for this evening's celebration. She let me lead and most of what was planned for Liam's birthday worked perfectly for our reception. While I had a different party in mind, they let me choose everything! And somehow it all worked beautifully for both occasions!

Once we were set, our wedding party walked out on the back patio to rousing applause and cheers from everyone. Jenny let them in on the secret just before we arrived back at the house and by the sound of it, everyone was happy for us.

I saw the joyful faces of Colin and Mark, the Prestons, MacLaughlins, Chef Dan and his new girlfriend, Meredith Cox, and Abby Marshall and her husband who Liam flew in from France. Rounding out the party were Jenny and her husband, and a few others from Liam's company and even my Aunt Cecilia. She was my mother's sister, well into her eighties, and the last of my own family. How Liam remembered that and got her here I will never know!

I smiled seeing the other member of our extended Crichton family, Sarah. She was also genuinely happy for us, and I was happy to have her here. We smiled at each other, and she nodded to me. I could not speak to what she felt in this moment at the wedding reception of her ex-husband, but I could only think that our new extended family was complete. Perhaps she thought the same, but I was still in shock about what happened just an hour before.

Liam's sons stood behind us and I believe cheered louder than anyone in front of us. Even Bryant squealed loudly at the noise and applause. I could not stop smiling and laughing at the thought of what had just happened and how my life had changed in an afternoon.

Each conversation and discovery about each other validated what we both felt in an instant—Liam and I belonged together. Everything since we met has pointed to that fact. Our feelings for each other were powerful from the start. They had only grown stronger in the short amount of time we had been together. And those feelings were magnified by family and our combined friend group. All I knew was that I loved every face before me this night. Every single one.

"*Corrine,*" Liam said, leaning in and putting his hand to my cheek, "*I know it has been an unexpected day, but are you happy, my love?*"

I kissed him and said through my unending smile while he grabbed me tight around my waist, "I am so happy! I told you that I was *playing for keeps* and now you are mine forever, and I am yours. Yours forever and always."

"*Yours forever and always,*" he whispered in my ear before kissing me again in front of everyone we loved and through rousing applause and cheers.

"*I love you, my Scot and my husband!*"

"*You must know that I love you more!*"

I just smiled up at him as he kissed me once more.

Forever and always.

+++

GRATITUDE

I would like to thank my friends and family for their collective support, guidance, and honest feedback as I spent the last three years trying to find my own voice as a self-published author. Along the way, I learned about myself, the art of creative writing, and the complexities of the self-publishing process. My learnings have both amazed and humbled me. I did my best to tell the stories I had in my head and learned how to make them better through the often imperfect and frustrating process of editing.

I am not sure that I can be *'retired'* for much longer, but I have found something that I love more than anything! The fulfilling art and creativity of writing will forever be part of my life. In fact, I told a friend in Scotland recently that I *must* do this, and I do! **I must do this!**

Researching and writing novels was what I was meant to do, and now I cannot imagine not doing it. I have worked seven days a week on my novels since May 2020, and I feel fulfilled in a new way. It doesn't feel like work. Success is relative, but I am proud of the stories and characters I created. And I am grateful for the opportunity to live the life I never knew I wanted and never thought I could have. I *must* do this!

Like you, I fell in love with Corrine Hunter and Liam Crichton in **Fun & Games**, and I ended the novel wanting to know more about how their relationship would continue. It is an honor to tell the rest of their love story and publish the sequel just fourteen months after the first. I would have released it sooner but had to find out how Scotland fared against Ireland at the 2023 Rugby World Cup in Paris. *[Chapter 15]* I was fortunate to watch the match live in Scotland during my latest and longest trip. The only thing that would have been better would have been able to watch the match live in the Stade de France in Paris with thousands of Scottish fans... and a Scottish victory, of course!

I would like to thank **Giovanni**, bar manager at **Bar Prince at The Balmoral Hotel, Edinburgh.** He and his incredible team—**Stefano, Enrico, Tom, Alec, David, Michalis, Rumi, Elliot, Raynaldo, Victor, Nicole, and many others**—always make me feel welcome and never hesitate to let me sit at the end of the bar with my laptop... even on a busy evening. I have always felt at home at this hotel, but my friends in the bar encouraged my progress on the completion and publication of five novels. I thank them all for caring for me and supporting me in the way that they have! It is no coincidence that the hotel and bar are central to Corrine's Edinburgh experience and her relationship with Liam. It is a warm and welcoming place!

At **The Gleneagles Hotel**, the entire staff are five-star all the way! From the very beginning, I felt like everyone was celebrating with me and cheering me on. On my current trip to Scotland, I would like to acknowledge my old friends at **The Century Bar—Cameron, Teresa,** and **Michele.** My new friend and avid book reader at **The Spa—Gillian.** And the incredible staff who took care of me every morning and even celebrated my birthday with not only a special candle-lit treat but a full rendition of *The Birthday Song* at **The Strathearn—Natalie and John.**

I continue to have gratitude for the talented **Jared Frank** (@visualether on Instagram). I love his collaborative spirit and admire his creative work in support of my novels. He embraced Corrine's story from the start and brought my unexpected contemporary series to life in more ways than I could ever imagine. Each cover perfectly captures the spirit of Scotland and the love story between Corrine Hunter and Liam

Crichton. Seeing the first two books together makes me so proud! Much like my **HOLD FAST Series**, the covers he created naturally and beautifully fit together, while simultaneously standing proudly on their own. I could not ask for a better partner!

I shared this sentiment at the end of **Fun & Games**, but the plot for my contemporary novels revealed an opportunity to honor stories that are central to my historical fiction **HOLD FAST Series**. I love continuing the manifestation of Glenammon Whisky and my fictional version of Clan MacLeod at Castle Dunmara on the Isle of Skye. These books also offered me an opportunity to share stories from Scotland's rich history—even in a small way—via another author.

Corrine Hunter and I are not the same, but we are connected in a way that allows for a unique circle of storytelling across literary genres and centuries. It is a connection that I can only hope to continue in the future.

+++

ABOUT THE AUTHOR

Cynthia Harris is the author of the **HOLD FAST Series** of historical fiction novels set in Eighteenth Century Scotland. With ***Corrine Hunter Is Playing For Keeps***, she continues to follow the love story between Canadian author Corrine Hunter and her Scottish love, Liam Crichton from her debut contemporary romance novel, ***Fun & Games***. All of Cynthia's novels are available in both paperback and Kindle versions on Amazon.

Cynthia built a career in storytelling. From leading advertising and marketing strategy for some of the world's most recognized consumer brands, international news organizations, and major league sports teams—to leading internal and external communication strategy and speech writing for technology, human resources, gaming, and entertainment executives at Microsoft—words have not only been her passion, but her livelihood. With her novels, Cynthia now focuses her time on finding and sharing her own voice.

A proud graduate of The University of Georgia, Cynthia made a home in the Pacific Northwest seventeen years ago. She keeps her gas tank full and her passport current, so she can escape to the incredible places near and far that allow her to revisit history, fuel her creativity, and find peace. But Scotland is calling, and she is currently looking for a new home in the country that she loves.

FROM THE AUTHOR

Thank you for reading! If you liked *Corrine Hunter Is Playing For Keeps*, the sequel to my debut contemporary romance novel *Fun & Games*, I'd appreciate your review on Amazon. Your feedback helps me improve, tells me what you would like to read in the future, and helps other readers discover my work.

If you want previews of future novels or want to learn about my journey as an author, visit me at **cynthiaharrisauthor.com** or follow me on Instagram **cynthia_harris_author**.

Contemporary Scottish Romance Novels

Fun & Games

Corrine Hunter Is Playing For Keeps
[Sequel to Fun & Games]

The *HOLD FAST* Scottish Historical Fiction Series

HOLD FAST
Book 1 Of The HOLD FAST Series

A STRENGTH SUMMONED
Book 2 Of The HOLD FAST Series

RAISE YOUR SHIELD
Book 3 Of The HOLD FAST Series

Coming Late 2024
TITLE TBD
Book 4 Of The HOLD FAST Series

Short Stories

Coming January 2024
The Regulars
Corrine Hunter's Observations From The Bar